NOTE ON THE TEXT

With apologies to Hungarian readers, I have rarely used diacritical marks, especially the two Hungarian forms of the diaeresis, for names of people (like Petofi) and places (Torokszentmiklos). Strictly speaking this is wrong. But they do tend to complicate matters for non-Hungarian readers and they add to the cost of printing. I hope I am forgiven by the purists.

JT

BREAKING
THE CROSS

Jack Thompson

authorHOUSE®

AuthorHouse™
1663 Liberty Drive, Suite 200
Bloomington, IN 47403
www.authorhouse.com
Phone: 1-800-839-8640

First published by AuthorHouse 11/21/2008

ISBN: 978-1-4389-1615-6 (sc)

*Printed in the United States of America
Bloomington, Indiana*

This book is printed on acid-free paper.

ACKNOWLEDGEMENTS

This story is another figment of my imagination. But it grew out of conversations I had in Budapest with a police officer who did just what the tragically fated Captain Peter Kovacs does – ferret out illegal immigrants and grapple with corruption on a scale even he had never imagined. It was 1989. I was making a radio programme (for BBC World Service) on the collapse of communism. My policeman was one of many people I was introduced to in Hungary, largely through the efforts of another journalist and the best of friends, Karoly ("Charlie") Patak, to whom I dedicate this book. Charlie had a list of contacts as long as your arm and he put it all at my disposal. Sadly he is no longer with us. But thanks to him I came back to London with fistfuls of tape and notes. Charlie also sent me to the seedy town of Ozd to investigate an explosion in a steelworks that killed a group of workers in suspicious circumstances. So that part of this story is true as is the existence of a band of Roma musicians, yet more good souls who gave me their time and the benefit of their wisdom. The rest is fiction, some might say fantasy. There is a far right wing political party in Hungary but, as far as I know, it doesn't operate a private army. And it doesn't hold Roma as slaves in concentration camps. But the House of Terror is there and there are forces at work who would certainly like to see the return of the so-called glories of the past. For all its membership of the EU and NATO, democracy is a tender plant in Hungary.

Jack Thompson
London July 2008

PART 1

Chapter 1

I always enjoy a meal at the Kispipa. Tucked away down Akacfa ut, where the lights are dim and the shutters locked for the night, it offers the genuine article and the tourists stay away. Tonight I've eaten bean soup Jokai style, pork stew, stuffed cabbage with plenty of paprika and Gundel pancakes, fluffy as cotton wool. Consumed with a genuine Bakaver which won't leave me with a head in the morning.

I'm dining alone, savouring the food and listening to Irvin's passable imitation of Oscar Peterson, his pudgy left hand never quite in synch with his right. That's jazz and the Kispipa's proprietor has every right to indulge himself. In any case the clientele like what he plays.

He joins me for a nightcap. He's lived through turbulent times and did a stretch in a communist jail. We swap the gossip, assassinate a few characters and Irvin names names. I take a mental note.

"Good night, Charlie. Take care," he says. "There are some funny people about."

"Indeed there are," I reply.

He laughs and I stagger off, tugging my collar up against the night wind.

My Opel is parked twenty metres away. I peer ahead, see no one but I know I'm not alone. As I fumble for my keys, a figure, faceless behind a balaclava, steps from a shop doorway. A mammoth fist catches me right between the eyes. I stagger and snatch at the cold steel of a wing mirror. The mugger comes again. This time the pile-driver smashes into my chest. I topple to the pavement. The keys skitter into the gloom. A sixth sense tells me to expect a kick in the ribs.

It doesn't come. In a half conscious haze, I hear the echo of feet from the deeper darkness of Akacfa. My befuddled mind picks off bits of anatomy that hurt like hell. I try to heave myself on to my good hand. It gives way.

"Shit! What's happening to me?"

This time the hand holds, as does the knee I'm using for a second pivot. I haul myself up the side of the Opel, lean against the door and fumble for cigarettes. Out come a dishevelled pack and a card of Kispipa matches. I light up and inhale deeply.

"I either die of lung cancer or assault and battery. What the hell."

There's no one around to hear me now. Two more drags and I throw the thing away. Then squat and scrabble about with my right hand. The keys flash from the gutter. I grab them and collapse on to the hard, damp tarmac.

I curse again and the outburst does me a power of good. I stand up straight, open the door and slump behind the wheel. My nose is bleeding. There's a box of tissues on the seat beside me and I dab my face until the flow's been stemmed. I look down and see a piece of paper stuck to my lapel. The print is faint and barely legible.

'Arrow Cross. Hungary for the Hungarians. Fight for your national destiny'.

And scrawled across it in English, 'Foreigners are scum. Get out now'.

I reach for the ignition and breathe more easily as the engine fires. It takes a painful half-minute to manoeuvre out of the space and I'm sure I hear the tinkle of glass as I nudge the car behind. But pain or no pain, I'm away, lights ablaze, tyres screaming. A sharp right turn takes me on to Lenin Korut. There's little traffic about. I drive fast, faster than the law allows. But I don't stop until I've bolted myself inside the apartment and poured a stiff Scotch. I sit for a while in my favourite armchair, relishing the aroma.

"Bastards," I whisper into the night.

I look at the Arrow Cross poster again, sigh, drag my body towards the bedroom and undress with care.

"I feel decidedly self-righteous," I say to the world at large. "And I shall take a long, hot shower."

Wrapped in a cotton robe, I splash another tot into the glass. My head is clearing and the words for a piece are taking shape at the back of my mind. An hour later, I'm reading through the copy.

"Personal and painful experience of the revival of fascism in Central Europe. Not bad. Not bad at all."

I'll file it tomorrow. Even Fred, that cynical old news editor presiding over the desk in London, will like this one. I, Charlie Barrow, lie on my bed and drift into slumber with what I know is a seraphic smile across my battered face.

Chapter 2

Captain Peter Kovacs inhabits one of the towers at the western terminus. It houses assorted bureaucrats, discarded pieces of railway property and thirteen policemen. Those having business with Kovacs head for Platform 1. Just before I reach the barrier, I look to the left for a door of peeling green paint. I climb the stone stairs to the third floor, knock twice and enter a set of dowdy rooms in which the squad lounge on worn sofas and drink bottled beer kept in a rusting fridge next to the filing cabinets.

Under the old regime, the police always had 'facilities' at railway stations. Travel was a privilege for the reliable few. Bourgeois traitors might take it into their heads to board a train for Vienna or some other Western capital. But with communism dead and buried, the role Kovacs and company must play has been reversed. Now they try to keep the unwanted out of the country.

"You should have reported it straightaway, Charlie."

Kovacs is being very stern. I hand him the poster.

"But there were only the two of us, Peter. He didn't rob me. He didn't take the car. I don't think he intended to top me. He just gave me a rather painful warning."

"When foreigners are the victims of crime in this country, the procedure is different. Anyway, let's concentrate on this bloody thing."

Kovacs takes the poster, holds it up to the light and rubs it between thumb and finger.

"Sloppy print and bad Hungarian," he mutters. "How's the English?"

"Simple enough. Tells me to fuck off - or else."

Kovacs reads through the poster again and gives a mournful shake of the head.

"Keep it," I say. "Give it to forensics."

"You do know who the Arrow Cross were?"

"Only too well, Captain. World War Two fascists who did some very nasty things to Jews, Gypsies and communists. And it looks as if they're back in business."

This attempt at a coy enquiry doesn't fool Kovacs. He knows all about me. We met for the first time soon after I arrived in Budapest. I'd driven out to Szentendre on the day Hungary's last communist government let thousands of East Germans cross the border, driving their Trabis out of Czechoslovakia. The road was crammed with a convoy stretching from Esztergom on the Danube southwards to the capital. Kovacs had orders to keep watch on this mass emigration, cool fraying tempers on a hot August day and make sure no single carload took advantage. He found me standing outside a service station where the Germans were spending their last Ostmarks on sandwiches and bottles of water.

Later, for Kovacs's benefit, I translated the headlines in the British papers.

"What's this? 'Magyar Cop Waves On The Trabis'. And 'A Patient Officer Watches The Exodus'." The big policeman laughed and our friendship was sealed. Kovacs learned the ways of the western media and I got some good stories.

He puts the poster to one side and shoves a departmental memo across the desk.

"It's the latest directive from the ministry."

I read that expenses claims will in future be scrutinised by a new section. They will take up to four weeks to process if the applicant is asking for a refund exceeding his monthly salary. A reply asking for comment on this change in the rules is required within a week.

"They expect me to say 'yes' to that crap. How am I going to sell it to my lads?"

Kovacs stares out of the window at the traffic, the yellow trams, the scurrying life of Budapest on a raw November day. Something is bugging him. Maybe it's because his girlfriend refuses to marry him.

"Toss it back," I advise.

"If they've changed the rules, it means someone's found a way of screwing the rest of us. They're on the take."

"By the way," I say. "I see you've been given a desk top."

Kovacs fixes his sights on the word processor.

"I'm still learning how to use the damn thing," he says. "I never thought a bloody machine would undermine my confidence. It either tells me I've given it the wrong instructions or it says it's going to wipe the lot if I don't stop."

I chuckle at his confusion. "All you have to do, Peter, is save the stuff every now and then. You can't wipe it."

"Don't tempt me." He lifts a finger but thinks better of it. "Sod it," he says. "They can wait."

The phone burps.

"Kovacs. Where? Yes, I know it. I'll be there in ten minutes."

He rises from his chair exuding latent energy.

"Got to go, Charlie. We must continue this discussion."

"What discussion? We haven't got further than a quick history lesson. Anyway, where are you off to?"

"Café Troika, corner of Jozsef and Rakoczi."

"Can I come?"

"I suppose so. I'll probably get bollocked for taking a foreign reporter along….."

"But you don't give a stuff, do you?"

We burst out of the office and collect five of the squad. The posse clatters down the stairs and into the station car-park.

In a flurry of grey, they clamber into a couple of blue and white Ladas. I join them, slamming the door, as we bump across the tramlines and hare out on to Lenin Korut, sirens blaring and lights on full beam.

"What did Petofi say?" This from Kovacs's assistant, Sergeant Sandor Ubul.

"He spotted two suspicious characters in the Troika. He was excited. And it can't be the coffee they serve in that place."

Lenin Korut is a broad boulevard, lined with elegant four and five-storey buildings built in the nineteenth century - shops, theatres, cinemas, publishing houses and cafes, once again the haunt of writers, actors and artists. It's thick with traffic. Progress depends on some bold and skilful driving from Ubul.

"Damn this rain," he says.

"Easy. Don't hit anybody, for all our sakes."

A bus driver shakes his fist and sounds his horn as the Lada cuts him up.

Ubul scowls. Ubul is always scowling. "No respect for authority," he mutters.

"Be conscious of your public duty, Ubul."

"I have read all about democratic accountability," he says. "I know all the jargon. It means - don't annoy pedestrians queuing for trams and be nice to Gypsies." Ubul sucks his breath. "Fucking Gypsies."

"I wouldn't say that beyond the confines of this motor car."

"And Charlie Barrow is listening. Aren't you, Charlie?"

I usually get on well with Ubul but I know he doesn't trust me. He eyes me through the driving mirror.

"You don't look well, by the way. What've you been poking your nose into now?"

There's no time to answer as we screech to a halt outside the Troika.

Corporal Petofi has them lined up. Three old men, five young women and a boy of about twelve. The women wear headscarves and soiled overcoats, the men torn suits and shoes without laces. The boy shivers in a thin wind-cheater and trainers.

Café Troika is a place for cheap meals - soup, dumplings and cabbage. It has an air of faded grandeur, with a lofty ceiling into which some plasterer has worked filigree motifs of leaves and flowers. It smells of stale tobacco and unwashed bodies. Petofi's charges don't look as if they can afford coffee.

"The old ones, the women and the kid - they have papers, of a sort."

"Of a sort?"

"They've got I.D.s issued in Kolozsvar, Captain."

"I admire your patriotism, Petofi, but I think we'd better call it Cluj. It's technically in Romania. The time may come however....."

Petofi shrugs at this rap across the knuckles. "This old boy has a Romanian army pass," he says. "All documents, at least four years old." He hands them to Kovacs.

"No passports," he goes on. "They say they came across three days ago in the back of a truck. No work. No homes. No food. No crops. No cattle. Their village was burned down by locals in revenge for the theft of a chicken."

Petofi squares his shoulders. "Hungary is their promised land. They are, after all, our kith and kin."

"You mean they're Hungarians from – Transylvania?" I ask tentatively.

"Correct, Charlie. And they will have to go to a camp until some local authority finds them housing." Kovacs sighs. "And these?" He nods towards two other men.

They're better dressed and better shod. They're in their thirties. They look like truck drivers or the sort who offer profitable rates of exchange at airports.

"Interesting," says Petofi, suddenly ten centimetres taller than his usual stooped self. "These two do have passports."

"Romanian?"

"Not Romanian." He pauses, enjoying the moment. "Croat."

Kovacs casts his eye over them, registers their insolence and notes how one flexes his right arm inside the sleeve of his jacket.

"Shouldn't that be 'Croatian'?" This from Corporal Lajos who has decided Petofi is getting a bit above himself.

"We don't get two of these every day of the week, Captain."

Kovacs grins at Petofi. "OK, I owe you a beer." He takes the passports.

The Croat moves and the pain is like nothing I've experienced since a leather football hit me in the scrotum during a match at school. I double up and fall to my left. Stars and coloured lights flash across my eyelids. But I see the Croats bolt for the door. Ubul and Petofi fling themselves forward but miss. Kovacs charges for the exit. He trips over a high stool. Lajos yells at the uniforms outside but never finishes the curse he means to heap upon them.

One of the Croats turns as he backs out of the café. The shot echoes round the Troika's walls. Lajos crashes on top of Kovacs.

Kovacs wrenches himself free, meets the stare, sees the dribble of blood and the hole in Lajos's shirt. The clientele abandon their food, scream and shout and scramble to get out. Except for the Transylvanians, who stay rooted to the spot.

"Christ, you idiots," Ubul hisses. "Didn't you see them?"

9

"There were too many people, Sarge. We couldn't get a shot in."

"Where did they go?"

"Down Nepszinhaz."

"Then bloody well radio everybody. Go on. Do it."

I sit on the floor, dazed, lame and resigned. Most of the Troika's custom may be desperate to leave, but some are curious enough to linger over the corpse. Petofi does his best to shoo them away.

The manager approaches to remonstrate with Kovacs, sees the body and holds a paper napkin to his mouth. Ubul is scowling again, possibly at the thought that he might have to take the blame for this fiasco. I know he'll have a go at Petofi who didn't do a proper job frisking the buggers.

"Two Croats on the loose and a dead police officer," intones Kovacs. "Great. Just great."

He takes off his parka, kneels and uses it to cradle Lajos's head.

"They'll show up again, Captain."

"How do you know, Ubul?"

"Petofi's right."

Petofi looks relieved.

"Two Croats with passports, who kill a policeman in broad daylight, are something special in Budapest."

Kovacs rises, looks down, holds out a hand and drags me to my feet.

"You OK, Charlie?"

"There's a clinic on Szobi," I croak. "I think I'd like them to inspect my equipment."

No one smiles. Kovacs offers me a lift. But I insist on taking a cab. I step over the motionless Lajos and walk slowly out the door.

***   ***   ***   ***

"So what did the bastard say to you?" It's seven o'clock. My manhood has been examined by a young doctor who assures me it's intact.

"It was only a kick, Mr Barrow."

"*Only* a kick?" The doctor smiles and dismisses me.

I crawl into another cab and join Kovacs and Ubul for a beer at Mitzi's. It's a pub on Rakoczi smelling of gherkins but the lady who runs it keeps her draught at the right temperature.

"He threw the book at me."

Kovacs is referring to Colonel Mihaly Kozma, large, bald, eyes like a fish, and very unpleasant. He'd picked up on the Troika shooting. Kovacs was summoned to his office in a building on a tree-lined avenue which the citizens of Budapest still call Andrassy ut 60 or The House of Fidelity. At one time or another it has been the headquarters of the Arrow Cross and the AVO, the communist police. Its basement contains the torture chambers used by both organizations.

"Kozma prides himself on his mastery of irony," says Kovacs. "But he doesn't know the difference between irony and cheap sarcasm."

He grimaces at the memory of his meeting.

"He asked me if I needed the whole police force and what's left of our armed forces to round up a couple of Croats on the run."

"I once had to listen to him for a whole hour at a police seminar," says Ubul. Ubul is an up-front policeman, with a boxer's nose and broad shoulders. Seminars are not his thing. "He had the brass neck to tell us that the AVO had been a credit to the nation. He had a go at the leaders of the Socialist Workers' Party. Said they'd given up too easily. And he didn't disguise his feelings about the new lot in power."

He pauses to light up and swig his Dreher.

"They tell me he was an AVO man himself."

"Well if he wasn't," says Kovacs, "he was certainly one of the *pufajkasok*, the 'quilted jackets', the people's name for the outfit set up to replace the AVO after '56. It was a reference to their Soviet uniforms."

"Otherwise known as the *Karhatalom* – Kadar's 'Armed Force'," adds Ubul.

"A smart operator?" I ask.

The two of them nod in tandem. "He's always known how to look after himself," says Ubul. "Did you get a chance to state your case?" He's still watching Kovacs's face.

"I said it wasn't the first time criminals had jumped an investigation."

"I know just what he said to you." Ubul folds his arms across his chest and sets himself up for a spot of mimicry. "'It's the first time in a long time, comrade Captain, that a police officer has been shot dead on the streets of Budapest.'."

"Very good, Ubul," says Kovacs. "You're in the wrong job."

"We're all in the wrong job." Ubul drains his glass. "Except Charlie Barrow."

I'm somewhat thrown by this uncharacteristic compliment. Ubul grins.

"I tried," Kovacs goes on. "I said Lajos was shot *inside* a café. But Kozma wasn't thrown by that. He actually said we should have executed the Croats there and then - 'as a lesson to the people'. I was daft enough to tell him that in his day the people had lynched policemen for doing just that. Then it got stupid. He said he didn't need lectures on the lessons of '56. So I lost my wool and said I didn't need lessons from him on how to do my job."

"I'm amazed you got out alive," says Ubul. He sits back, savouring a vision of the scene at Andrassy ut. "I think he's scared."

"Scared?" I raise an eyebrow. "He's too powerful to be scared."

"He thinks he is," says Ubul. "But he's tired. He's frightened of the future. And he's getting old. Next time you get the chance, look at his face. It's got that haunted look. He survives because he has enough in his locker to embarrass a lot of people."

I gaze at Ubul with new respect. "I must get you to expand on that," I say.

"It'll cost you."

"He's given me a week," says Kovacs. "Technically it comes within our job description - rounding up 'illegals'. If we screw up, Ubul, someone else gets the glory."

"We won't screw up, Captain. We never do."

"And of course you don't do it for the glory." I smile at them.

"However did you guess?" they chorus.

PART 2

Chapter 1

The power is back on. A single bulb hangs from the ceiling, throws shadows round the apartment walls, patterning the bas-relief of the rough breeze-block. In one corner two men sit on plastic chairs, huddled round an ancient radio. The Grundig wheezes short-wave signals at them through valves still holding out against all the odds of wear and tear.

I hear this story many moons later. From Coro, a Gypsy lawyer, a rarity in Hungary. Coro beat the system but not before the system nearly killed him.

He said he often wondered how old Uncle Zeleno managed to preserve this relic of the 1940s, its dial bearing strange names like Droitwich, Hilversum and Reykjavik. But Zeleno was clever at playing the recluse. Not even the Securitate suspected him of any interest in the world beyond his miserable hovel. Two days ago, he looked across the muddy courtyard and saw the bastards rounding up his neighbours. They were made to kneel in the dirt.

"Look at them," said the bruiser in charge, massive shoulders encased in black leather. "Bloody Gypsies. I bet none of you have been near soap and water for weeks."

The Securitate checked a few papers. Then left out of boredom. The neighbours crept back into the building.

Zeleno still remembered the days when Nicolae Ceausescu forced the Roma to abandon their wandering ways, work in factories and live in concrete blocks on the edge of towns where onion-domed churches and the grander houses were left to rot. Coro's mother and father resisted and were tortured and shot after a farce of a trial.

Zeleno took Coro under his wing, ordered him to hold his tongue and go to school.

"I did as I was told," he said, "and learned to read and write."

There were few books other than the collected works of President Nicolae and his maniac wife, Elena, but the local priest spotted his intelligence. He slipped him precious tomes from his secret library. Coro pored over a Bible and three slim volumes of poetry. He listened with his uncle to the BBC, the Voice of America, Radio Liberty and Deutsche Welle. And times were changing.

"There've been demonstrations in Timisoara," he said.

"I know. And that's not all." Zeleno twisted the dial and found another station. They heard a Romanian voice commenting soberly on events in Poland, Hungary and East Germany. And more about a man called Gorbachev who was trying to change things in the Soviet Union.

"Trying to take the fear out of life," said Zeleno. For fear lingered like a damp mist in Romania, crept through cracks in the wall and under the door, followed you relentlessly in the street and hovered at your shoulder in the bread queue.

The next night they listened again, this time to a broadcast in Hungarian about life in the West.

"It isn't perfect," said Coro. "They talk of crime, unemployment, drugs."

"But they admit their faults."

Coro smiled at this. His uncle would never visit that wonderful place where people were not afraid to speak out.

He would never travel, drink superior liquor, or smoke better tobacco.

"But I shall go," he said out loud.

Zeleno read his thoughts. "Yes, I think you will."

Coro did. After a journey through hell, he told his story and let me write it down.

Chapter 2

Two days later, Bucharest goes mad. The radio can't stop talking about it. The people sweep Ceausescu from his throne, shoot him and his wife in cold blood, storm the Securitate and Party buildings, hug one another, laugh and weep and laugh again.

A garrulous woman from downstairs knocks on their door. They try to hide the radio behind their back-sides.

She laughs at them. "No need for secrets now," she says. "Come and watch television."

They see images of Bucharestis holding icons and crosses, celebrating the coming of Christmas for the first time in years, openly, out on the streets and before the altars of churches the dictator hasn't had time to demolish.

That night they drink lots of cheap brandy and, despite the winter cold, sing and dance in the yard outside. Then they fall silent and remember those whom Ceausescu's police humiliated, abused and slaughtered.

In those months of unbridled chaos Zeleno urges his nephew to get out of Romania. But Coro can't bring himself to leave. Who will look after the old man? He doesn't trust the neighbours. They may be Roma but they're sly enough to take advantage, cheat him out of his food or steal his clothes – and the old radio.

One day in November, Zeleno loses patience.

"Here's money," he says thrusting crumpled notes into his nephew's hands.

"Where did you get that from?"

"Mind your own business. Go and buy a ticket. Go, for God's sake, for my sake, while the trains are still running. Go and find out if what the radio says is really true."

Coro hesitates.

"I shall die here," says Zeleno. "A dried-up old Roma in a paltry little room."

Coro wants to protest but Zeleno is unstoppable.

"I should be out in the open, watching a campfire flicker in the dusk. But it's too late. You must get out. Find others who will travel again, as I used to do, across fields and rivers and into the hills."

Coro watches his uncle for a long time, watches his face twitch through innumerable emotions, watches him glare and weep and throw up his hands. Then he embraces him. They drink a sentimental toast to friendship, love and eternal bonds.

Early in the morning, Coro leaves on a train bound for the customs post at Nadlac, the last town in Romania before the freightyards at Mako, five kilometers inside Hungary.

Chapter 3

The wheels make music. But Coro can't dance. He can't even move. Crammed into a beehive of humanity rolling through a day of glaring sun, he shuts his eyes against its beams. Broken by the slatted blinds, they leave a pattern of stripes across his exhausted features.

The train beats out a monstrous rhythm, accompaniment to a cacophony of wailing children, the snores of old men, the chatter of women fending off fear with aimless conversation. He hears this endless chorus only from afar but smells the stench of unwashed bodies, vomit and urine, rotting fruit and cheese, remnants of meals unpacked from plastic bags and repacked.

His eyes are heavy and sore. But he can just make out the faces of those sitting opposite. An old couple, the man completely bald with liver spots spattering his forehead, the wife's face scarred with the lines of a lifetime's labour. He tries to focus on it as if it were a map that might tell him where the beehive is heading. But the strain's too much. His eyes close again. He screws the lids down tightly.

"We are in a train that makes music. My head tells me I am dancing."

But he stays trapped by fellow travellers, dozing Romanian workers, dreaming of paradise, a cornucopia of jobs, fields to till and walls to decorate with icons, the doleful eyes of a Christ who will fill the hungry with good things and send the rich empty away. For has he not put down the Mighty from their seats? Nicolae, Elena and their henchmen are gone. The old man leans towards him.

"We took this train so that the prophecies of Mary, Mother of God, could be fulfilled in another country," he says.

Coro stares at this innocent interruption to his thoughts.

"Dream on," he tells the old man. "Dream of milk and honey, of houses decked with the flowers of good fortune. I hope your dreams come true."

*** *** *** ***

Inches from his half-open eyes, he sees rough grass and nettles. A sharp pain knifes into his ribcage.

"Up. Up. You scum."

He turns his head and sees a boot, black, scuffed and muddied but well cobbled with metal lace holes.

"Up. Up." The voice rises to a scream. Coro hauls himself on to weary arms and hands. A huge man with a beer gut stands over him.

"In line. Over there. Come on, you shit."

Looking round, Coro sees a dozen young men, standing or leaning against the bogies of a freight car. Their faces are thin and drawn, their hair irreparably tousled. Like him, they wear cheap shirts and cheaper jeans.

"You want work? I give you work, a week's work," says the beer gut. "You pick onions, peppers and garlic in my fields. I give you bread and soup. You work ten hours. No shirking. You work shit and you go back on the train to Cluj."

The benefactor gestures to an even bigger man, wearing even bigger boots.

"My friend, Feri," he says. The man holds a gun and a bull-hide whip. He points to Coro.

"You. Gypsy boy. You work hard, huh?"

"Where am I?" asks Coro.

"You speak Magyar. Where are you? Who cares where you are? This is Hungary. This is Mako. You just crossed the border in your filthy Romanian train. You want to work?"

Coro spits. "Fuck off."

A boot finds his groin. He doubles up. The whip cuts through his shirt. He ducks. The butt of the gun misses him by a whisker. He joins the others near the freight cars. The benefactor and his sidekick can't stop laughing. Coro knows they're half mad and permanently drunk. They'll beat their labour force to pulp if the fancy takes them.

"He's frisky, Feri. Keep an eye on him."

He strides up to Coro and grabs his chin just above the Adam's Apple.

"You try that again and Feri beats the shit out of you. Got it?"

Coro stays silent.

"I said – you got it?"

Coro nods. The grip relaxes. He takes his chance. Darting under the buffers, he sees the rest of the railyard almost empty of rolling stock. He staggers over the tracks to a road beyond a signal cabin and runs like hell.

The commotion behind him dies down. The benefactor and his companion are too fat and too pissed to give chase. In any case, they have their quota. And a cruddy little Gypsy boy won't get far. But Coro never stops running until he's well outside Mako. He doubles back to the railway and pulls himself aboard a train of cement wagons, trundling into Hungary. Hours later, with the light fading, he drops off as the train rattles by a bend in the Tisza River. His back smarts from the whiplash. He's cold and hungry. Yet he can't resist shouting into the wind.

"I am free."

This is the land of the Alfold, the great, flat plain of Hungary, field upon field of prairie grass, wheat and maize, rivers and streams, reed beds and bulrushes, weeping willows, blackbird, swallow and cuckoo.

Coro walks through the twilight. Evening has turned into the early darkness of a cloudy summer's night. The breeze ruffles tall poplars lining a narrow dirt road. They hiss and sway, threatening rain. Two crows fly out across a field, squawking their rivalry for territory.

Coro has no money.

"Beg, steal or hunt?" he murmurs to himself through chattering teeth.

He shuffles on past banks of long grass and stubby bushes. Then sees a fluttering light. Dogs bark. But do not growl. The light becomes fire throwing a glow that frames a cluster of four or five silhouettes. There is the mutter of conversation. They are gathered in a clearing away from the road. As Coro approaches, the dogs' barking subsides. They sniff his ankles and wag their tails. He stands still, hands in the pockets of his jeans, offering them no excuse to attack.

"You must be Roma, or they'd have had you by the throat," says a voice in Hungarian.

"I am Roma," he says. *"Phrala thaj Romale."*

"Likewise, Brother," the voice replies.

The dogs withdraw and amble off into the darkness.

The acknowledgement comes from a stocky man wearing a trilby, dark trousers, a chequered shirt, green waistcoat and what the English call Wellingtons. He carries a whip which Coro knows he would have used if the dogs had given contrary signals.

Coro walks slowly into the firelight. Four faces scrutinise him, unsmiling but curious.

"He's cold and hungry," says a woman.

"Then get him something to eat and something to ward off the chill."

The stocky man hasn't taken his eyes off Coro.

"Come closer," he says.

Coro kneels to warm his hands at the fire. He flinches as a coarse blanket is draped over his shoulders. He turns his head. She has soft, dark eyes, a small, straight nose, high shaded cheekbones and a firm mouth that can't quite hide a smile. Her jet-black hair is swept back beneath a patterned scarf. From the lobe of her ears hang large golden rings. Coro stares and then is aware of his discourtesy. But she gives him no time to apologise.

"I shall bring you soup."

She slips away. He stares again, this time into the flames, trying to recall in some sensible sequence everything that's happened since Uncle Zeleno gave him the cash to buy that train ticket. He remembers the sweltering journey, the incident at Mako, the stitch in his side as he ran from the railyard, jumping ditches and barging through thorns, then clambering into the cement wagon. He recollects the wind that ripped through his shirt and froze his ribcage even in late summer, the cautious walk through the fields and the flickering campfire.

Suddenly she is there again handing him a wooden bowl out of which rises the enticing smell of vegetables and herbs. The broth wipes away his stomach pains and slowly restores a sense of well-being. She comes again with bread, fruit and a pitcher. The rough red wine adds to his reviving self-esteem.

"Take your time with that," says the man in the overcoat.

Coro lets every spoonful, every bite from the hunk of bread, every sip of wine, linger on the tongue and slip slowly down into his empty insides. He wants to weep with relief. But he knows that won't impress his hosts. He breathes deeply and relaxes his shoulders.

"You're feeling better now?"

Coro looks into the man's face and sees a strong jaw surmounted by a flourishing moustache and enquiring eyes, not gentle but not unkind.

"Yes," he replies. "I thank you."

"You're welcome."

The man produces a crude pipe from the pocket of his greatcoat and fills it with tobacco kept a small pouch pulled from another pocket. He takes time over the ritual of lighting it. The wind stirs the match flame. It rustles the tall grass and churns up flurries of dust and the embers of the campfire. When it subsides, there is only the snuffling of dogs and the hoot of an owl.

"I must tell you my story," says Coro. "I must tell you how I got here.….."

"Not now. You are exhausted and I too am tired."

Coro is about to persist but the man holds up a hand.

"No. We must sleep. The dogs will keep watch. We are safe. At least for tonight."

Coro frowns at this caveat. He's tempted to ask questions but catching his host's tone thinks better of it. They part. The man slips into shadow. Coro doesn't really see where he goes. He takes his blanket and walks into the gloom of the reedy grass to relieve himself. He finds shelter in the bole of an oak tree, pulls the blanket over him and drifts into sleep so sound that no images of the recent past disturb him.

PART 3

Chapter 1

I tap out the words on my old typewriter.

A Budapest policeman was shot dead today at a café frequented by illegal immigrants. Corporal Istvan Lajos had gone to the Cafe Troika in the heart of the city responding to a call from the manager claiming that a group of Romanians had failed to pay for the food they had eaten. The shooting happened after another policeman called for back-up from the special unit assigned to check on those suspected of entering Hungary unlawfully.

A senior officer said Lajos was killed by one of two men, thought to be of Croatian origin, as he and other members of the unit examined papers and questioned a number of customers. The man pulled a gun and fired one shot at point blank range. Lajos died instantly. The man and his companion ran off into nearby crowded streets.

Police want to interview two men of medium height in their mid-thirties, wearing dark trousers and zip-up jackets. They say 'illegals' from Croatia, Serbia, Romania, Ukraine and other parts of the former Soviet Union are responsible for a rising crime rate in Budapest and other towns in Hungary. They often cross the border with forged or outdated documents and with little or no money. The Hungarian government has accused some of them of being members of criminal gangs running prostitution, money-laundering and protection rackets or trafficking in drugs

"My superiors won't thank you for bad publicity, Charlie, but you're on target."

Kovacs has dropped in for a nightcap after the get-together in Mitzi's.

I translate the copy into Hungarian and run it past him.

"Tudtam, hogy nem fogsz unatkozni. I knew you wouldn't be bored."

"Where did you learn your healthy command of my language, Charlie?"

I smile. "I think you know the answer to that, Captain."

Kovacs sips his whisky and waits for me to confirm what his own files have already told him.

"They gave us a hell of good grounding at the armed forces school," I explain. "If you didn't make your way through each stage to the satisfaction of your fanatical superiors, you were sent back and assigned some God-awful clerking job in a barracks not of your choosing. I wasn't having that. So I worked hard and passed my exams. After two years military service, translating all sorts of stuff, I decided to combine my Hungarian with the study of Russian for which I was offered a place at one of England's oldest and noblest universities."

"Then you were spotted by those who thought of themselves as the true guardians of your country's interests and security?"

"Yes. It was good fun at first. I did some fascinating research into the arsenals of the Warsaw Pact countries, some of it by listening to people who came out of here in '56."

I rub my five o'clock shadow. "That was my undoing."

"How come?"

"The powers-that-be decreed that my skills as an interrogator were more important than my command of two of the communist world's most difficult languages – and my knowledge of its more unusual weaponry. They sent me to Northern Ireland."

The apartment is silent except for the usual noises-off in the street outside.

"I spent five years there. I faced IRA and Protestant paramilitaries in soulless interview rooms, wringing the shit out of them. Then I jacked it in before it destroyed me."

I sigh at the memories.

"It had already done for my marriage. After an interval considered decent enough by the Service, I was allowed to use my contacts and pursue a new career."

"The noble trade of journalism."

"That's not what everybody thinks, Kovacs." I pause as he grins back at me. "But I hated deskwork and newsrooms. And night shifts. One day I packed my bags. Hungary and Britain were becoming ever more generous with visas for one another's citizens. So, I pitched up here, among the stuffed cabbage and the paprika – not to mention the concert halls where they play my beloved Bartok with unique reverence."

"Too difficult for me. No tunes."

I'm not going to argue the point. "Sit back and finish your Scotch while I phone the desk." And Kovacs watches, amused, as I vent my exasperation on the newsroom in London.

"Look Fred, I'm sitting on one of the best stories I've ever run into. Why don't you people wake up to what's happening here?"

I wink at Kovacs. The editor to whom this tirade is directed is a man of forbearance who knows me only too well. He promises to consider the offer. He'll ring back.

"I shall flog myself to death trying to explain it all," I say.

"Why don't you throw in a line about secret armies, corruption inside government, silencing journalists with liberal leanings and anti-Semitism lurking in dark corners?"

"Are you offering to supply that information?"

The phone squawks like a throttled chicken.

"I am willing to be persuaded," says Fred. "So, persuade me."

"I can speak the language, Fred. I can swear in it."

"I'll vouch for that," says Kovacs quietly.

I raise a finger to my lips.

"There's a lot happening here," I tell Fred. "And I want a chance to write about it."

"I agree, Charlie," says the patient voice at the other end. "There's definitely enough for a series to give readers the mood of the place, conspiracy and rumour, with a good sprinkling of history and so forth. I might even fly out myself and sniff the air."

I wink again. Kovacs is still smiling.

"But if you're going to write about the resurgence of fascism, Charlie, you're going to need proof. If you want to get anything into my foreign news pages, you'll have to provide incontrovertible evidence. Names, dates, meetings, rallies and interviews – on the record."

I replace the receiver.

"If you're out on any more busts like the Troika, will you give me a call, Captain? If police officers are going to get shot in the line of duty, I want to be there."

Then I wince.

"I'm sorry. That's crass. I keep tripping over the fine line between doing the job and the need to respect people."

"I know how you feel," Kovacs replies. "But tip-offs have to be discreet."

We freeze and listen. Someone is outside in the stairwell. Kovacs moves swiftly to the door. We watch as the letterbox is pushed open. A piece of paper drops on to the mat. He swings the door open. There's no one there – just the fading sound of footsteps.

Kovacs picks up the paper and reads out loud. " 'We told you foreign reporters were scum and liars. This is our final warning. Get out now or suffer.' "

The words are scribbled in English. And again the Magyar legend. 'Arrow Cross. Hungary for Hungarians. Fight for your national destiny'.

"Menj a halal faszara. Go to Hell."

"Colourful language, Charlie."

"Fancy another Scotch?"

"I ought to be getting home. But, yes. After that little episode, I will. No more than one more."

I lean forward and pour the whisky. Kovacs scrutinises the poster again. Then he looks up at my bookshelves. I have a large collection in at least five languages.

"Ah, my library. Books I have read several times out of sheer enjoyment and dedication to their authors. And books I know I should have read but have never had the stamina for."

"What's this?" asks Kovacs. He's pulled down a thin volume with a worn dust cover depicting a stretch of water and stylised animals.

"That is a treasure of the English language, Kovacs. There is an appropriate line somewhere in there. 'The hour has come.' As Badger said to Ratty and Mole."

Kovacs thumbs through the book.

"You have in your hand *The Wind in the Willows.* Pure, sweet nostalgia. A classic, and not just for children. Whenever I look at its spine, I'm tempted to indulge in some comfortable time-wasting instead of doing the job I'm paid to do."

Kovacs hands the book back. I replace it with reverence. Then wheel round in anger.

"Damn the bastards."

I go back to the shelves and extract another book

"This has a more a menacing title," I say. *"The Circle of Hell – An Account of the Soviet Siege of Budapest 1944-45.*

It is the work of a distinguished academic at the Budapest institute of military history." I toss it over. "That's what I *should* be reading."

The policeman looks at the title.

"Yes, I know it well," he says. "It contains all you need to know about the Arrow Cross. I shall leave you to get on with it."

"No. Don't go just yet. Tell me what it says. I'll take in the detail later."

Kovacs looks at his watch. He knows the poster has unnerved me. He takes a deep breath.

"Towards the end of 1944, that strange man, Admiral Miklos Horthy, Regent of Hungary as he called himself, came to his senses. He'd played along with Hitler in the hope of regaining territories in Slovakia and Romania – a reward for sending Hungarians to their deaths at Stalingrad. But Hitler didn't lift a finger. So Horthy changed sides. But the Germans were ahead of him. They occupied Hungary, threw Horthy out and installed the Arrow Cross."

Kovacs turns the pages. I wait for him to find the relevant passage. He stabs at the book with his forefinger.

"The Arrow Cross was led by Ferenc Szalasi. The Nazis ordered him to assist in the annihilation of Hungary's 750,000 Jews. His interior minister said the solution to the Jewish problem should be such as the Jews deserved. 'Let not a single Jew believe that he or she can circumvent the lawful measures of the Hungarian government.'

"These 'measures' allowed Arrow Cross thugs to roam the streets unhindered. For three months they looted, robbed, tortured, raped, beat and killed Jews, Gypsies, communists, anyone they considered an opponent of the regime, anyone who could not produce the right papers or come up with a big enough bribe."

"You see, Charlie, I had grandparents who saw all this. They remember the Arrow Cross massacre at the Jewish hospital in Buda. They remember the day when victims were thrown into the river to drown or freeze to death."

He downs his whisky.

"Then my family went through '56 and another betrayal, by people who called themselves communists. And yet they would tell you, if they were still alive, that not even the Soviets and their Hungarian henchmen behaved as badly as those fascists."

I produce a packet of Marlboro's. "Go on."

"You can read it for yourself. Tale after tale of atrocity, of killing and terror, until the Red Army reached Budapest and laid siege to it. The Germans did a thorough job on the city. They blew up all the bridges across the Danube and killed 25,000 people."

Kovacs leafs through the book again.

"I have pored over this many times, Charlie. It's worth learning by heart."

He reads on.

"In the months to come, People's Courts took their revenge. Many Arrow Cross and other collaborators were executed. But many fled into Austria and beyond to Germany. They were never brought to justice.

"The so-called 'little men and women' of the movement who stayed behind also thought they knew how to survive. In the years up to the final inauguration of a Hungarian People's Republic in 1949, they quietly ditched their right-wing prejudices and entered the lower ranks of the burgeoning communist party. But they had backed the wrong horse."

It's my turn to gulp Scotch.

"As communists like Matyas Rakosi, who had seen out the war in Moscow, did the bidding of Stalin and took control of the Hungarian party, the home grown variety, whether genuine Marxists or converts, were violently purged.

"Yet some inevitably slipped through the net, working quietly away at whatever tasks had been assigned to them. After '56 they emerged as trusted members of the nomenklatura. They have always swum with the political tide, making up the shoals

of bureaucrats we are apparently still fated to be governed by. And as communism collapsed, a few grew even bolder. From fish they have evolved into the frogs and toads of a new fascism, croaking old Arrow Cross slogans with a new vocabulary and an enthusiasm that should frighten their fellow Hungarians. The question is whether their fellow Hungarians know enough or care enough."

He slams the book shut. I almost drop my glass. He lays it down on a small table with infinite care, as if it were holy writ.

"Charlie, you look shattered. Come and have supper with me and Andrea."

"Are you sure?" I ask, willing him to say 'Yes'.

"I'll take that filthy piece of paper. Get your coat."

Chapter 2

Andrea is serving *paprikas csirke galuskaval*. Chicken with paprika and pastry. She is monumentally beautiful. Jane Fonda with a winsome smile.

"Eat," she commands.

I am relieved and hungry, only too ready to do justice to this meal. But Kovacs merely pokes at the dish of white cabbage. His appetite seems to have deserted him. Perhaps he still sees the trickle of blood from Lajos's mouth. Or maybe he's ruminating on his meeting with Kozma.

"Think about Lajos if you must," says Andrea, eyeing him as one who understands his moods. "But not for too long. It won't help his wife and kids. You have something else you want to tell us, haven't you?"

Kovacs affects his hound-dog look, designed to elicit sympathy from the woman he loves. She isn't insensitive, simply pragmatic.

"I was lucky to find you, wasn't I?" he says shamelessly.

"Don't change the subject, Kovacs. You're embarrassing Charlie."

"Far from it," I protest. "You two are a sight for sore eyes."

She lowers her gaze and shakes her tawny hair. They are very much in love. I know that he's ready to go to the altar or at least to the local marriage parlour. She isn't. He's already told me that Andrea won't take it any further even after a year of living together. It brings hurt and happiness in equal measure.

"No girl friends these days, Charlie?" she asks artfully.

"Too busy," I reply. "No sensible woman would want to share my lifestyle."

"What a pity." She smiles.

Andrea is a journalist, deputy editor of a prestigious weekly. Like Kovacs, she doesn't keep office hours. It's a life of early starts and late night meetings, overseeing the work of others, keeping them up to scratch, checking facts and allegations. It's her job to make sure the magazine doesn't indulge in the sort of crude muckraking to which much of the Budapest press is prone, selling porn to children, lashing out at Jews and Gypsies and running libel with impunity.

"Have you been travelling lately?" I venture.

"Too much, Charlie. To the provinces and beyond, to Prague and Vienna. It's exhausting. Evenings of *paprikas csirke galuskaval* and a bottle of decent wine are rare."

I nod in sympathy.

She rests her chin on her hands and narrows her eyes. "Peter?"

Kovacs sighs deeply. "I'm dining with two journalists who are going to follow up every word I utter. Kozma will kill me."

"Kozma will kill us all if he gets the chance," I say.

"Your pessimism knows no bounds," says Kovacs.

I make no comment and Andrea wills him with a stern face to get on with it.

"We've been getting reports. All of them from Balaton. The last time you and I were down there, Andrea, was in June. And what did we see?"

"Much the same as usual. Camp sites. Sailing clubs. Hotels, old and new."

"Mums and dads and kids," says Kovacs. "Ladas, Trabis, mobile campers, barbecues and windsurfing. The good worker's family holiday with the addition of our somewhat more affluent neighbours from the West, doing the same with slightly more style."

"You paint an accurate picture. Whimsical even. Perhaps we should swap jobs." When she teases him, he knows he's in her good books.

"But there were imported frolics," he goes on. "Casinos, Ladies – and gentlemen – of the night. Drugs. Not what our former political masters would have put up with. And not exactly the stuff of nice family holidays in the sun. All that beach tennis, volleyball, a decent dinner and a bowl of water for the dog."

"My, we are getting sentimental." Andrea laughs softly.

"I am trying to sustain the accuracy," he says and shifts uncomfortably in his chair. "We know from the records of our overburdened colleagues in Fured that they had two murders, five rapes or attempted rapes and God knows how many assaults, muggings and robberies last year. The heavies moved in. The so-called protectors of small business. Blokes with wide shoulders, gold chains, mobile phones, BM's, Mercs and Suzuki jeeps."

Kovacs recalls having to raid one of Budapest's less salubrious hotels. A slightly hysterical tip-off from the station at Fured had put him on the track of a gentleman who had been less than discreet in the bar one night. What had he not done to a certain restaurant manager for failing to provide 'services'.

"Like drinks on the house and the assignment of one of his waitresses, a pretty young blonde from Ukraine, to 'other duties'?" I ask.

"How did you know that?" Kovacs snaps at me.

"It was in the papers."

"You see. Talk to hacks and what happens?"

41

"Oh, come on," says Andrea. "You're not giving away state secrets, for pity's sake."

It was this arrest and the information extracted from it that opened Kovacs's eyes to the changing nature of the resorts along the shores of Hungary's inland sea.

"He was convicted and given a short spell in jail. And now he's making people's lives a misery again."

"How?" I ask.

"We know he's trafficking in 'illegals'. We know he's a pimp. I've had his white Suzuki followed for hours on end. But he's learned a trick or two, including a disinclination to further public indiscretion."

"So you can't get the evidence to charge him?"

Andrea sweeps the used plates on to a tray, pushes it towards Kovacs who wanders off into the kitchen.

"Leave the dishes," she calls. "I want more accurate verbal pictures from you."

"I haven't got any." He walks back into the room brandishing another bottle.

"Well, I have," she says. He pours us more wine and Andrea settles herself into an armchair. "The hoteliers of Hungary are up in arms. The other day, for my sins, I went down to Fured to cover a conference of hotel managers. God, it was cold. The lake was frozen round the edges, the ducks were slithering about all over the place and the central heating at the Forum was either off or battling to survive. The food was awful and I got one Scotch out of them."

"We get it plushier of course," Kovacs quips. "Fresh air and fun and, if you're lucky, you get kicked in the balls or killed."

"Listen, Peter. These people are scared. They gave me roughly the same story as you."

"As long as you don't quote me….."

"Have I ever let you down?"

"No." His answer is quick and firm.

"The piece is ready for next week's edition. It's attributed to people in the trade."

"I shall look forward to reading it," I say. More copy is taking shape behind my eyes.

"Move it on," she says. "But don't be surprised if you're accused of undermining Hungary's tourist trade."

There's a pause and I'm beginning to think I ought to leave. But Andrea has decided to flush a few more thoughts out of Kovacs.

"Peter knows I've always used any information he's let slip only after checking other sources. Besides, it's important to have aspects of police work made public through the press. That's why he talks to you, Charlie."

"She's right," says Kovacs. "Our academy training was polluted with an ideology that's now been discredited. But it's been hard for policemen to adapt. The old system's falling apart. I, and a few others like Ubul, have grabbed the chance to improve our lot. We air our grievances. It isn't just about pay and conditions. We want to rub out the image of a police force as agents of the Party. Kozma has warned us against it. But new men in the ministry are looking to make the rule of law work. And crime is on the increase. Detection rates are falling. New freedoms spawn new villains."

"Very elegantly put," says Andrea charming him with another smile.

I turn to her. "Who did your hotelier friends blame for the mayhem and chaos in Balaton?"

"Some blamed renegades from the Party. 'Turncoats with contacts' one called them. Sacked cadres using their influence to settle scores. Others talk about 'outsiders'. But they either didn't know who these people were or were too frightened to tell me more."

"They're frightened all right," says Kovacs. "The outsiders are Croats, Serbs, Slovenes, Chechens, Russians and Ukrainians. They've cottoned on quickly to making money in our lovely country. And they have friends. Some of them in high places."

"And they're determined to do more than make money?" I suggest.

"Oh yes. They want to run the place like some latter day Wild West."

"Come on," says Andrea. "You're making this up. Croat gangs employing Hungarian deviants, or the other way round, charging round Hungary like Al Capone mobsters, running protection rackets and drugs syndicates? It's a joke. It's got to be."

"I only wish it was," he says darkly.

She looks at his pockmarked face and the premature worry lines that frame his mouth. This time the hound-dog look is genuine. He is party to some very special, painful information at which, so far, he has only hinted.

"Come here." He moves over to her and she kisses him gently on the forehead.

"Good night, lovely people," I say, polishing off my wine and rising from the table.

Andrea holds out another hand and I receive a peck on the cheek.

"Take care, Charlie."

"People are always saying that to me."

Chapter 3

My mouth is dry. I pace round the flat wondering what to do next. I think about a late-night foray to the Kispipa. But Andrea has fed me well. It would be pointless.

There it is again. The scuffle of feet and the sough of heavy breathing. The letterbox flap opens and another piece of paper floats down on to the mat. My hands tremble as I stoop to retrieve it. The same words. The same message.

I fling open the door. The welcome mat is soaked in blood and gore. Sprawled in among this, a black cat, quite dead, its throat cut and its belly slit open. I throw up.

It takes me five minutes to disgorge Andrea's supper and much else besides. I lean against the wall, indulging in the last throes of retching and coughing.

It occurs to me later that none of this, neither the noise nor the smell, attracts the attention of my neighbours.

Leaving the door ajar, I withdraw to the kitchen and drink as much tap water as I dare until my innards are distended beyond endurance. I breathe deeply so that my intake of air and my pulse slowly return to something like normal.

I find a bundle of waste sacks under the sink. Then a brush, a pan, a mop and a bottle of disinfectant. I boil five kettles of water and pour them into a plastic bucket.

I scoop the corpse and the welcome mat into a sack, dragging it downstairs and hurling it as far as I can into a heap of plastic bags piled some twenty metres from the front door of the apartment house. Then spend three quarters of an hour with bucket, bleach, water and mop frenziedly removing all traces of the mess and smell spawned by the cat and my own vomit.

I close the door and undress there and then.

I throw my clothes into the laundry basket and head for the shower.

Later, in the stillness of a November night, trembling like a shell-shocked squaddie, I open a bottle of Dreher and sit in front of the typewriter. I go through the copy I read out to Kovacs. I check everything, facts, grammar, punctuation, style.

"You'll get it in the morning, Fred," I say to the piece of paper in front of me. "Stimulating material to freshen up your international pages."

I rummage through the clutter of my desk until I find the key to my safe. I reach inside and pull out the revolver I managed to smuggle into Hungary months ago, a purloined relic of my days with Her Majesty's armed forces. I pull the top off another beer, extract a plaid rug from my wardrobe, wrap myself inside it and sit in the leather armchair that normally gives me a sense of security. The gun lies under the rug on my lap. The room is warm but I can't stop shivering. I pull the rug round me and peer at my copy of *The Circle of Hell*. Then look at the rug again. My eyes close and I don't even hear the beer bottle clatter to the floor.

Chapter 4

It is early afternoon.

"You're brooding," I grunt.

"So I'm brooding."

Kovacs has spent the day hoping and praying for a call from some uniformed young officer telling him he's seen the Troika killers. To relieve the tension he's waded through a heap of reports on 'illegals' stretching over several months. He's turned up one reference to Croats, held at the Letenye border post on the River Mura in September. The descriptions aren't detailed enough for him to pin down any of them as his two villains. But the border police and Customs have made a special note that, for all their outward affluence, their Audi saloon and their neat haircuts, they included a couple of stroppy individuals who tried to pull a fast one with inadequate travel documents instead of valid passports. They were turned back. But in the laconic words of one seasoned old officer at Letenye, who was to say they didn't sneak across somewhere else later on? River or no river, the border was hardly impenetrable these days, especially at night.

Kovacs puts the file to one side. The phone buzzes at last. It's Accounts wittering on about their memo on expenses. I can hear the rasping voice at the other end.

"Have you clarified the position to your staff, Captain?" asks a woman who is obviously going to brook no nonsense.

"Not yet," he answers. And before she can butt in, he tries to explain the somewhat unusual nature of the squad's operations. "My men work long hours. And they put themselves at risk. And so do I. There hasn't been time."

"That is no concern of mine," she says. "I advise you to find the time."

"Listen, lady. One of my men was killed yesterday in the line of duty."

There is an awkward silence.

"Will his widow receive the compensation due to her under the terms of our new contracts of employment?"

The silence endures.

"Well, will she?"

The woman gathers herself for the final onslaught. "It is not for you, Captain, to question the integrity of those dealing with such matters. And I hope in return that we can count on *your* integrity as you spend the ministry's limited resources."

He stays just the right side of politeness but gives himself the satisfaction of slamming down the phone so that the lady will know how he feels about her unwarranted Stakhanovism.

Ubul is with us, listening with a face like thunder. He grabs a portion of the frontier post reports and retires to the outer office. Rescuing a beer from the fridge, he slumps into one of the ageing armchairs and sets about a crude sifting process. But he can't concentrate. His fuse blows and he blunders back into our presence.

"You've tapped the end of that bloody biro three million times. You've smoked at least ten fags, which for you is outrageous. And there must be something fucking fascinating in the grain of that desk, because you haven't stopped staring at it since I came in."

Kovacs draws on another cigarette, throws the butt on to the lino and crushes it with excessive zeal. Then he tosses the pack to Ubul.

"Thank you, Captain. I will."

"Keep 'em. You're right. They're doing me no good."

Kovacs runs his hand across his chin, feeling the stubble. Rain splatters the window and a wind howls through gaps in the wooden frame.

I stay silent. I have been invited to examine more Arrow Cross posters. They've been collected from lamp posts and doorways all over the city.

"Forensics haven't come up with anything on your original handbill, Charlie. No dabs and they can't trace the printer they used."

"We should be so surprised," grumbles Ubul. He's just about tolerating my presence. But I have no intention of going away.

"Ubul, how long have we known one another?" asks Kovacs.

"Oh boy. Here we go. Another session of 'I don't know how much longer I can put up with this'. Do me a favour, Peter. Please."

Kovacs shakes his head. "I see, Rozsi's been at you again, has she? Wants *you* to jack it in. Get an honest job. Marry. Have kids. House up near Szentendre and so forth."

"Something like that," says Ubul. "And by the sound of it, I'm going to get your version of the same song. I can write the words now. Andrea wants you out of the force. Transferred to a desk job in the ministry. Nights at the opera.....and so forth?"

"She might be right. They both might be right. I don't fancy another day when I lose a brother officer. And I don't want another heart-to-heart with Kozma."

"There's more to it than that, Peter. And it *has* got something to do with yesterday."

Kovacs looks again at his sergeant. Ubul. Stolid and solid. Wily peasant mind in cop's clothing. And clearly a good friend. For how long? Three years?

Three whole years since they'd been flung together at the behest of Kozma's political bosses.

Kovacs told me how he was appointed to the job by a senior interior ministry official.

" 'Illegals', Kovacs."

The official had pronounced the word with evident distaste.

"We don't want them. We don't want a refugee problem in Hungary. They may pass through, onwards and upwards, so to speak. But we don't have the money to put them in decent camps. Capitalism means unemployment, official unemployment. We never admitted to joblessness in the old days."

"You mean it wasn't allowed," Kovacs had quipped.

"I shall pass over your facetiousness. Right now we are not having Hungarians from Romania taking jobs that Hungarians in Hungary can't have, if you get my meaning. Never mind Gypsies and real Romanians and God knows what other riff-raff are waiting in the wings."

So Kovacs was given his orders.

I deem it my task, even my right, to question the illogicality of government policy.

"No wonder this country is in such a bloody mess if its supposedly better educated brethren think like that."

"Quite right, Charlie Barrow," exclaims Ubul from his corner. And it is Ubul who now points up the illogicality of their current assignment.

"When we set out on our merry little jaunt yesterday, you told me that Petofi had spotted – what was it you said? – 'two suspicious looking merchants'."

"That's what I said."

"And when we get there, what happens. Wham, bang and thank you. A gun pulled. Lajos dead as horse flesh. You are summoned to Kozma's office. Now that tells me that our two villains are a mite special. And I am not an investigator of *special* cases, Captain. I am merely an investigator of illegal immigrants."

Kovacs stares ahead again.

"Peter. Are you listening to me? What's the score? Who are these two…..Croats?"

Kovacs has opened his mouth to reply but Ubul has more to offer.

"Let me in. Or I might just turn nasty and uncooperative. And with Kozma breathing down your neck and you taking an unnatural interest in Charlie Barrow's mugging," – he nods towards me – "you need me and those poor buggers in that office out there more than ever."

Ubul folds his arms across his gut. He may abuse his boss but I know he almost worships him. He's told me so. Because he's the first officer he's worked for who really cares about the job, cares about his men and cares about getting the right result.

"You bottle it up too much, Captain."

"And I don't seem to trust anyone, do I? Not even you."

Ubul shrugs but doesn't do him the favour of responding.

"OK. Sit back and listen. I shall give you both a lesson in political history. Do not yawn or look glassy-eyed. Because you've asked for this. And if you want to help me in your various ways, you need to know, mark, learn and inwardly digest everything I tell you."

Ubul unfolds his arms and leans forward. "Try me," he says. "Just fucking try me."

"And me," I say affecting truculence.

"We reburied the great Imre Nagy in June 1989 and that was the end of communism in this country. The following year we had an election." Kovacs is relishing the prospect of getting this off his chest. "We chose the Forum. A coalition of the Right. And that nice librarian, Mr Antall, became prime minister."

Ubul sniffs at this. "We were to have the brightest colours, the most majestic heraldry, the jolliest bunting, and very little else," he says. "I remember those words. They were spoken by a very erudite member of the opposition."

"And once upon a time," I interject, "today's opposition were Kadar's communists."

"Who now call themselves socialists," says Ubul.

"Have you two finished?"

Ubul sits bolt upright. And scowls again.

"We haven't done that badly," Kovacs goes on. "Given our propensity for making a mess of almost everything we've ever done, we Hungarians have made this thing work…..sort of. I've been reading the figures. Still with me, gentlemen?"

Kovacs makes the beams of a cathedral roof with his fingers.

"We have had more foreign investment than our nearest neighbours – even more than the Czechs. We have lovely shops in Vaci utca. We have imported some nice cars from Germany and Japan. There's more food in the markets – better quality – even if it is expensive. But we are poor. We have a massive foreign debt which the communists accumulated and used to finance consumption and keep the people happy. Yet three million Hungarians live in poverty. That's about a third of us. And you know and I know that crime is on the up – precisely because of that poverty."

"Figures? Data? Statistics?" I ask.

"Robberies by two hundred percent in five years. Murder by ten percent. We are unstable. And that means any fool of a demagogue, any crook with a gramme of intelligence and ambition can make a killing, sometimes literally, if he puts his mind to it."

"So, what can we do about it?" Ubul asks.

"We can stay awake, alert, informed and prepared."

"Go on. You've told us nothing yet."

"The Forum is out of its depth," says Kovacs.

"That's fairly obvious," I mutter.

"It hasn't the experience or skill to govern. And it's falling apart because it's being pulled apart, by well-meaning liberal conservatives on the one hand and a bunch of fascist thugs on the other. It won't last the course."

"So you're a prophet, Captain. Then prophesy."

"Give me back those fags."

Ubul deliberately extracts a single cigarette and holds it, like a father offering his child a sweet. Kovacs smiles, takes it, lights up, inhales deeply and blows the smoke towards the ceiling. Ubul pointedly watches the blue cloud spiral into the fetid air.

"Do you like Jews. Ubul?"

Ubul's eyes flash. "I beg your pardon, Captain."

Kovacs repeats his question.

"What are you trying to pin on me?" Ubul shoots back. "I made a quip in the car about Gypsies. And that was all."

"I'm not interrogating you. I'm asking. Do you like Jews?"

Ubul rises, walks round the room like a caged lion, stops back at his chair and holds Kovacs's gaze. I make as if to leave. But Kovacs holds up a hand.

"Stay where you are Charlie. And listen to this carefully."

"Since you ask," says Ubul, "no, not much."

The phone breaks the tension. Kovacs looks at it as if it's about to bite him. Ubul reaches over and gently lifts the handset. Apart from confirming that the caller is through to the right office, Ubul says nothing for at least a minute.

Kovacs stretches his legs, sees Ubul's eyes widen and his chest and shoulders expand.

"Stay with it, Petofi. Do nothing till we get there."

"What's going on?" asks Kovacs.

"Well, it isn't Croats this time. It's our fellow countrymen. And by the sound of it, a full contingent of riot police and some of your less respectable Forum supporters. Plus a few foreigners. Which makes it our business. All kicking the shit out of one another in a suburb of our glorious capital city. Grab your coats. And your gun, Captain."

PART 4

Chapter 1

For a split second Coro thinks he's back on the train. A bright sun shines straight into his eyes. As sleep ebbs away, he blinks furiously, tries to lift a hand but finds himself tightly wrapped in the blanket.

He shuts his eyes again but the glare is so powerful he's forced to roll on to his side and bury his face in the grass. A confusing memory of where he is and how he got there pushes itself into his consciousness. He is suddenly depressed by the thought that his night of security and relative comfort is over.

He unravels himself, sits up and looks around. A new fire has been built up to accommodate pots, pans and canisters. Beyond it he sees a long, low tent with flaps held back by rope. His host waves to him from the threshold. The old man's exchanged his waistcoat for a sleeveless khaki jacket but his baggy cords are again pushed into his Wellingtons. As he gets up, two younger men and four small children, gabbling wildly, move off behind the tent. He walks over to the fire, pours something into a tin mug, strides towards Coro and hands it to him.

"You slept well."

Coro sips the strong, hot coffee. "Thank you, yes. A deep sleep, the deepest I've had in a long time. No dreams." He flashes a smile. "And no nightmares."

"Good. Very good. When you have washed and eaten, we will talk. Unless, that is, you wish to be on your way, no questions asked."

Coro has not even considered the possibility.

"I have nowhere to go. I am Roma. You are Roma. I need all the help I can get."

Feeling he should say more, he adds, "Thank God I found you."

"Thank God indeed." It is almost a reprimand for blasphemy.

Both men eye one another, the elder examining the younger who holds his gaze but tries not to look defiant.

"Go behind that tent, my friend. You will find a mobile shower and a WC. There are soap and towels."

The old man laughs. "You thought we were a bunch of travelling tinkers, didn't you? Layabouts. Idlers. Rough and ready. Unclean. Oh, we travel, especially in summer. And we travel in what those who are not Roma would call a civilized manner. It amuses me to think that they always expect us to be unwashed, unkempt and *un*civilised. Even you assumed the worst."

"It was dark," says Coro. "I saw only you - and the fire - and the food and drink you gave me."

"And my beautiful granddaughter?"

Coro lowers his eyes. The old man affects to take no notice.

"Behind the poplars," he says, waving towards a line of trees. "Three vehicles for three families. Or three branches of the same family. And by the way I am Kalman Olah. And you are about to ask why I let you sleep in the open when I could have offered you space in one of my campervans."

"No, please," Coro protests. "I was too tired to ask questions. In any case, as you said, I slept well."

"True. I have a reputation for being tactless. Forgive me."

There is an awkward pause in which Coro is unsure of his next move.

"Before you wash," says Kalman, "and now that you know my name, I need to know yours."

Coro rummages in the pocket of his shirt and brings out his rail ticket and an old identity card. He hands them over and walks beyond the tent towards the shining, silver vans parked in an extended semi-circle.

"The one at the end." Kalman Olah has followed him. "Don't worry. I'm not going to lock you in. Take your time. Then we shall talk over some food."

The warm water trickles over Coro's battered body. He rubs soap into his hair and armpits. An impulse to be cleansed as well as clean has overtaken him. But he is careful to avoid using the bar of soap on his lower body. He has never washed like this before. It is not the Roma way. But Kalman Olah and his clan are not type-cast Roma. And questions are forming in Coro's mind.

Kalman has anticipated them. Later, as they eat fried eggs and drink more coffee, he says, "You want to know how a group of 'Gypsies' " - he spits his distaste at the word – "normally the poorest of the poor, are so well organised? And what are they doing in the middle of the Hungarian countryside living in well-equipped caravans, the sort rich *gazos* use to go on vacation?"

"Something like that, yes," says Coro.

"Understand this," he says firmly. "We are not *Romungro*. We are pure Roma. In the family we speak Romany, not Hungarian."

"So I've noticed. Is it important?" asks Coro sticking to Hungarian.

Kalman ignores this. "We have money because we work hard. We are musicians."

"Musicians?"

"Yes. Why be so surprised? In Vienna and Budapest, every café, every restaurant, needs a Gypsy band. Sometimes we are billed as an 'orchestra'. But what can you expect from a lot of ignorant purveyors of overcooked food and mediocre wine?"

He snorts, picks his teeth and lights his pipe.

"I, Kalman Olah, and my three sons can play so-called Gypsy music till the cows come home. The same adulterated tunes, the same tear-jerking melodies bereft of all their original irony and pathos, and stretched to their emotional limit. We can churn them out for as long as a group of drunken German tourists, imprisoned in an expensive eating house, want us to. In the new political era we have become a smart business playing rubbish to an undiscerning public. Even I take pride in the tricks the Roma play on outsiders."

Coro grins and stays silent.

"By October we have had enough," Kalman goes on. "We take a break. The Olah clan resorts to homes on wheels, the biggest and best that years of musical drudgery have allowed us to buy. But I am a sentimental old fool. I prefer to think that I can still be Roma and sit round a fire, smoke a pipe and potter about with my dogs and my grandchildren. So I follow the others in my ancient Mercedes and sleep in that tent. An old fool, Coro. But an old fool with money in the bank - and an Austrian bank at that."

He takes his pipe from his mouth and coughs until his throat is clear. Then slurps his coffee and runs a large, multi-coloured kerchief over his ample moustache. By which time his sons have emerged from the campervans. All three are spitting images of their father. They draw up an array of furniture, a makeshift wooden bench, an old dining table and the latest in trendy patio chairs. Two of the sons prefer to sit on the ground. None of them interrupts the old man but all of them inspect Coro.

"But we are serious musicians, Coro. Apart from the trash we play for a living, we are involved in a real artistic enterprise. The Budapest Gypsy Orchestra. They started in 1985 and we were asked to join two years ago."

He preens himself. Coro tries not to look totally bemused.

"Some fellow came to a restaurant we were working in Vienna. Auditioned us there and then. If we'd known he was listening with an attentive ear, we would have played something special. Anyhow, he liked us. So now we play Liszt and Kodaly."

The old man beams at Coro who hasn't got a clue what he's talking about.

Kalman laughs again and the sons join in. The children have wandered off to play and Coro notes how the women have approached to listen from a distance. The man he takes to be the eldest son speaks for the first time.

"So, Coro. You've heard our story. What about yours?"

The early morning breeze rumples hair and clothes and stirs the ashes left by the fire. The children's voices drift in from the fields, mingled with the barking of dogs. Coro drinks the dregs of his coffee and puts the mug down on the corner of a bench. Then speaking slowly, he takes them with him, back to his days as a wandering farmhand, dodging Ceausescu's police.

"I ended up lifting packing cases in a factory. For hours on end, until my back ached and I thought my arms would drop off. I quit and walked for days until I found my uncle's family living on a housing estate outside Timisoara."

His pace quickens as he tells them of his inauguration into the secret world of short wave radio, the change of regime in Bucharest, and his journey on the train.

When he gives them a graphic account of his beating at Mako, one of the sons hawks vigorously.

The women draw closer. Four are clearly the wives of Kalman and his sons. Three others have to be Kalman's granddaughters, their sisters or cousins, including the one who has caught Coro's attention.

"So now you need money, papers and some new clothes?"

Coro shrugs

"Do you know anything about the plight of the Roma in Hungary? Do you know what the *gazo* police will do to you if you're caught?"

Kalman Olah explains how illegal immigrants who are not obviously kith and kin Hungarians from Romania, Slovakia or Yugoslavia are sent back without ceremony.

"If you'd worked for the man at Mako, you'd have stayed for as long as he needed you. Then you'd have been deported. But since you've got this far into Hungary, you could lose yourself in one of the Roma settlements. The authorities allow the settlement bosses to issue documents giving Roma what they call 'right of abode'. Some Roma don't like having community leaders imposed on them but the *gazos* insist. And once they give you that piece of paper, life gets a bit easier. But there's no guarantee of a job. You'll have to live off the settlement's charity or work for other Roma, fetching and carrying, tending horses and pigs. And they pay peanuts."

Coro's thin face wavers between pride and despair.

"At least you speak Magyar," says the eldest son.

"And you could work for us," says another.

There is a collective gasp of surprise.

"But what could I do for you? I'm no musician. I have no skills."

"Of course you're not a musician. But musicians need support. And *we* need….."

"A roadie….," shouts the youngest son.

"Cerbo knows all the jargon," says Kalman. Then he answers Coro's question before he has a chance to put it.

"A roadie, Coro, is an assistant, an organiser, someone who helps hump the equipment around, sets it up and makes sure nobody steals it."

"And deals with the *gazo* sharks who try to cheat us," adds Cerbo.

"But look behind you, Kalman Olah," says Coro. "I see three smart campervans and a Mercedes. No one's been cheating you out of much. You are good businessmen as well as good musicians. I know nothing about music or business. I know nothing about anything."

The eldest son steps forward.

"I am Jenoe," he says. He places his hands on Coro's shoulders. "We want someone to do what Father has had to do for many years. He's getting sick of it. And too old. Don't argue, Father."

Kalman raises his hands in mock surrender.

"But he's a good judge of character, Coro. He doesn't think you've been spinning a yarn and neither do I."

"Thank you for that."

"There's no need. You have brains and guts. We need more brains here, and a spare set of guts." And he laughs as robustly as Kalman.

"And I need you," says Coro.

The deal is done. They all embrace and crack open a bottle of brandy.

"Baxt, sastipe te del amen o Del. May God give us health and luck," exclaims Kalman.

The women come forward to be included in toasts to the future. Kalman's well-endowed wife grasps Coro's hands and kisses them. The children scamper back from their game aware that something special is afoot. The dogs yelp, pant and whirl round in a frenzy of dust. The Olah clan decide to go on a busman's holiday. From the depths of the campervans they bring fiddles, a double bass and a cimbalom. Kalman fetches his clarinet. Then he remembers Coro's shame at his shabbiness.

But the women need no second bidding. They rush to the vans and return with a sizeable collection of shirts, shorts, jeans and footwear. Coro catches garments in mid-air and retreats to Kalman's tent. The males of the clan are on the portly side but Coro's new wardrobe fits him well enough. He emerges to be greeted with a barrage of wisecracks.

At first he can only watch the revelry. But then a dream comes true. At a nod from Kalman, the girl with the soft eyes, shaded cheekbones and delicious smile, comes forward and draws him into a flamenco from which there is no escape. Kalman observes them closely, as they dance but never touch, their shyness changing not to the vulgar familiarity of the young *gazos* in the cities, but to an exchange of delight and respect.

"Take care of that young man, Judit," the old man calls out. "Don't run him ragged. I need to talk to him again."

They swirl past him as the music gathers pace.

"But not yet," he says *sotto voce*. "Dance, Coro, with the prettiest of them all. And give me an excuse for another bout of sentimentality."

Judit pulls up abruptly.

"He cannot dance for long, Grandfather. He hasn't the energy."

Coro knows he's blushing, although he has never blushed before in his whole life. Suddenly the memories flood back – the violence at Mako, his escape, the journey and the welcome from these, his own kind. He runs from Judit, runs as fast as he can so that they won't see his face and his helplessness. Judit runs too but is called back by Kalman. The music and dancing die down.

"That young man needs to weep," says the old man. "Too much has happened to him too quickly. Leave him alone for a while."

It isn't until late in the afternoon that Kalman sends Judit to find Coro.

He sits on the grassy bank of a stagnant stream well away from the camp and stares into the haze of a waning day. He hears the rustle of grass and feels her hands rubbing gently at his scarred shoulders. She rests her chin on the back of his head. He turns. His face is streaked with the lines of his sobbing. She kisses his cheek and folds his arms around her. Again they do not move until the sun sinks beyond the Tisza and the evening returns to the tops of the willows. Then she leads him away to a place where the joy of the morning changes to an ecstasy neither of them have tasted before.

Chapter 2

Coro journeys for a week with the Olah clan. They're taking a break from the tribulations of music-making and are not in a mood to travel fast. The days are long and leisurely, the weather good, the driving confined to mornings. At noon they pitch camp and dine, wholesomely if not lavishly, on fish or game, usually laid out on the old table in the shade of a tall tree. The younger children scuttle off, returning every now and then to snatch cheese or fruit for their own private feast in some nearby meadow. It is, Coro admits, an idyll that is lasting longer than he has any right to expect. He senses that Kalman is responsible for a healing process born of deep anger at the treatment meted out to one of his own kind.

Coro's reserve commends itself to the family.

"He's no brash youngster," observes Kalman to his wife. "He isn't full of himself. He takes advice, wants to learn, works at his chores. Doesn't expect to be waited on hand and foot." The wife agrees and amuses herself by watching Coro's flourishing relationship with her granddaughter. But Judit does not throw herself at Coro and, even after their first long encounter, he is careful not to give the impression that he wants to be with her all the time.

Yet he does. He longs for her touch and smile. Judit catches his mood and rewards him with discreet signals to walk with her in the evening, to sit and talk, or keep a companionable silence on some river bank. They take as much time as decency allows.

On the road, Coro accompanies Kalman in the battered Mercedes. They have a companion, Kalman's favourite dog, a *mudi* with its dark, shaggy coat. It sits in the back, its snout pushed out of the window, enjoying the slip stream.

"Never answers back, that dog," says Kalman.

Coro takes the hint and lets the old man chatter on.

Kalman says his chief concern these days is the condition of his people, their rights, their duties, their treatment by governments in general and officials in particular.

"We have a Roma parliament here in Hungary. Eighty members elected by all sorts of groups and organizations. The *gazo* president has given it his blessing. He's even offered his advice. He's told them that education is the way forward. Roma children must have the same opportunities as other Hungarians. He's right. The only problem is - how do we do it? There are so many Roma communities and settlements scattered all over the place. They're easy targets for the *gazos*, who don't want our kids in their schools."

"So what can you do about it?" Coro asks.

"We've got one college where a few Roma teenagers can study with their own kind. But even that causes problems. Some of our people don't like what they call 'segregation'. They want 'integration' or 'assimilation'. They say it's the only way to stop the *gazo* politicians who'd like to keep us in ghettoes and blame us for every crime in the land. They jabber a lot, these people. But it's better than fighting among ourselves. And there's been plenty of that in the past."

Kalman stops the car.

"I want to smoke," he says. "Out in the open. The others will catch us up."

Then come the disclosures that shatter Coro's idyll.

"What we have to worry about is the raids, the beatings and shootings – the thugs with shaven heads."

Kalman blows smoke into the morning air. It lingers like a wraith. There is no breeze. Not a whiff of wind from any quarter. The smoke rises slowly and dissolves. Coro is mesmorised. But Kalman snaps him back into reality.

"Which is why I take certain roads and not others," he goes on. "Why I avoid towns as much as possible and why I steer clear of the police. They have a nasty habit of passing on information to the hooligans. They tell them where we camp, where we eat and sleep – and where we're moving on to."

He sticks his pipe back in his mouth and just as quickly pulls it out, tapping the bowl on the bonnet of the car.

"We've been in fights, Jenoe and I – and the others. But we know how to look after ourselves. We're not emaciated little men without jobs and prospects. We have food in our bellies, muscles in our arms, money in the bank and healthy families. But I tell you, Coro, most Roma do not. The men work as unskilled labourers on building sites in Budapest or Miskolc. They live in miserable hostels. Once a month they take the train and come back to their families in those damned settlements. Wretched places. Mud brick. Breezeblock and corrugated iron."

"Just like Romania," Coro muses.

"Except that Hungary is supposed to be the promised land. But there are *gazos* without jobs. Too many of them. They're jealous. And they loathe us with a poison that's spreading."

He lights his pipe again and looks across a field of grain and sunflowers at the wide horned cattle grazing on the horizon. They smell the wild flowers. The flies buzz round them. A crow caws from the top of a tree and flies off with a clatter of wings.

This time Kalman bangs his pipe on a fence post.

"Tomorrow, we pay a visit to some friends near Torokszentmiklos. They don't know we're coming and I don't want to phone ahead. But they'll know what to do. And you might have to stay with them for a while."

Coro wants to know exactly what that means. But he daren't ask the question in case the answer buttresses his worst fears. Kalman watches his face as he tries to hide his feelings.

"When you're fixed up, you'll rejoin us and be our roadie."

Kalman laughs but Coro is only partly reassured. The rest of the convoy arrive. Jenoe climbs down from his cab leaving the engine running. He jogs across the road, anxious to pant out his news.

"There's been trouble in Szolnok," he says. "Skinheads went for some Roma boys in a bar. Turned into a brawl. One of ours pulled a knife. Stabbed a big guy. No action taken against the *gazos*. But they've detained two Roma."

"How did you hear about it?" asks Kalman.

"The radio, Father. We have them in the vans and you've got one in the car. Why don't you listen to it?"

"The only news I want is what I get from our own people. They're the ones that matter. That contraption is just a nuisance. It interferes with my thoughts."

Jenoe rolls his eyes. Kalman sees the gesture and winks at Coro who's remembering the times he and uncle Zeleno gleaned all their information from the airwaves.

"These attacks are getting more frequent and this isn't just thugs looking for a chance to beat up the feeble and defenceless," says Jenoe.

"We've always been on the receiving end of violence," adds Kalman.

"Yes. But these skinheads are different. Someone somewhere is stirring them up."

"And has a reason for doing it. Which is why I'm in a hurry to get Coro his papers. He needs something to wave in front of a nosy policeman if he gets caught in a fight and finds himself spending the night in a damp and dismal cell."

PART 5

Chapter 1

It's a football pitch, of sorts. I see two sets of rusting goalposts. On Sunday mornings, fifteen and sixteen-year-olds from the nearby estate argue over the ownership of this scruffy patch of earth. Then for ninety minutes, they play out a serious fantasy. They are the heirs of Puskas and Hidegkuti, those warriors of old who beat the English on their own ground in London. Their fathers, if they have fathers, tell them about it – frequently – remarking morosely that Hungary has never had a decent side since the faded triumphs of the fifties.

But there's been no football on this particular raw evening. The youngsters tried to start a rough and ready game while the light lasted. But they were chased off by men with shaven heads, knuckle dusters and chains. By the time Ubul is rolling the Opel on to spare ground next to the goalposts, we can smell the smoke and the tear gas and hear the frenzy.

"Duck," he shouts.

Kovacs just has time to slam the door. A bottle skims his right shoulder and smashes itself to pieces on a wheel arch. Another follows, shattering the vehicle's nearside window. Calculating on a lull in proceedings before the next salvo, Kovacs and Ubul run to join a group of about twenty uniforms beating the shit out of a bunch of skinheads. I watch from behind the flimsy shelter of the Opel's battered bodywork.

"For Christ's sake," yells Kovacs. "Take it easy. You'll kill the buggers."

"Who the hell are you?" asks a young officer through a bloody nose.

"Who the hell are you, if it comes to that?"

Kovacs flashes his ID. Ubul follows suit.

"Either turn round and get of here, fast, or do something useful," says the officer. "If you want to survive, borrow a stick and a shield and wade in with the rest of us."

Kovacs ducks again as another shower of bricks and bottles clatters against a police van. A front line of uniforms, two on horseback in full riot gear, pushes the skinhead mob into a corner formed by two high walls. Kovacs catches Ubul's eye and shakes his head vigorously.

"No. No guns. Don't even think about it."

"I knew you'd say that." Ubul growls his deep disappointment into the collar of his parka. Two skins with wounds which will require special treatment from skilled doctors are being led away. They still have enough energy to shout obscenities at the police, Gypsies, Jews, communists and anyone else they can include in their litany of enemies.

Kovacs's attention is drawn to three men lying motionless, heads half submerged in a pool of filthy water.

"Get them out of here." The young officer seems to take the sight of the bodies as a personal insult. "Get them out. For God's sake."

Three uniforms scramble to do his bidding.

"Christ, lieutenant. They're blacks – niggers – negroes."

The uniforms struggle to turn the three face up.

"Move it," screeches the officer. His frustration has ballooned into outright rage. Kovacs and Ubul step into the puddle, seize a pair of ankles and pull hard. One of the blacks groans.

"Cushion his head, Ubul."

"With what?"

"With your parka."

"Oh thanks. How many more bits and pieces of my wardrobe do I have to ruin in the line of duty?"

"Just shut up and do it," says the lieutenant who's tugging at another pair of ankles.

Ubul advances on him. "Sergeant Ubul to you, Sunshine. Sergeant….."

Kovacs steps between them. "That's enough."

Ubul doesn't stop.

"I said – enough, Ubul."

"I'll have your guts……" Ubul backs off like an angry dog.

"Lieutenant. You still haven't told us who you are. But I'm telling you right now, whoever you are – these three *we* take to hospital and you won't ask why."

"And leave the rest of us to do the dirty work? No way. I repeat – who the hell are you?"

Kovacs shows his ID again and lets the lieutenant take a good look.

"Kovacs. Illegals." A pause. "*Captain* Kovacs." The challenge invites reaction.

The officer merely shrugs. "Csucs. The name's Csucs."

"Oh good," quips Ubul. "Now we all know one another, maybe we'll get a fucking sight more respect."

Kovacs rounds on him.

"For the last time, Ubul, shut it. Do something useful, like the good lieutenant says. Look after these three for a start."

Ubul slinks away to join the uniforms lifting the blacks into a minibus.

They have to move fast. The cornered skins have regrouped and found fresh heart. With more bricks and

75

bottles, they have rushed the uniforms who find themselves trapped with their backs against a line of police vehicles.

"Get in that thing and go, Ubul. Stay with those guys. I'll catch you up."

Ubul opens his mouth to protest, thinks better of it and scuttles into the minibus just as its doors close against another volley of concrete and glass.

Csucs sees me standing by the Opel.

"Who the fuck is that?" he asks.

"That," says Kovacs, "is an accredited journalist. He has perfect right to be here which is why it would be a good idea for us to play this by the rules, even if those bastards aren't of a mind to."

I haven't moved during this exchange. Kovacs knows he's taken a risk bringing me and I don't intend to make life any more difficult for him. He's fulfilling his promises and I'm sticking to my side of the bargain. In any case, two television crews have rolled up and are already in the thick of it.

There's a flash to our left. The skins have resorted to primitive fire bombs. Flames catch the jacket of a young uniform whose closest colleague leaps to help him. Together they roll in the dirt. It breaks a bone or two but preserves him from the pain of third degree burns.

Another flash of flame. The splintering of glass again. A rush of air and the innards of a patrol car are ablaze. Someone wrenches an extinguisher from another vehicle and wrestles with its controls.

"Work, you bastard. Work."

He hits the lever. A stream of foam fights a losing battle against the inferno. The driver fries.

The skins advance.

"I've changed my mind," shouts Kovacs, pulls his gun and fires into the air.

The lieutenant looks at him for a split second and does likewise.

Two uniforms take their cue. The skins hesitate.

"Next time, over their heads," yells the lieutenant.

The TV crews are having a field day. I marvel at the courage of the cameramen.

The riot squad regroups and charges again. The skins flee back to the wall. Uniforms grab them, beat them savagely and not even Kovacs is going to stop them. Behind him, Csucs hears sirens. Someone has finally summoned a fire tender and ambulances. But the patrol car burns ever more fiercely. If the flames reach its tank, few of us might live to tell the tale.

Csucs races back to his own car, grabs a loud-hailer and bawls like fury for everybody to get the hell out, even the skins pinned against the wall. But the skins don't hear or don't care. They push forward again.

Gunfire rattles through the din and fury.

"Oh, shit. No," I cry.

Kovacs freezes, straining not to believe what he sees. Three skins lie dead, undoubtedly dead. Suddenly, there's no more frenzy, just the crackle of flames, the strobing of blue lights and the panic of feet. Then voices welling up, as the trapped skins try to climb the wall in a frantic mixture of mutual help and self-preservation. The uniforms stand and watch. One finds another extinguisher. The burning car is doused.

Paramedics race to get at the driver. There's a slim chance he's still alive.

"Who the hell fired that gun?"

Csucs is about to wade into the ranks of his own men and beat the daylights out of the first to get in his way. Kovacs hauls him back and shakes his head. The lieutenant kneels in the mud, hiding his face in his hands.

A cameraman zooms in on him but he does nothing to avoid the intrusion. Kovacs thinks of intervening, hesitates and decides against it. There is a curious hiatus like an interval in the theatre. Stretcher bearers pass to and fro. The last of the detained skins are frog-marched and shoved into police vans. Most of the mob has gone over the wall.

The chill returns. The rickety goalposts stand like drunken sentinels.

Csucs lifts his weary features.

"Tell me, Captain Kovacs." He's calling on all his reserves of self-control. "Why are 'Illegals' so interested in a riot by skinheads and assorted scum on a seedy stretch of waste ground in my patch?"

Kovacs puts his gun away and looks down at his muddied footwear.

"My information, Lieutenant, is that this riot of yours didn't just happen. It was planned and deliberately provoked. And it wasn't provoked by those yobs and their racist slogans but by people who did a timely vanishing act long before it turned nasty."

"All I heard," says Csucs, "was that a group of skinheads had gathered for a rally. Nobody asked permission. That made it an illegal gathering. I assume it's the sort of occasion when speeches will be made to rouse the faithful. Well, they certainly did that. And now the faithful have martyrs."

He sighs.

"And so do we."

He makes a vain attempt to wipe dust and grime from his jacket. Then looks defiantly at Kovacs.

"You're telling me a lot of it happened before I came on the scene?"

Curious, I think, how we use these dramatic metaphors. I watch the tear gas waft into the cold air.

"The people who started this pulled out some time ago," says Kovacs. "I don't know who they were but I can guess."

Csucs walks in a circle, kicking gravel. "What will you do with the blacks?"

"Do with them?" Kovacs asks, surprised at the question. "Make sure they stay alive. Then when they're fit enough, question them. Why were they here, tonight of all nights? Who are they, for pity's sake? Students? Workers? I thought all our Third World friends had gone back home. A cut-and-dried case for 'Illegals', Lieutenant."

"You get the interesting stuff. And I get the shit. Christ, I didn't even know we'd brought the bigger firearms along. *I* didn't authorize them. I'm not senior enough. But I'd like to know who did."

"You might never find out," says Kovacs. "Your lads look as if they'll clam up, especially after they saw what happened to that poor sod in the car."

He decides Csucs needs a little encouragement .

"Lieutenant, I have no wish to cut you out of anything that has a legitimate connection with all that's happened and your gallant attempts to handle it."

"Don't patronise me, Captain."

Kovacs ignores this. "Look, if you want to come to the hospital with me….."

"No, forget it. I've got enough to do here."

A TV reporter is hovering. Kovacs doesn't want to give interviews. Csucs knows he'll have to.

"I'd be obliged if you'd let me know what happens to your charges," he says.

"I'll do that."

Kovacs shakes his hand and prepares to make for the wreck of our Opel. The fleet of police vehicles pulls out.

The kids will have to wait a while before they play any more games on this pitch. It's already been taped off.

"Let's go, Charlie. I think you've seen enough. And you can drive."

I turn the key and the Opel responds.

"Good, sound German engineering," I mutter. "But it's going to be bloody cold without that window."

I swing the car round, catch a glimpse of Csucs talking to the reporter, bounce across the hardened mud and head for the main road. There's a thump on the roof. In the mirror I see a bottle ricochet off the boot.

Chapter 2

At the hospital on Robert Karoly ut, Ubul briefs us in full.

"Their first names are Yohanes, Efram and Michael. They're Ethiopian. Yohanes is *compos mentis* and very ready to talk. The others are under sedation."

"What's he said so far?" I ask

"His Hungarian's a bit rough but he speaks English. He calls himself a 'mature student'. He says he's a relic from the days when governments like his sent their brightest and best to study in various parts of the Soviet empire. And they had to be politically reliable."

"Looks like these three have been a little less than politically reliable."

"Exactly, Captain." Ubul pulls out a pad and consults his notes.

" 'We anticipated the downfall of the Marxist regime in Addis Ababa, learned enough Hungarian to keep going in Budapest, quietly organized an extension of our visas with an unsuspecting official and, without fuss and bother, pursued our studies at the Semmelweis medical university'. Clever sods, aren't they?"

"Careful, Ubul. Don't let your prejudices show."

"Prejudices? What prejudices? I wish I could recruit lads like these into the force. They're brighter and braver than most of the buggers we get."

"He's won you over, Ubul."

Ubul's scowl reappears but he reads on. " 'We sussed out the political direction in which Hungary was moving. We did not want to go back to Africa. Not yet at any rate. Much to our surprise, the ministry responsible for our study programme kept us on the books and paid our tuition fees plus an accommodation allowance'."

"Some bureaucratic practices are clearly unstoppable whoever's in charge."

Ubul ignores my intervention.

"To eat, they had to find jobs. They've cleaned buses, collected garbage and dug holes in roads. Now they're working as orderlies – here in this hospital, no less."

"Let me talk to him now," says Kovacs. "Or better still, let Charlie talk to him."

Ubul scowls again. "He can try. It's taken me the best part of an hour to coax that lot out of him. He says he's avoided the police up to now. He's scared."

"Which is why I want Charlie to have a go."

We move into the side ward where Yohanes lies on his back, staring at the ceiling. The handsome face is scarred with cuts and bruises.

"Yohanes?"

The African's eyes roll sideways as I introduce myself.

"This is Captain Kovacs," I say in English, nodding in the officer's direction. "I am a British journalist. He wants me to ask you some questions. But he wants you to know that you and your friends will stay here overnight. You will have police protection. There'll be an officer at the door of this ward all the time. No one will get to you."

I hope Kovacs can keep that promise.

"In any case, you're in no condition to be moved."

Yohanes makes a sudden impassioned plea. "We want to go back to work when we're well again. And we want naturalisation." He delivers this with an impressive if slightly manic command of both languages. And he wants to tell us more.

"We were walking to our apartment. It's on the fifth floor. The skinheads picked on us as an afterthought. They'd already piled into a Gypsy family accused of every theft in the area for the past six months. Their blood was up."

"And they were looking for someone else to attack?"

"Yes. They threw us to the ground. I took a blow to the head."

He lifts a hand to an ear and winces.

"Efram and Michael were punched and kicked. It lasted for about five minutes. I passed out. I don't know how we ended up in that filthy water. They must have dragged us there. The water revived me but I didn't dare move. Then I lifted my face to see if we could make a run for it."

A young doctor with tired eyes walks in.

"Well?" Kovacs stares hard at him.

"They're OK. But they'll need rest and more treatment for serious head wounds."

"I'm afraid you'll have to put up with one of my men on the main door."

The doctor shrugs and leaves. Yohanes slumps back into his pillow. Before we realise it, he's fast asleep. Kovacs beckons to Ubul and me and we set off down the long corridor.

"I'm damned if I'm going to write a report tonight," says Kovacs.

In the dim light of the hospital entrance, they light up. A team of paramedics wheels in the victims of a road accident. A woman in a green plastic raincoat walks past, her arm round the shoulder of a girl I presume is her daughter. Both are weeping silently. Outside, it's raining a tacky drizzle.

Ambling to the car, Kovacs says, "Guess who I saw at our little fracas."

We both look at him like kids expecting sweets.

"He stood well away from the action. Looked like an extra in a James Bond movie."

"Surprise us then," says Ubul.

"Kozma."

We're stopped in our tracks.

"Are you sure?" I ask, gawping at him.

"As God made little apples. And standing next to him, Charlie, was that bastard who kicked you in the balls at the Troika."

"I think," Ubul hisses, "I think we should go back to your lesson in recent political history, Captain."

"What do you mean?"

Kovacs has failed to detect his sergeant's mood. But I've seen the look on his face.

"Peter. You're buggering us about. We experience an evening of violence and high drama in a Budapest slum. We are enrolled as temporary members of a riot squad that sees one of its number killed by a petrol bomb. We rescue three young black men from certain death. I ruin a uniform and you, the first decent pair of shoes you've ever worn."

Ubul is warming up fast.

"And now you tell us, we can all go home to a nice warm bed. And by the way, the man who gives us our orders and signs the authorisation for our salaries is actually conspiring with known criminals, even with illegal immigrants, to provoke mayhem and chaos on our own patch."

I'm thinking I'd better get out of the firing line.

"Well, fuck you, Kovacs. Drive yourself home."

Ubul tosses the car keys at Kovacs and runs off towards a taxi rank.

"Sergeant. Come back. I order you," shouts Kovacs.

"You can order till hell freezes over, Kovacs."

Ubul has turned on his heel. He sprints towards a group of cab drivers taking more than a mild interest in the rumpus.

"You can't let a night's work end like this," I say to Kovacs.

He runs on, trumpeting Ubul's name into the damp night air.

"OK. I'm sorry," he gasps as he reaches the line of cabs.

Ubul is clambering into a back seat. The driver hesitates as he opens his own door. Even at this distance, his eyes tell me he doesn't relish being party to a punch-up between two men decidedly bigger than himself. There'll be damage to the cab. It'll be very boring and lose him a night's trade.

But Ubul knows he's already lost the battle of wills. He climbs out, shoves some notes into the driver's hand and faces the breathless Kovacs.

"You come one step nearer and I'll bust your nose. I won't give a sod if Charlie Barrow is a witness to assault and battery. And I don't care if I'm disciplined and fired."

I get between them. It's not the wisest move I can make but I have this crazy notion about moral obligations.

"Out of way, Charlie," says Ubul. "This is between him and me. And incidentally, you're around too often for my liking."

"I think I've realised that, Sergeant."

"Good."

He's calming down and he hasn't blown all his gaskets.

"Kovacs. I want a pledge from you," he says. "A promise that you tell all. To me. Fucking everything about this case."

Kovacs is about to speak but gets no further than a gesture of compliance. Ubul catches his breath.

"I also demand a commitment to the purchase of a new parka, new slacks, two shirts and a pair of shoes out of departmental funds. And right now I want one of your expensive German cigarettes – the ones you get from Charlie Barrow."

I'm already fishing about in my pocket.

"And you will buy me a beer at Mitzi's because I bloody well deserve it."

I toss the smokes at him and he catches the pack like a practised English cricketer.

"If I put my hand on my heart," says Kovacs, "you'll only accuse me of poncing about."

"Captain. I may have my lighter side. But this time I'm not kidding. Promise me, you bastard. Promise me."

"Sergeant Ubul. What would I do without you?"

"Precisely, Kovacs. What would you do without me?"

I'm already walking away. After this little lot, three is definitely a crowd. And they don't try to stop me.

PART 6

Chapter 1

The room is long, large and featureless. It has whitewashed walls of breezeblock, high windows and a concrete floor. The air is circulated by a creaking fan, its flex trailing to bared wire ends fixed into the wall by a couple of matchsticks. The place serves as an office by day and a gymnasium in the evening when the settlement's young males play crude games of soccer or volleyball.

Coro takes in the faces lining up to present grievances and petitions to a middle-aged Roma sitting at a rickety table. Here are the old, the pale and the careworn, pathetic yet hopeful, the faces of the long-suffering who spend most of their lives waiting passively for permits, dockets, hand-outs and an inkling of encouraging news. Coro and Kalman have come early in the day to see the man at the table.

"The boy's business is urgent, Tivadar." Kalman tells Coro's story with judicious embellishments and discreet omissions. The old man has warned him that, good as his case is, engaging the Roma leader's sympathy will be an up-hill struggle. A few twists and turns in the narrative will not be out of place.

"Just keep a straight face, Coro. And fix an eye on Tivadar. It'll help to break him down."

"Everybody's business is urgent, Kalman Olah."

Tivadar's drooping moustache heightens the air of cynicism he feels it necessary to convey to those asking favours.

"Don't mess me around, you old fraud. This is special."

"He's an illegal immigrant, Kalman Olah. That's all there is to it."

"Which is why he needs the right papers. From you. Now. Yes?"

Tivadar leans back in his chair, bends to the right and rummages in a battered leather portmanteau. Like someone playing patience, he lays out what Kalman knows is a set of application forms for a residence permit. One white, one pink, one blue. He leans back again and produces two scruffy pieces of carbon paper. With elaborate ceremony he inserts them between the forms.

"What's all that shit?" asks Kalman.

"That 'shit' is very necessary shit. If the police or some clever dick of a magistrate decide to check my records one day and find I've been doling out permits like confetti, you won't have a friend to do your bidding next time."

"But he can't put down that he was born in Romania, you fool. He can't say he studied there, worked there, crept across the border without a passport. Can he?"

"What he writes on the forms is his business. I don't care about the details. Just as long as I have something to show the authorities when they come snooping."

"However did a Roma turn himself into a faceless bureaucrat?" Kalman sighs the sigh of one whose acumen makes him despise those of his kind who show no energy or enterprise.

"Look," says Tivadar. He pauses before continuing. "I know what you have done for our people. I know we owe you a lot. But….."

Coro listens hard. He understands that Kalman Olah is no ordinary Roma. What he hasn't realised is the extent of the old man's network, his contacts with *gazo* officials, politicians and business people.

"Some of them quite like us," Kalman tells him later.

"And they're willing to help?"

"A few are. But it's hard work. I've had to spend a lifetime dealing with hard-nosed café proprietors and hoteliers, artists and academics. I've lobbied and cajoled them. I've put pressure on and squeezed cash out of them. My bankers in Austria have taught me how to invest, create trusts, and pay as little tax as is decent."

Kalman says he has no conscience about tax-dodging.

"The state doesn't do much for us. Why pay up when there's next to no return? At least the government has said it will match every forint we can raise ourselves with one from the national treasury. That's how we got our college built. And the clinics in the settlements."

He bears down on Tivadar.

"Yes, you owe me," he says. "And what you owe me right now is a nice, clean, piece of paper giving this man the right to live in your poky little village. We'll stick a photograph on it – a picture of his handsome, young face, Tivadar."

The bureaucrat looks down at the table, fiddles with his fingernails and scratches an earlobe.

"What is it?" asks Kalman. "You're hiding something."

The fan hums. Two sparrows fly in through a window, their chatter bursting into the tension. Tivadar summons up his courage.

"We have a sick child here. She needs treatment. The clinic can't….."

"For God's sake. Why do you keep holding out on me, you brainless man? What do you need? What's wrong with the child? Why do we have to waste time bargaining like this when it isn't necessary?"

"She's six years old," says Tivadar timidly. "She fell into a coma three days ago. Her father's away in Szeged. Her mother is feckless. Her sister came to me yesterday." He nods towards a teenager watching them from the doorway.

"So the girl needs a doctor."

Kalman is almost breathless with rage.

"Here's your bargain then. Show me the house. You, girl, show me where you live."

Kalman stalks out into the dusty yard pursued by garrulous villagers who scurry behind him as if he's the pied piper. Coro tries to fend them off but they're not going to be denied. The girl leads them down an alleyway of dried mud to a shack with dun, concrete walls. At the door, Kalman swings round and hisses at the crowd.

"Go and gossip somewhere else. The sick need peace and quiet." And to the girl, "Show me."

They stoop into a single room. The door and window are open but the air is stifling. Coro gags at the stench of urine and sweat. In a corner, on a bed of dishevelled clothes, the sick girl lies, apparently asleep, barely breathing. Kneeling beside her is a woman, gently wiping the child's forehead with a moistened cloth. She doesn't look up as the strangers enter.

Kalman bends low and speaks softly. "Mother. She must go away. She is very ill. Do you understand?"

The woman turns and stares with reddened eyes and sees nothing beyond the old man's smile.

"Stay here, Coro. I'll bring the car to end of the alley. We'll take the girl to Szolnok. There's a hospital there and the doctors are good to us."

The mother gives out a sudden wail. Tivadar hangs his head.

"Fix this family up with some extra food," Kalman orders. "Take them to your office or to some neighbours. And have this place swept and cleaned. Every germ in Christendom must find a welcome in here."

Tivadar nods his assent.

"And never, never, do this to me again," says Kalman. "You don't need to bargain for this kind of help. And I don't need to bargain for residence permits when death hangs in the air. But you do know what I expect of you when I get back from Szolnok, don't you?"

He strides off.

Coro lifts the child from her bed and carries her to the end of the alleyway. Kalman has the Mercedes ready with the engine running. He opens the rear door, takes the girl from Coro and eases her on to the back seat. He closes the door as gently as he can. But once in the driving seat, he guns the accelerator, turns the car in a wide arc and heads for the highway. Coro risks a glance and sees energy and fury combined.

"I know. This is faster than I'm used to," says Kalman "But don't ask me to slow down."

Hours later, they're travelling much more sedately, making their melancholy way back to the settlement. They head for Tivadar's office, dim now in the evening light, to report the death from spinal meningitis of one Margit, daughter of Anna and Gyorgy, sister of Rosa, a bright kid, they said, before she fell so desperately ill – a kid who laughed a lot, already knew her letters and, with her sweet voice, sang the lays of her tribe.

"I suppose you're still blaming me," says the official.

"What's the point, Tivadar? It's a harsh lesson to learn."

Tivadar stares at the piles of paper on his desk. But remorse is not in his character.

Coro passes a sleepless night. Time and again, with the aid of a torch, he peers at the document Kalman Olah has procured for him, a card in a plastic holder saying he's a resident of Ketpo Roma settlement in Jasz – Nagykun – Szolnok county in the Republic of Hungary. He's no longer an 'illegal'.

But the visit to Ketpo has stirred uncomfortable thoughts. Is this the way Roma are expected to live, in soulless hovels in the middle of nowhere under leaders as desiccated as Tivadar?

"If I'm forced to spend time with them, maybe I'll learn something," he says to himself.

He stares into the night and listens to the wind.

"Forget it. Stick with Kalman Olah. Be his 'roadie'. He's your best chance."

Chapter 2

The weather has cooled. By dawn, grey clouds hang over the river. There's no breeze and the reeds and sunflower stalks hardly move. Kalman has resorted to his greatcoat. He and Coro exchange the briefest of greetings, eat an aimless breakfast and wander up and down the dusty patch of ground in front of their tents, mugs of coffee in one hand, cobs of bread in the other. Even the dogs have caught the mood. They squat where they can, snouts tucked into paws, morose and wary. The rest of the clan stay in the campervans. The odd muttered remark floats on the sullen air. Coro can't make out the words but he can guess their meaning.

"If the old man's in the same frame of mind as the dogs, I'm in trouble." He lets the thought expand in his head. "Perhaps, after all, they think I've brought them bad luck."

He's had his first row with Kalman.

"You stay at Ketpo for a month and establish your right of residence. Tivadar isn't a generous man but he'll make sure you get work and earn your keep. God knows, that place needs able-bodied men to do the heavier jobs."

Coro says he doesn't relish the prospect.

"Of course you don't," says Kalman. "But Tivadar has his eye on you. He wants to offload some of his more tedious bureaucratic tasks. You can read and write. You can make sense of the jargon in those documents the authorities keep throwing at him. You'll be busy enough. The time will pass quickly. Before you know where you are you'll be back with us."

"What about Judit?"

"What *about* Judit?"

"You know I'm smitten, Kalman."

The old man smiles and thanks his stars that Judit was too young when the son of an Austrian restaurant owner recently asked if he could marry her. Judit told Coro the story.

"In any case, he was *gazo*," she says. "But they want me to marry now. They don't say so to my face. Isn't it strange that big, strapping men can't bring themselves to talk about delicate subjects? They always have to wait for some crisis to push them into decisions. But my mother drops hints, Coro. She's almost as taken with you as I am."

She runs off, laughing over her shoulder. He's overwhelmed again by her dark, silken skin, her slender waist, even her mockery. He's wretched about her.

Kalman's question rouses him from his reverie.

"Do you want to talk?"

Coro looks into the wrinkled face. Kalman beckons to a wooden bench. The dogs, glad that some human is making a positive move, follow, tails wagging in slow motion.

"I know what you're thinking, Coro. You thought life for the Roma here wouldn't be as bad as I'd painted it. Nothing could be as desperate as Romania. And now you know it is."

Coro bites his lip and looks down at the ground.

"You feel guilty because you've had the luck to meet the Olah clan. And we are different. We're not shiftless and dependent. And we've been good to you. But now you think you ought to abandon us and dedicate yourself to the feckless and the poor."

Coro holds up his hand. "You're not being fair, Kalman."

The old man lets him gather his words.

"I have drowned in your generosity," says Coro. "I love your zest for life. I'm impressed by your enterprise. And I've fallen in love with your granddaughter."

"But you do not think your future lies with us? Being a 'roadie' isn't good enough?"

"I don't know what to think. I'm as confused now as I was the day I jumped from the train and walked into your camp. But I do not want you to think that I am throwing your kindness back in your face."

Kalman lights his pipe and steadies himself for a mental ordeal.

"I know," he begins firmly and slowly, "that you are the best thing to happen to this family for many months. Ask them. Ask Jenoe and the others. Ask my wife. Do you know why they are not jealous of you? For they could be. They might easily have seen you as an intruder. Jenoe might look on you as the thief who stole his daughter. But no. They saw in you the person who saved me from tumbling into mean old age. When Jenoe said I was getting sick of all the organizing, the bargaining with *gazo* restaurant owners, all the arguing and planning ahead, he was telling you that I'd become a burden to the family, a dismal old dog who never laughed any more, never danced at festivals with his much put upon wife, never had a kind word for the gaggle of beautiful grandchildren they've given me."

Kalman is smiling at last.

"Do you know why we had such a celebration that first time, when we brought out all the instruments and Judit made you jump about like a young stallion?"

He pauses to inhale. The clouds have parted a little and a watery sun is breaking through. The dogs wag their tails again.

"Because we were glad, not just that you'd survived – a Roma who'd beaten the system. But because *I had survived.* I was purged of a sickness. Relief, Coro. Uncontrollable relief. We were happy again. And we were happy because you were sharing our happiness."

Kalman pauses before uttering the truth he's afraid of.

"You are my new son, Coro."

His hands shake and his eyes grow moist, not with the rheum of old age but with tears he rarely sheds.

"I know it sounds maudlin. But that is your value to my family. Ask them. Go on, ask them."

Coro looks round and sees the whole clan standing in front of the campervans, watching and smiling, while Judit and her grandmother walk towards the bench. Kalman's wife ruffles his hair, seizes her husband and embraces him. Judit takes Coro's hand, looks at him wistfully and, flaunting custom, plants two gentle kisses on his flushed cheeks. The children run forward, dance round them and scamper off again pursued by barking dogs.

And suddenly there is talk of a wedding. Grandmother and Jenoe's wife are already discussing the preparations. Kalman Olah lets them jabber on and watches Coro's face. The boy is dazed. He holds on to Judit's hand as if his life depends on it.

"Perhaps it will be Judit who guides Coro out of his confusion," Kalman says to no one in particular. Women these days are so forceful, far more determined to have their way. He can't decide whether he approves or not. So many things have changed in a life of war, persecution, poverty and revived fortune. And the women have suffered most.

Kalman gazes at the sky. The morning has brightened. He puts another match to his pipe and pulls his greatcoat more squarely on to his shoulders. His favourite *mudi* has ambled back and flopped at his feet. It looks at him with soulful eyes. And Kalman nods back.

PART 7

Chapter 1

I am running down the middle of a long, dark boulevard. It might be Ulloi, or Kerepesi, or Rakoczi. There's no traffic unless you count the tanks parked on either side. It's the middle of the day. But a seamless canopy of smoke blots out all natural light. I run because I am the quarry, knowing that if I trip over the debris, the broken bricks, the twisted metal and the charred beams, I shall be caught, dragged to a lamp post and hanged.

They're gaining on me. A crescendo of yelling fills my ears. I try to keep my eyes on the far end of the street, a target that gets no nearer, despite my pounding heart and bursting lungs.

I see a flashing sign. '*KISPIPA*'. Shall I head for the door? The acrid smells are momentarily displaced by the imagined taste of soup and dumplings, grilled fish and gherkins.

My way is barred by a group of men in helmets and greatcoats brandishing pistols and machine guns. I stop. A sudden inferno erupts in the building to my left. The rising thunder of collapsing walls makes even the troops cower. But the mob crowds in on me. Someone takes aim. Another shouts.

"Nyilas. Nyilaskeresztes."

I snore and splutter and am suddenly awake. Words form fitfully on my dried lips.

"Nyilas – Arrow Cross."

I smell alcohol and sweat. Spilled beer has stained the carpet. The dampness in my armpits tells me it would be a good idea to take a shower.

First though I shall brew fresh coffee. I pinch the bridge of my nose and heave my aching frame out of the chair. The plaid rug falls away and both the book and the gun thump on to the floor.

I peer at my watch and discover it's early evening. I've slept through the best part of the day. I recall a restless night, tossing and turning in the armchair, fearful of another silent visitor and a second message pushed through the letter box. I took the gun again and kept it on my lap.

Did I wake at daybreak? I remember that I tried to read *The Circle of Hell*. I drifted off and fell into a deeper sleep that brought on the nightmare.

"Must get organized," I mutter, heading for the bathroom.

There is smell in the air. It leads me to the door. I see it just in time, an envelope, once white, now stained by the shit inside.

"Oh, Christ, no. Not again."

I swing open the door. But there's no dead cat this time. Just another piece of paper. And a similar message.

"Right, you swine. That's it. No more backing off."

I try the phone. Fred in London is in a meeting and Kovacs is out.

I clean up the mess, and consign the paper to the waste bin. Then shower and shave, and find a clean shirt. The pile is going down. I'll have to sort out the dirty linen for Zdenka. Thank the Lord for Zdenka. She comes twice a week, takes away the washing and leaves the place spotless. Such order as there is in my life is her doing.

I found her through the man who runs the local *trafik*, the corner kiosk where I buy Marlboro's and metro tickets.

"I'm looking for a woman," I said artlessly.

"Aren't we all?" he responded.

Among the many adverts for so-called teachers of English, piano tutors, painters, plasterers and plumbers, I spotted one boldly announcing that 'a superior cleaner' was available. She took in laundry. Her rates were 'negotiable'.

"Know her, do you?" I asked.

"Don't know any of 'em. But I think that one's Slovak. Came and argued the toss over the price of the ad. A pain in the arse."

Zdenka turns out to be a formidable lady in her mid-forties. Her Hungarian is heavily spiced with the idiom of her native language but we get on well. She lives in a block in Zuglo. Her pride and joy is her washing machine. Hence her offer to do my shirts etc. She doesn't exactly mother me but gets indignant if I try to help her with the housework.

"Such a lovely place, Mr Charlie."

I decide the only way to hang on to this gem is to pay her more than the going rate.

"My God," she says. "You got money to burn?"

"No. But I know a good thing when I see it."

She smiles a very winning smile.

I shall have to explain to her that pressure of work prevents me from preparing the usual pile of soiled clothes which I normally stuff into a cloth bag. This hangs behind the bathroom door, reminding me of school. C. Barrow, House 3. My aunt, who had more domestic skills than my socially climbing mother, sewed on the label just before I set out for that miserable first term.

I try Kovacs's numbers again.

Where the hell is he at this time of day? I'm missing something here. But short of motoring all over Budapest and enquiring at every police post, there's nothing to be done.

And I've given up on Fred, who by now will be in some watering hole or slumped inside a filthy railway carriage heading for London's south western suburbs.

My innards are rumbling loudly enough to cause social embarrassment. I think longingly of the Kispipa. I could be knocked on the head as soon as I step outside. But I can take the gun.

At which point I recall my nightmare. There is one more call to be made.

Professor Gyula Bokor, author of *The Circle of Hell*, answers his phone promptly. I explain my mission. He's wary at first. Like many Hungarian academics, he despises journalists, categorising their writing as half-baked, superficial and misleading. Gyula Bokor was fired by the communists and thrown into jail, to be re-instated in his teaching posts when the Kadar regime recognized the benefits of relative liberalisation. He is not accustomed to speaking without careful thought. His recent book has brought him some fame and not a little fortune. It's been called an honest assessment of Hungary's role as both Hitler's and Stalin's ally. But it's also provoked unseemly vituperation from the New Right and the Old Left as well as nasty pieces of paper through his letterbox.

"I've had a couple of those," I say. I decide to keep quiet about the cat.

This changes the professor's mood. "Be careful, Mr Barrow. These are dangerous people. Really dangerous people."

I ask again if he'll see me.

"Would you like to pop round tomorrow to my office in the university?"

"Admirable. And thank you."

"I keep a good *barackpalinka* in my sideboard. It should warm us up on a cold November day," he chuckles. "And steady our nerves into the bargain."

I judge him to be a likeable soul who might be willing to give me much of what I need to satisfy Fred's demands for detailed background. I promise to be there at two.

I grab my coat and draw back the bolt as noisily as I can. I step on to the landing. No one. I clatter down the stairs into the lobby. Still no one. I walk to the car, unlock the door and half expect it to explode in a final obliterating fireball. Memories of Belfast are crowding in again. Training and instinct make me scan the gloomy street. There's the odd pedestrian and the traffic moves normally. No suspect shadows. No unnatural movements. And no offensive handbills stuck to my windscreen. And yet the moist evening air depresses me.

I drive to the Kispipa but park this time in the light of the Hotel Emke. I prefer to walk at a measured pace into the darker part of Acacfa with a hand on the gun in the pocket of my overcoat.

I am about to turn into the Kispipa's entrance. A figure moves smartly across my path from another doorway. I draw the gun and whip the butt across the balaclavaed face, once and back again. He hasn't time to move.

I strike hard at his windpipe, just as I was taught all those years ago on that mightily useful self-defence course. My victim hardly groans as he falls in a heap at my feet.

"My turn this time, you bastard."

A car approaches but moves on with a quick flash of its headlights.

I look right and left, tuck the gun back into my pocket and walk as calmly as I dare into the restaurant. Ten minutes later, sipping a steadying Scotch at the bar and listening appreciatively to Irvin's rendering of *Georgia On My Mind*, I note the entry of a slightly harassed young police officer. Irvin stops playing, intercepts the cop and follows him outside. A couple of minutes later, he returns alone, nods to his head waiter who comes over for a short tete-a-tete. Irvin joins me at the bar.

"Trouble?" I ask.

"Er…..no. No trouble."

"What did the cop want, Irvin? Not been paying the right protection money?"

Irvin is not amused and I quickly backtrack.

"Sorry," I say. "Out of order. Uncalled for. My apologies."

"I run a good place, Charlie, don't you think? Respectable, reasonably priced. I rarely have…..trouble."

"But…..?"

"Sometimes, some fool of a drunk tries to push his way in." He lowers his voice. "This one fell flat on his face before he could get through the door. Or somebody hit him. He was out. Stone cold. The policeman couldn't understand why he was wearing one of those woolen things over his face. If he was out to mug somebody, he definitely missed his chance."

Irvin risks a slightly hysterical giggle.

"They bundled him into the back of a squad car. Odd, isn't it? By the way, did you see him outside? Couldn't have been far behind you."

"Me? Good Lord, no. Never set eyes on anyone. Too dark out there."

"Yes," muses Irvin. "I must get that entrance light fixed."

He brightens up and raises his glass.

"Cheers, Charlie. I accept your apology. Have one on the house."

Irvin resumes his version of Hoagy Carmichael. I dine alone again. If I wasn't wondering where Kovacs is, I'd be relishing every mouthful with my confidence restored.

The *maitre d'* comes over. "A call for you, Mr Barrow."

I slide over to the bar and he hands me the phone.

"Charlie?"

"Sergeant. Where are you?"

"Mitzi's," says Ubul. "Join me."

Chapter 2

Ubul sits in the usual corner nursing a beer. A cigarette smoulders in one of Mitzi's large pot ashtrays.

"This is a surprise," I say. "I thought you'd ruled me out of the charmed circle."

"Sit down," he says. "Want one of these?" He flicks his fingers.

"Where's Kovacs?" I ask.

"You tell me. I've been trying to get hold of him for most of the day. But he's gone off on his own. He isn't even answering his pretty little mobile phone."

"So what's this all about?"

"I want to share some thoughts with you, Charlie Barrow. Thoughts that came into my head after that little argument you witnessed last night."

"Go on then."

"I asked Kovacs to tell me all….."

" 'Fucking everything' is what you said."

Kovacs, he goes on, came up with a frightening tale.

"Not housebreaking, car theft or mugging. Nothing commonplace. Not even illegal immigration. This was about vicious protection rackets, gangs who wreck shops and cafes and pubs like this one."

"So, why are you telling me this?"

"Let me finish. Kovacs named," he says this with fervent emphasis, "*he named* politicians and ex-party cadres who've been bought off to push certain issues in parliament, to rant and rave against Jews and Gypsies and gays. Jews, because they're taking over the economy, the media, art and culture."

"Bollocks," I say.

"Shut up and listen," says Ubul.

"Gypsies, because they're the scum of the earth," he goes on. "And gays, because, since macho fornication is approved conduct for the true Magyar male, queers, poofters, TV's and fancy men dilute that image – the image of the New Hungarian, who's going to get rid of all this insipid, democratic nonsense, make Hungary great again and call in the forgotten legacy of Miklos Horthy and the Arrow Cross."

"That's strong stuff," I say downing half my beer.

"I haven't finished." He calls for two more. "Kovacs told me about his contacts, people he trusted at the top – old communists who were feeding him information about people they called 'deviants'."

"An odd euphemism. Without sounding pompous, can I ask what these people are deviating *from*?"

He hasn't understood the question.

"Ubul, as far as I am concerned, former communists can only deviate from ways that were essentially bad in the first place. Why are Kovacs's contacts necessarily the good boys while those they don't like are naughty and wicked?"

"You journalists are full of shit, aren't you?" Ubul wears his usual scowl and I suddenly realise I may have played a very bad hand. "Full of high-falutin crap."

"That's nearer the truth than you suppose." I tell him about the messages and the dead cat.

"Godfather stuff, eh?"

"I think that was a horse's head. But no more sick-making than my moggy."

I draw deeply on my cigarette. "Carry on."

"Kozma."

"Ah," I exhale. "And?"

"Kovacs knows enough about our boss to bring him out in a cold sweat and keep him awake in the small hours."

"Kovacs or Kozma?"

"Don't fuck about. Kovacs is a troubled man."

"I'd guessed that."

"Kozma has blocked investigations into crimes to which he is party through pay-offs and favours. He's in league with all kinds of villains – foreigners – Croats, Serbs, Slovenes, Russians, Chechens. They keep popping up in funny places."

"Like second-rate eating houses and the less salubrious parts of Budapest. Last night's riot for example?"

"Right."

"Any evidence?"

"No. Nothing that'll stand up in court. Kovacs said his contacts were too scared to go public."

"Nothing to back up *any* of his allegations?"

"Kovacs says he's got documents and bits of paper which Kozma would probably wish he didn't have. But they don't amount to a body of proof that'll shaft the bastard."

"So if Kozma gets wind of this, all it takes is a call to the minister and you're screwed."

He looks at me with what I think is renewed respect.

"Well, at least that's not high-falutin," he says.

"Did he tell you his Balaton saga, about frightened hoteliers, drugs and porn and brothels in enchanting lakeside villages where families once took innocent holidays?"

"Yes. It all fits."

"Let's go back to these contacts of his. Apart from those nice ex-communists."

"He has friends in the other parties. They've also been passing on what they know."

"And what do they know?"

"The Right has got people into some of the top posts in radio and TV. It's their job to fire reporters and producers who won't toe the line. Some of those guys worked quite happily under the old system. So they're tainted, even though they're good professionals."

"You're telling me that Kovacs has his sources in both camps?"

"He may be just a cop but he's not averse to a spot of lobbying and political speculation. He thinks they might get together and work within a coalition."

"But that's a dirty word with fascist rabble-rousers and unreconstructed Reds. You know as well as I do – you never work with the enemy. You do all you can to destroy him. If you're in a position to milk the system, Left or Right, you either cling on to what you've got, like a nice house in Buda which the party gave you for loyal service, or you cheat and thieve your way to the top, buying up state assets and selling them off at a handsome profit. And you don't pay taxes."

"You seem to know a lot already, Charlie Barrow."

"I do my research, Ubul."

"Oh, is that what you call it?"

We quench our thirst again. Ubul lights up. The smoke curls along the yellowed walls. He chews his lower lip.

"What was your response to all this?" I ask.

"I told him he was in deep, deeper than the average cop should be. His neutrality as the new brand of officer, servant of the people and all that, is compromised. I mean, it has to be a kind of positive neutrality – neutrality on the side of the angels."

Ubul uses his large hands, opening and shutting fingers and thumbs like a fan. They claim my attention. I'm the client before the hypnotist.

"But how can you be neutral when you're chasing villains, Charlie?"

"Villains who can't be dealt with according to the law as it stands?"

"Or according to the law as our new democrats would like it practised. Justice *and* Retribution. Both at the same time. Kozma is guilty *before* he's tried and Kovacs will make bloody sure the judge knows that *before* the case is even heard."

"Dear me. He has upset you."

"No he hasn't. He apologised for keeping me in the dark thus far."

Ubul smiles at the memory of his little victory.

"Then he asked me if I'd go along with him – all the way."

"And you said…..?"

" 'Have I got any choice, Kovacs? Like you said, what would you do without me?' "

He stubs out his cigarette and zips his parka up to the throat. There's a murmur of chat among the regulars in another alcove. The traffic rumbles outside the frosted glass. The pub isn't cosy any longer.

"See you at the hospital at eight. And don't forget to pay, Charlie."

Chapter 3

Yohanes has recovered. He's his talkative self again. Which makes it hard for me to keep up with him at this hour of the morning. He wants to tell me everything, about the times he and his friends were the target of crude jokes from the skinheads, how they were spat at as they rounded the corner at the end of the block, and how they had to paint out the graffiti scrawled across their door.

"That can of emulsion was an expensive way of salvaging pride," he says and frowns at the memory. "It went on for months. They were only isolated incidents at first. Then it was obvious the threats and slogans were part of a campaign to get us out of there."

He sighs and shifts into a more comfortable position on the bed.

"They found out what time we finished work and lay in wait. There'd be two of them at the bus stop. They'd follow us, shouting things we couldn't understand, though we knew what they meant. Then there'd be three or more at the end of the access road and still more at the entrance to the elevator. The group would grow, chanting and jeering, pushing and shoving, just enough to jangle the nerves but not so violent as to make us lash out."

"But you did lash out in the end?" I ask.

"At first we tried laughing at them, you know, trying to make a joke of it. But that only made them worse. Then we said we wanted to talk. We asked them why they were against us. 'You're black,' they said. 'Niggers and foreigners. You've got our jobs and you want to fuck our women. You're scum.' "

"Enough to try anyone's patience," I chip in lamely.

"One night, Michael lost his temper. He was jostled. He hit back, hit hard. The guy doubled up. The others backed off. They were stunned. They never thought we'd have the guts to do it. But it didn't last long. They came for us and we had to run."

"Where to?"

"We just made it to the elevator. It's so slow. When we got to our floor, three of them had rushed up the stairwell to meet us. We had to fight. Michael did more damage. He broke a couple of noses. Efram and I just punched and kicked as hard as we could. Eventually they backed off again after a woman in one of the apartments screamed at them to stop. And told us to get out."

"Were there any more fights?" I ask.

"A few. We talked about moving. But we couldn't afford to really. As foreign students, we'd been assigned our place by the ministry. And they paid the rent."

"That was clever of you."

He smiles.

"One night though, about a month ago, we walked across that patch where the riot took place. The skins hardly glanced at us. They whistled and yelled but nobody moved in on us. They were listening to this man standing on a crate. I couldn't understand half of what he said. And we weren't hanging around."

"What did this man look like?"

Yohanes ponders the question. Then his eyes grow bright.

"He had powerful shoulders, fair hair and a moustache. But he was a long way away."

He pauses and frowns.

"But I do remember the other man."

"What other man?"

"He was standing to one side. He wore a black raincoat. He was big too. Bald. And I remember his eyes. He never blinked. Like a fish."

"You sure of that?"

"Is he important?" asks Yohanes.

"Oh, he's important all right."

Ubul's face is poking through the curtain drawn round the bed.

"I'm not quite finished here, Sergeant."

"Oh yes, you are." He grabs my arm and pulls me into the corridor.

"It's Kovacs isn't it?" I whisper. "He should be here and he isn't."

"He phoned late last night and said he'd meet us here. After I put the phone down, I remembered something I should have told him – about a speech by that right-winger, Szarka. I tried his numbers again. Apartment and mobile. Three times. No answer. I gave up and went to bed."

Ubul rubs a thumb nail against his teeth and scratches an ear.

"Come on. Let's get round to his place," he says.

There's a cry from inside the ward. "I've got more to tell you," Yohanes protests.

Ubul isn't listening. And neither am I. I hare after him, down the corridor, through the main door and out into the car park. The tail of the Opel shimmies over to the right as he swings into the traffic. Petofi is in the back seat.

"Did you tell any one about this?" Ubul growls at him.

"Nobody, Sarge. Not a word. Honest to God."

Petofi is much chastened by the scene that meets us as Ubul slams on the brakes.

"Then why do I see two patrol cars and a big black Mercedes, all of them with blue lights flashing like a clip joint? And in front of the building in which Captain Peter Kovacs has an apartment? Something has gone wrong."

Wearing a face like thunder, Ubul steps up to the line of police tapes.

"Er, sorry, Sarge, but….."

"But what?"

"The boss, Sarge. Colonel Kozma. He says no one….."

"Colonel Kozma can go fuck himself."

The young officer is not about to argue. Ubul leaps up the stairs like a demented circus acrobat. The door to Kovacs's apartment is wide open but a burly type, state security written all over him, bars the way.

"You are…..?"

"I am," – Ubul gathers himself – "I am Sergeant Sandor Ubul of the Illegal Immigration Squad. And I am informed that my superior, Captain Peter Kovacs is…..in some difficulty." Ubul's boxer's nose is within an inch of his interlocutor's chin. "I have come to assist him."

They glare at one another.

"Who the hell are you?" asks Ubul.

"Don't play the comic with me, Sergeant. You can't go in. That's all there is to it."

Ubul is probably about to commit a serious offence when Kozma appears in the doorway.

"Who is it, Urbach? What's all the noise?"

Ubul is momentarily stunned by Kozma's looming presence but he's in no mood to conduct negotiations through third parties.

"Let me say it again," he intones. "Just in case anyone is in doubt. I am Sergeant Sandor Ubul of the Illegal Immigration Squad and I want to see my superior officer,

Captain Peter Kovacs, outside whose residence I happen to be standing in the reasonable knowledge that he is at home. All in the line of duty…..Sir."

Kozma eyes him with all the disdain he can muster.

"Your superior officer, Sergeant Ubul, is under arrest. It is not necessary for you to have access to him. He is in my charge. I suggest you return to the Western Railway Terminus and get on with your work, which, I am led to believe, is the apprehension of unlawful entrants into this country…..although I am also led to believe that you, and indeed Captain Kovacs, have not been too successful in your mission of late."

"Arrested?" In subsequent conversations, Ubul will confess that at this point his hold on sanity slipped a notch. "On what charge?"

The three words are pronounced deliberately slowly. Ubul has clearly decided he needs time to think and there isn't a lot left to him.

"I have told you." Kozma's voice is a panful of menace. "It is not necessary for you to know any details. Go away."

Ubul gulps, steadies himself and wades in.

"Colonel Kozma. You see standing behind me one Corporal Petofi, also of the Illegal Immigration Squad, bearer of an illustrious revolutionary name but not, as far as I know, related to the great poet of that name."

Kozma sniffs impatiently.

"Behind him," continues Ubul, "one Mr Charles Barrow, a British journalist working for some highly reputable international newspapers."

I nod.

"Now," says Ubul, "apart from the fact that they are witnesses to this little encounter, may I also point out that Mr Barrow and I have tried by every lawful means to get Captain Kovacs to answer his telephone. With no success. Which is why we've come knocking at his door, so to speak."

Anyone watching Ubul's face will have concluded that he is enjoying himself.

"Like me, Mr Barrow has a legitimate interest in seeing the good Captain. It is my…..er……humble opinion therefore that it would not be in any of our interests for you to send us packing. Whatever the pretext under which you have, as you put it, arrested Kovacs, I suggest you share it with us."

Ubul pauses. Petofi's jaw drops a mile. I simply smile.

"Don't threaten me, Sergeant. Apart from the fact that your journalist friend has no right to be here, I am in a position to do your career as a police officer considerable damage if you persist with your insolence….."

"And I, Colonel Kozma, am in a position to…..how shall I put it…..to influence the course of your own career as chief factotum in the Interior Ministry, especially since I have witnesses to your clandestine presence at a riot two nights ago in Angyalfold, an event which you certainly did not attend in your official capacity."

This, Ubul tells me later, is the moment when he and Roszi might have kissed goodbye to that nice little house in Szentendre.

Kozma looks at him for ever. The eyes do not blink.

But Ubul has never been one to cower in front of life's stoats.

"Come in, Sergeant. Just you." This at a slight movement from Petofi. Ubul shakes his head and Petofi backs off.

"I ask you again, Colonel. On what charge are you holding Captain Kovacs?"

Kozma bridles at the question. Then relaxes with a fearsome grin.

"Murder, Sergeant." No one moves.

"Who's he supposed to have murdered?" I ask. Ubul needs moral support. I look straight at Kozma with what I hope is an unwavering professional stare.

"We found Captain Kovacs unconscious under his dining table with a gun in his hand."

"When?"

"Early this morning. And we also found the body of a man in the kitchen. It has not been difficult to….."

"I want to see for myself." Ubul crosses the threshold unhindered. For a reason we can't fathom, Urbach takes his leave, running down the stairs like one possessed and out into the street. The door doesn't quite close, drifting slightly ajar. Petofi and I retreat to the far side of the landing. I bring out my Marlboro's. We light up in silence. Petofi takes a long drag and slowly opens his mouth.

"Fu….."

I put a finger to my lips. "Keep your counsel, officer. It may be needed in court."

***   ***   ***   ***

The door stays ajar. We edge over to eavesdrop. Voices are raised.

"Your distaste for that weapon terrifies me, Colonel."

It's Kovacs.

"It'll go off by itself if you don't get a tighter grip."

"My distaste will not be exceeded by your own discomfort, should you move one jot from that position, Kovacs."

"He's got a gun on him," whispers Petofi an inch from my earlobe.

"I can work that out for myself," I hiss. "Shut up and listen."

"What's Ubul doing?"

"How the hell do I know?"

Kovacs again. "You do use language in a remarkably odd way, Colonel. By the way, may I have a drink of water?"

Kozma gives orders to someone in the room.

We hear the tread of feet on wooden floorboards. Then silence. Then more footsteps.

"Your acolyte in the suit and shiny shoes does well, Kozma. You should employ him as a valet."

"You are in no position to jest. There is a dead man in your kitchen. He has been shot in the chest….."

"And you put him there."

Kozma cackles raucously. "My dear Kovacs, what is the use…..?"

"Kozma. You will listen to my version of events. Sergeant Ubul is a witness and so is your assistant."

"That can wait," snaps Kozma. But Kovacs doesn't wait. We hear him punch the air with words, bellowing an account of what has happened. Kozma tries to shout him down but finally subsides into listening or affecting to listen.

We hear both men breathing noisily like boxers at the end of a bout.

Petofi coughs and Kozma flings the door open waving his gun. We duck but Kozma fails to fire. I see Kovacs lying on the floor. Shiny Shoes is retrieving the water glass. Kovacs shifts his weight on to his left elbow and Shiny Shoes is surprised to find himself full length and face down with Kovacs twisting an arm up his back.

Ubul steps in behind Kozma and quietly relieves him of his weapon. Then he kneels down and takes over from Kovacs. Shiny Shoes is on the point of crying out at the damage being done to his shoulder.

"Be a good boy," says Ubul. "And do stop making a fuss."

Kozma has backed into the room and Petofi and I have followed. Petofi guards the door. I move over to the window overlooking the street.

"Your friend needs to go back to the unarmed combat class, Colonel," says Ubul. Kozma shoots a venomous glance at his assistant. Kovacs is on his feet and dusting himself down.

"Now, Colonel, why don't we all sit down in a civilised manner and talk this over? Establish some facts. Dispel allegations and mutual recriminations and all that sort of thing? I think for a start we should make a combined examination of the corpse we seem to be lumbered with."

"You go nowhere near it." Kozma finds it difficult to control his lower lip.

"Colonel, I think we all know enough by now to assert that your clumsy attempt to pin a murder on me won't wash."

"The bullet in that man's chest is from your own gun, Kovacs. Yours are the only prints on it."

"How do you know that? Forensics haven't been anywhere near that gun yet. The poor sod was shot all right. But more interesting right now is - who bounced me last night? Who took the gun from my unconscious hand and who tricked him into becoming an accessory to his own death?"

Ubul and I exchange glances. Now we know why Kovacs didn't turn up at the hospital.

"You can't prove that," says Kozma. He steps towards Kovacs, then realises he no longer holds a gun. Ubul moves in front of Kovacs and Shiny Shoes stays very still.

"Any more than you can make a murder charge stick," Kovacs answers.

He leans casually against the back of an armchair. "An honest examining magistrate will carve you up, Kozma. Angle of entry, distance, prints on gun showing lack of pressure. What time is this supposed to have happened? I know roughly when I was hit. And here you are, ten hours later, flinging your accusations around in front of a motley collection of your own men. You must be pretty desperate to have staged this little farce."

He stands up straight and clicks his heels. "Comrade Colonel."

"In any case," says Shiny Shoes, "he was shot in the back."

They turn as one. Shiny Shoes swivels his head to meet their collective gaze. There's a distant buzz of chat somewhere outside. The central heating has indigestion again. We hear a car horn and an overflying jet.

"Out of the mouths of….." Ubul breaks off and walks into the kitchen. I follow.

The body is lying on its right side. Kovacs gestures to Shiny Shoes to get up and move into the narrow space between sink and cupboard.

The man kneels, turns the corpse on to its face and points to the burn in the jacket.

"Do you want to see his papers, Sergeant?"

"I don't need to," says Ubul suddenly very weary and wondering where all this is leading.

"Oh, I should if I were you." From his pocket Kozma's assistant produces a passport. Ubul peers at it.

"REPUBLIC OF CROATIA – JANKO DOBROSLAV – D.O.B. 26/03/55."

"It's the bugger who kicked me in the balls and probably killed Lajos," I say.

The apartment door slams.

"Your lord and master has deserted you," says Kovacs.

"For Christ's sake, Peter, why did you let him go?" Ubul storms back into the sitting room.

"Because he's more use to us on the run. And right now, I don't think I could have got away with detaining him. We're still on weak ground here."

"Why didn't he have better back-up?" I ask.

"Arrogance and self-confidence," says Shiny Shoes. "I'll tell you all about it if you'll let me."

"You and I certainly need to talk," says Kovacs.

"For the record, Captain, I didn't do this." He points to the dead Croat.

"I think I believe you. But you're in one hell of a mess." Kovacs is all adrenalin again. "What's your name?"

"Janza, Captain. Pal Janza."

"In that case, Pal Janza. Make some coffee."

We hear the screech of tyres and the roar of a powerful engine.

"Petofi, go and organise a tail."

Petofi scurries out. I hear shouts from outside, open a window and lean out to see him confronting a small crowd.

"Go on. Shove off. The lot of you," he yells.

Then he remembers the first law of policing in a democratic society.

"Ladies and Gentlemen. I beg your pardon. The operation is over. Please don't waste your time hanging around. Thank you very much indeed."

I laugh loudly as they shuffle off muttering collective scepticism at his assurances. Petofi looks up and makes a very rude gesture.

PART 8

Chapter 1

It's Coro's last meal with the clan but as merry as ever. In his honour there is hare and goose and fish livened with paprika, parsley root and bay leaves. And fruit. All washed down with sweet white wine.

Coro has begun the occasion in his regular chair, in the middle of the table to Kalman's left. But as the light fades and the conversation ebbs and flows, he finds himself manoeuvred into a seat next to Judit. There follow the inevitable toasts to success, happiness and long life. Grandmother drifts into sentimental song, spinning the verse to suggest that their guest will soon be a full member of the family.

Coro and Kalman have shelved their problem. Kalman has told him that if he does five or six weeks at Ketpo, that'll be ample time to reflect and make the right decisions. Tomorrow he'll give Coro a lift to the settlement.

"Then," thinks Coro, "you'll abandon me, hoping that desolation brings me to my senses."

Coro feels the touch of a hand and sees the half-smile he was granted all those weeks ago. Judit rises from the table. Jenoe produces his violin and the others bring out more fiddles and a double base. Kalman unleashes his clarinet. They dance their version of the *hora* and the *sarba*. Coro and Judit face one another with hands on hips, never touching but close enough to send the obvious message to the whirling circle crying "Hai, hai" into the evening air, as Jenoe bows the climax of his tempestuous melody.

The ring breaks and the couple dance away along a dusty path, out into a meadow beyond the carab trees.

Their pace slackens. Alone now, they kiss delicately. Judit draws him down into the long grass and their lovemaking is unyielding until both lie half-clothed and desire more of the same.

"Should we be doing this?" asks Coro

The clarinet pierces the night with a long bitter-sweet tune of Kalman's own making. The others intersperse chords from ancient modes. And the women sing verses drawn from their savage ancestry.

Coro and Judit dress and wander back to the camp. It's deserted now except for the dogs that come panting to greet them.

"So it is done," she whispers.

"Are you sorry?" he asks.

"How can I be sorry?"

Coro holds her in his arms.

"What's worrying you?" she asks.

"I want you to come to Ketpo with me. But I know your grandfather won't allow it."

"Neither will my father," says Judit.

She rises and he marvels at her pert breasts, perfect hips and that dark, rich skin. She rouses him again. He responds and glories in it. But the ghosts won't go away. And in the morning, when Judit begs Kalman to change his mind, he is adamant.

"I cannot have you living in a place like that," he says. "It's a hellhole."

"But you're ready to condemn Coro to a six-week sentence."

"You know the reason, Judit. He has to establish his right to residence somewhere. It might as well be there."

"But he has this conscience, grandfather. He might stay at Ketpo out of a sense of duty. He's got this idea in his head about helping others out of their poverty and ignorance."

"He's misguided."

Coro breaks the silence he's been trying to keep.

"If I did not recognise your generosity," he says, "I might call this blackmail."

He's astonished at his own words. Kalman's eyes flash.

"Call it what you like," he says. "This separation is your duty, an obligation you and Judit will fulfil."

Judit storms off in tears.

"Now, let's get in the car and go," says Kalman.

Chapter 2

Tivadar has assigned him a shack abandoned by a family who've moved on. It has two rooms and an outside yard. It stinks of detritus. He spends a whole day trying to clean the place with borrowed mops and buckets. Water has to be carried from a communal stand pipe at the end of the alley. He has no soap and no disinfectant. He tries to make a bonfire of the garbage they've left behind. Children come to watch and laugh when he can't get the stuff to burn. A neighbour, a wizened fellow who speaks little but grins a lot, offers a mugful of kerosene in exchange for a loaf. The fire raises a pall of smoke, bringing complaints from his neighbours. He ignores them.

At night he lies awake and listens to the autumn wind whistling and moaning through gaps between the corrugate iron roof and the rough concrete walls. Among the belongings fetched from the Olah camp is a thick sleeping bag. He thanks his stars there's no need to use the lousy mattress he's inherited. He thinks of Judit and weeps quietly.

By day he forks dung in the cattle pen. He was offered the job by a *gazo* who works the fields next to the settlement. No one else will do it. The men in Ketpo are either too old or too idle. Coro seizes the chance to do a deal which gives him a meagre income. The farmer has told the Roma to use the surplus manure for their own fields.

"But they're lazy," he tells Coro. "They come home once a month from building sites and unskilled factory jobs and spend their wages on drink or gambling. They beat their wives and children, shout abuse at all and sundry."

"And insist on their conjugal rights," thinks Coro, "so that a legalised form of rape produces growing families living in ever greater squalor."

Most of the men snigger at Coro.

"Get yourself a proper job," says one. "There's plenty of work in Szolnok."

He tries to ignore them.

On the morning Kalman drove him to Ketpo, the old man harangued Tivadar about work and wages for Coro. The official pledged the earth but Coro learned quickly that he had no intention of making more than a perfunctory effort to keep his word.

Wages come in the form of credits at the settlement store. But it doesn't take Coro long to discover that these are not buying him as much bread, fruit and cooking oil as the tokens rendered by others. He bides his time until the day Tivadar asks him to make sense of an official document on railway permits for Roma workers. Coro studies the piece of paper, letting the minutes tick by.

Tivadar loses patience. "Well, what does it say?"

"All in good time." Coro turns from his reading and leans across the official's desk.

"Tell me, Tivadar, how much bread is one of those blue tokens supposed to buy?"

"Tokens? Bread?" Tivadar affects some mental arithmetic. "One token – one loaf. Simple."

"Then I'd like to know why old mother Ildiko and that fat bastard Karcsi get two loaves for a token."

"What are you talking about?"

Coro doesn't answer. He's still leaning across the desk.

"I didn't know that," says Tivadar changing tack.

"Oh yes you did. Because *you* get two loaves per token. Or your wife does. Ildiko was daft enough to brag about 'getting the same as the boss'."

Tivadar is working hard to stare him out.

"You're a liar and a thief, Tivadar."

"Watch your mouth….."

"I'll watch it all right next time I see Kalman Olah….."

Tivadar scoffs at the challenge.

"…..or the delegate from the Roma parliament who comes here once a month," Coro goes on. "I've watched you. You won't let anyone else talk to him, will you? Well, I'm going to talk to him. I'm going to tell him – not only do you cheat on tokens, you cheat on wages as well. You keep all the tokens and all the cash in a safe at your place. You reckon to control all the money coming in and going out of this place. You're crafty. But not crafty enough."

Tivadar splutters, trying to keep a semblance of dignity and authority.

"I've been lifting shit in that midden for five days now," says Coro. "It's bloody hard work. But the *gazo* who employs me at least pays something like the going rate. I stink at night because I can't get a decent wash in that slum you've given me. Then you have the cheek to ask me to look at all the stuff that comes in from the county authorities, the police, the railways, so that I'll take the rap if there's a misunderstanding. And I do it for tokens, bloody tokens, Tivadar."

Tivadar tries to rise but Coro rests a hand heavily on his shoulder.

"Now, I'll tell you what I'm going to do and what you're going to do. I will go on being your administrative assistant. And you will pay me cash down for the work I've done and more cash at the end of the week. Forints. Ready money. No more useless bits of paper."

"A hundred an hour," Tivadar mutters.

"A hundred my arse."

Within minutes Coro has walked away with some notes from Tivadar's personal reserve, a signed agreement to pay him for further scrutiny of papers and documents and a verbal pledge to be responsible for any mistakes.

"Oh, and by the way," he adds. "The police want to know how many men you distribute travel warrants to in any one calendar month. I hope you've been keeping proper records."

The shack still stinks and it's still cold at night. But Coro now cooks himself one good meal a day on the Camping Gaz bequeathed to him by Jenoe. He also buys decent coffee which he shames the storekeeper into ferreting out from the back of his stock room.

For four long weeks he never leaves Ketpo. But there comes a Saturday when he decides to walk out of the village, past ploughed fields long harvested of corn, in the hope of catching a bus on the main highway to Torokszentmiklos. The walk gives him time to think of Judit again. But the tedium of the road and the wide open vistas bring only painful memories of the days he spent with the Olahs and visions of his girl and their night of lovemaking. He crosses the railway leading north-west to Szolnok. The klaxon of a locomotive hauling a train of boxcars reminds him of his harrowing introduction to this country. He trudges on and reaches the highway at a lonely T-junction. He's assuming a bus will roll up at some point and take him to the nearest town. But the road carries little traffic at this time of year. Coro is starting to wonder if his excursion has been a good idea after all

Even before he's committed himself, a figure slides out from a roadside shelter. It's a girl wearing a white blouse, short skirt and black boots up to her bare thighs.

"Hullo, darling. Where are you off to then?"

He stands, stunned by her boldness, her raised eyebrow, the way she holds her cigarette and points it at him, her flimsy clothing, her incongruous presence on a cold day in the middle of this wasteland.

"Why don't you come with me, handsome? We could have some fun together."

He says nothing.

She advances, places one hand on his shoulder, spins him round and waves with the other. A battered four-wheel-drive Niva appears from nowhere, brakes hard and pulls up alongside them, skidding in the roadside grit. Two men get out and amble towards him. Their heads are shaven and they wear boots. He knows exactly what they are and starts to run. But the walk's made him weary. He stands no chance. One of the skinheads brings him down and rolls him in the dirt.

"You're coming with us, Gypsy boy."

Coro bites, kicks and scratches like a cat. But they're too strong. A final blow to the head and the fight's gone out of him. The skins drag him by the armpits and bundle him into the back of the Niva.

"In you go, you little bastard. One more for the pot. Big Gyuri will be pleased."

"Just get in, Gabi, and shut your face," says the prostitute taking charge. "We've got a long drive. Fucking good job I spotted him. Otherwise we'd have gone back with bugger all and Gyuri would have belted us. Keep your eye on him. He'll come round before we get to the house. Tie him and gag him."

The other skin lets in the clutch and the Niva plunges forward. A whirlwind of dust and the T-junction is deserted.

PART 9

Chapter 1

Kovacs holds a council of war. We sit at his dining table. Kovacs at one end, Ubul and Janza facing one another. I'm included on the strict understanding that I don't file a word until I get the go-ahead. Aware that the gods are smiling on me, I am more than happy to comply.

Kovacs has given orders for the Croat's body to be taken to the ministry's mortuary.

"Get the 'path' boys on to it," he tells Petofi. "And quickly. Watch your back. God knows what Kozma will try. What news of the tail?"

"The Merc's been seen heading north east," Petofi answers. "He's been using his siren and his lights, so all the patrols assumed he was on legitimate business. No one's followed him. In any case they'd have a hell of a job keeping up."

Petofi departs. Kovacs shrugs and looks at the three of us in turn.

"One dead cop and one dead Croat. I suppose I could have made up a trio of corpses."

"But you don't think Kozma would have gone through with it?" I ask.

Ubul is watching Janza whose brain is clearly working overtime, assessing his prospects.

"I don't know why he didn't kill you there and then, Captain," says Janza. "It doesn't mean he won't find another way of getting rid of you."

"So, if he'd ordered you to do the job yourself, you'd have obeyed him?" Ubul's eyes drill into Janza.

"I might have had to. I still might have to. Unless I assume that Captain Kovacs can wangle my transfer from state security to a police unit."

This boy is too candid and too confident. He looks at Kovacs and wills him to respond.

Kovacs is careful. "We're assuming Kozma is actually guilty of a crime, aren't we? Just because he held me here, even on a false charge, we have nothing else on him, nothing to justify chasing round the country and bringing him in."

"We've got a body, for Christ's sake," says Ubul. "What more do you want?"

Then as the irony strikes, he adds, "Of course you're absolutely right, Captain. Nothing at all." But he can't resist giving his boss an old-fashioned look.

Kovacs drags Ubul's pack of Marlboro's across the table, pulls one out and lights up very deliberately. "Tell us how you got the job then, Janza. Before I recruit anybody, I like to have their CV in front of me. And I know damn all about you."

I surreptitiously produce notebook and biro.

"I'm 26," he says. "Born in Budapest and a graduate of Eotvos Lorand university. My father was an official in the finance ministry, a party member but, like many others, token in his commitment to the system."

Ubul sighs deeply. "Do you have to talk like an intellectual giving a lecture?"

Janza doesn't blink. "The old man's about to retire to a house near Szombathely. The privatisation agency has endorsed his title to it. My mother taught Russian. That's not a skill to admit to these days. But it might come in useful again. You never know. And I have a brother working in the United States."

"Qualifications?" Kovacs asks.

"A law degree." At which Ubul coughs on his Marlboro.

"Recruited how?"

"By some characters in the interior ministry who'd clearly vetted the student body. I passed all their tests."

"Although, as the Captain says, you need a refresher in certain physical aspects of the job." Ubul's jibes are getting nowhere.

"I've worked on various desks," says Janza, "including the old Department III/III, responsible for what was called internal protection. It usually meant sussing out likely political protest before it happened."

"Ah yes." Ubul rests his chin on a hand and glares at Janza with undisguised contempt. "Department III/III," he drawls. "I've often wondered what happened to those bastards." He blows smoke over the top of Janza's head. "I had an uncle who was tortured and killed after '56, punished for organising a strike."

Ubul narrows his eyes and explains for my benefit. "III/III, Charlie, had the job of countering hostile elements. In other words, shopping them to the political police."

"Yes, I know. They had a file on me." I lean back and grin at them.

Kovacs laughs at Ubul's surprise. "Let the man finish," he says. He's as desperate as I am to know about the inner workings of state security. But it's better to let Janza go at his own pace.

"Kozma pulled me in for special duties. These were never clearly defined."

"Your boss has a lot of fingers in a lot of pies," says Kovacs.

"He's an old-style cadre. Offically drawn lines between government departments mean absolutely nothing to him."

"Especially those intended to define the functions of the justice and interior ministries?" I ask.

Janza takes another cue. "Kozma has twisted the arms of a few judges in his time. He's been in the business long enough to know how to bake pies at the right temperature and which oven to choose."

I scribble that one down.

"Go on," says Ubul. "Don't be shy."

Janza allows himself a smile.

"What's so funny then?" Ubul shifts in his chair.

"Easy." Kovacs steadies the tiller. He's aware that the crew of this ship are not as one on the direction in which it should be sailing. Janza squares his shoulders, cracks his fingers and proceeds to speak from an extraordinary memory of cases and events unexplained and unsolved. Later, even Ubul admits he's impressed.

"First, drugs," says Janza. "Hungary is a major transit route for narcotics from Afghanistan, Turkey and the Middle East to Western Europe. In 1988, the last full year of communist rule, the police managed to seize only six kilos of cannabis, heroin and cocaine combined. Then the borders were opened to let East Germans escape in their Trabis and the figure jumped in a year to a thousand kilos. In October, 250 kilos of hashish were found in a truck on the Romanian border. It was on its way from Turkey to London. A couple of weeks ago, thirty six kilos of heroin were unearthed at a flat in Kelenfold. Which suggests that the habit's taken hold here as well. The latest find? 150 kilos of heroin in a Dutch container. Same spot. Romanian border. Same origin. Turkey."

He pauses to sip lukewarm coffee. He has our full attention.

"The twist in the tale is that after the stuff is confiscated, most of it simply vanishes. I can put names to a few addicts but there are no really big fish on my list. I can also identify some whose lifestyles have become unaccountably flashier. But it would be hard to prove they're pushers or dealers."

"And Kozma has this information?" Kovacs asks. I look up from my notebook.

"He knows the general picture," Janza replies. "But he doesn't soak up detail too well. What he does do is keep tabs on suspects like old mates in the ministry, ex-party men, and women, local secretaries turned entrepreneurs, and a few Department III/III people."

Ubul lights up vigorously again and Janza takes the hint.

"As you know, parliament has looked at a law authorising the publication of informers' names - *rendorugynok* - and those of officials given access to agents' reports. But it's run into trouble in the courts. The judges say all this has gone too far."

"Because they may be on the list themselves?" I ask.

"Precisely. Our new democratically elected government tends to agree with them. Ask yourself why. Whatever the answer, agents' names stay state secrets."

"Does Kozma know any of these judges, closely?" I ask.

"Of course he does. He knows them all – closely."

Kovacs sits back and ruminates.

"In 1989," continues Janza, "the departing communists generously handed over to the new government a list of agents, informers and others who'd done work for III/III." He speaks his next words with care.

"They include newly elected members of parliament supporting the government."

Ubul whistles. I want to ask more questions. Kovacs gives me the nod.

"So, senior people in the new parties have moved like grease lightning to block all calls for this so-called Agents' Law to be implemented, especially when those calls have come from within their own ranks. Have I got that right?"

"Exactly, Mr Barrow."

I'm engrossed in my notes but still concentrating on his words.

"It's a classic conspiracy of silence," says Janza, "between the new regime and the old. I suppose I should be grateful that this government has declined to support the publication of names. But those who want this out in the open are not after people like me. What they want are survivors from '56 and the Kadar years. Scapegoats. Which is why they've arrested four former members of III/III."

"Explain," says Ubul.

"You know the story. During the Revolution, they fired into a crowd at Mosonmagyarovar near the Austrian border."

"Have you seen these lists yourself?"

"Some of them, yes. Kozma's name is on at least one of them. He gave an order to shoot – at Mosonmagyarovar and elsewhere."

"Jesus," breathes Ubul.

"So, he's being protected," says Kovacs.

"You think you saw Kozma addressing the crowd before the riot in Angyalfold," says Janza. "And you think you saw our friend in the kitchen, and a man who harangued a crowd of skinheads. Can you be sure of that?"

"I know I saw Kozma. Who's the third man?"

"I'll tell you in a moment. Let's take this one step at a time."

He pauses. Sips coffee again. Steadies himself.

"A month ago, the Supreme Court reduced sentences passed on nearly fifty skinheads convicted on charges of assault and grievous bodily harm. They'd attacked black students. They'd also waded into a group of Gypsies. It happened about a year ago somewhere out in Sashalom. The gang-leader originally got two years. Most of the others, six months to a year. But none of them went down. All the sentences were suspended."

"Kozma put pressure on?" proffers Ubul.

"Spot on, Sergeant."

Ubul looks pleadingly at Kovacs. "Got any *palinka*, Peter? Coffee won't do."

"Bottom cupboard. Left-hand side."

"Who's protecting Kozma?" I ask.

"Protection," says Janza, "comes in two forms. There are those with a stake in the new system but they know they were manipulated by state security. There's ample evidence that some of the new parties and some of their so-called independent newspapers were created on the initiative of Department III/III. What we call the peaceful transition of 1989 was probably the most successful scam it ever engineered."

"That's a depressing nugget of information," I mutter.

"I'm afraid communism did not die a spontaneous death, Mr Barrow."

He moves on.

"Now there are those who simply want to destabilise the new set-up and kill it off. Both lots need help from the likes of Kozma, officials with power and knowledge. And the ultimate aim of all these wreckers is a takeover."

"So I've been told," muses Kovacs.

"I'm in no position to ask who told you, Captain. But give me credit for guessing that what *I've* told you confirms some of your information. You have friends in high places."

Kovacs is not about to fall for that one. "Do I indeed, Janza? Well, given where you've been these last few months, you probably know who's been talking to me."

Janza is treading warily. But we've got this far and neither he nor Kovacs can back off now.

Janza supplies his own answer. "If I'm to be of any use to you, Captain, if I'm on board, and we four, including Mr Barrow, who has all the information to blow this thing out of the water - if we're to are to bring Kozma down, then we pool what we know."

He says this without a trace of disingenuousness. I sense the self-assertion again.

"My material, Janza, is broad brush stuff," says Kovacs. "You have detail. And judging by the look on your face, you're keen to tell us more."

Ubul has poured four generous measures. Janza raises his glass. To our surprise, he proposes a toast.

"To Truth."

We toss back the fiery brandy.

"And Survival," I add.

"In the circumstances, Charlie, that's very apt," says Kovacs.

He asks me to tell the story of my mugging and the threats I've had. I include my research on the Arrow Cross.

Kovacs turns to Janza. "Now, go on," he says.

"You asked me about protection. Last week, for the very first time since I'd worked for him, I saw Kozma close to panic. He called me into his office at lunchtime. The radio was on. He was transfixed."

Janza exercises his prodigious memory again.

"Radio Budapest, 4th November. The minister supervising the secret services has asked the chief prosecutor to dissolve the right wing People's Justice Party. The party is already under investigation following allegations that it has committed incitement against minority communities. It openly promotes the ideas of the Arrow Cross, the fascist organisation led by Ferenc Szalasi, which took power in 1944 and killed or deported thousands of Jews, Roma and others it regarded as its political opponents.

"The minister has also asked the chief prosecutor to enquire into speculation that the PJP either has links with officials in key government departments or has been trying to recruit members from among their staffs....."

"Why was Kozma so taken aback by that?" asks Kovacs.

"Taken aback? He was livid. He demanded to know who had advised the minister. He ranted and raved and threatened to shoot whoever was responsible."

"But I ask you again. Why?"

Janza took a deep breath. "Why would he have been at the riot in Angyalfold?"

"Are you telling us he's personally tied in with the PJP?"

"I can elaborate on that if you want," says Janza. "Unless of course I'm boring you."

"Mr Barrow certainly isn't bored. Are you bored, Ubul? Don't play us for fools, Janza. Just spit it out."

"By the way," Ubul chips in. "We asked you - who was the other guy at the riot?"

"Artur Szarka. Self-styled chairman of the People's Justice Party."

Kovacs slams the table. "Shit. I should have known that."

"On the 9th of November," Janza continues, "Szarka gave an interview to one of the papers. He openly admitted that party members wore uniforms – boots, black trousers and jacket, green shirt and black tie, and an armband with a four-point star. Similar to the Arrow Cross emblem but not identical. He said the PJP has a thousand skinhead supporters. They were disciplined, he said. He used the term 'army-like'. If the PJP won power, it would nationalise all land and dismantle the prisons. Those who committed crimes in future would be isolated from society in settlements."

"I know who I'd stick in his settlements."

Kovacs grins broadly. "Ubul has his pet hates, Janza," he explains.

"And so have I," I grunt. "The PJP would be first on my list."

"Good grief, Charlie," cries Kovacs. "Where have all your good British democratic instincts gone?"

Ubul pours more *palinka*.

"Szarka unashamedly takes every chance to praise the memory of Ferenc Szalasi," says Janza. "He claims the Arrow Cross leader came to power through the will of the people. Then he rambles on about today's 'pseudo-order', a sort of pampered section of society exploiting the jobs-for-the-boys principle. Like one-time party officials. Or 'Jew boys' who've become heads of banks, or industrialists who lend one another vast sums. If the loans go down the drain, they get bailed out by the state with taxpayers' money. Szarka says there are as many as two hundred thousand members of this new *nomenklatura* with access to all the goodies, while the rest of us live in conditions that just get worse."

"Who's to say he's not right?" Kovacs recalls his own data on crime and poverty.

"Yes, he might be," I interject. "Hitler was right in one sense of the word. He gave the Germans self-respect, jobs and sound money. Mussolini made the trains run on time. But look what they did to your country – and mine. Look what they did to your city, for God's sake."

"This bullshit he spouts, Mr Barrow, isn't important," says Janza. "It's what he and his people do, or might do, that matters. He's nothing on his own. He'll probably fade away after the elections. Unless the moles deep inside the Forum government or the old communists who back him with laundered cash – unless they turn him into a credible candidate."

"You almost wear your heart on your sleeve with that statement," I reply. I watch Kovacs smile.

Ubul isn't smiling. "What happened here last night, Janza?"

For the first time since our meeting began, Janza fidgets and hesitates.

"Answer the question," Kovacs orders.

"Kozma called me at home about ten yesterday evening. He didn't explain why I was needed but he made it pretty clear that, however inconvenient it was, I had to be at Andrassy ut in thirty minutes. When I got there, I found Kozma pacing the room like a caged bear. Sitting in the corner was the man we now know as Janko."

"We should be so surprised," says Ubul.

"I'd never been out on 'special ops' with Kozma. I used to get the subsequent paperwork, the stuff he couldn't be bothered with. This time he went to his desk, pulled out a gun and tossed it at me. At least I didn't drop it. I'm not that rusty, Captain."

Ubul makes plain his disdain. "You're stalling, Janza."

Kovacs waves the interruption away.

Janza presses on. "When we entered the vehicle pound, Kozma didn't tell me or Janko where we were going. The black Merc sidled up like some beast in the night. Two patrol cars moved in behind and off we went. It was only when we got here and I read your name-card on the door that I got any inkling of what Kozma was up to. But when I asked him for more information, he just told me to shut up and do as I was told."

"How did you get in?" asks Kovacs.

"Kozma used a set of keys. He seemed to know which one would work. He told me to wait on the landing. He and Janko moved in here. After about five minutes, Kozma came out again and said he and I were going back to the office."

"And then?"

"Janko's call came about two in the morning. Kozma gloated over news which he didn't share with me. He pulled a bottle of Scotch from his desk draw and downed two sizeable slugs. Then he sent out more patrols and said he and I would follow later. We spent the next two hours working on a version of events including an accusation of murder against you, Captain, and a eulogy for teamwork leading to the capture of a criminal within police ranks. We went over it with a fine tooth-comb until Kozma was satisfied there were no holes in the story. Then he let me go to the toilet."

"Janko told him that he'd belted me?" Kovacs rubs the back of his neck.

"Yes. We set out again with that tough, Urbach, in tow. When we got here, we found Janko drinking coffee and you under the table."

"And Kozma takes the gun from Janko, distracts his attention and fires?"

"Exactly. Janko pitched forward and never moved again. Kozma told me to drag the body into the kitchen. He wiped his prints off the gun and put it in your right hand."

"What time was this?" Ubul asks.

"About six thirty."

"So what did you do between then and when I arrived with Charlie and Corporal Petofi? That's two hours for God's sake."

"Kozma said he wanted Captain Kovacs to come round in his own time. You didn't stir until about eight, Captain. I did the clearing up while Kozma paced up and down brandishing his own gun. He also told me go over the cover story to make sure I'd got it right. I know it sounds crazy, but that is what happened."

"Then we showed up?"

"Kozma hadn't reckoned on that."

It's my turn. "He thought he could convince us that Kovacs had been caught in the act. I've interviewed enough suspects in Ireland to recognise the signs. Delusion. What he didn't count on was Kovacs's own bloody-mindedness and, saving your blushes, Captain, your courage. He thought you would cave in because you'd been clobbered and had a filthy headache. Kozma has a propensity to panic brought on by the strain and stress of his double life. That's why he's bolted."

"So what do we do now?" Ubul rubs his chin and realises he needs another shave.

"Watch out for straws in the wind," I say. "Take note of events and pronouncements,"

"What the hell are you talking about, Charlie?" asks Ubul wearily.

"Pronouncements, Ubul. Like your worthy president's recent attack on Szarka. He's already called him a lunatic in public. Makes good speeches, does the president. About democracy taking root in people's minds and their instinctive acceptance of the rule of law."

"Crap," snorts Ubul.

"I don't think so," I add, "with the greatest respect. The head of state is a wise old bird. He's watching straws in the wind too."

"Like what?" asks Kovacs who's observed Ubul and me like someone in the crowd at a tennis match.

I nod to Janza.

"Like opinion polls and local elections results. How the good folk of Miskolc voted for a socialist mayor not so long ago. Note, a socialist."

"But it didn't end there, did it?" I say.

"No. Someone, somewhere in the ministry of interior went against the trend and ordered the police to keep tabs on Szarka's rallies. They put the wind up him. Followed him for ages. Made no attempt to disguise themselves. Stopped him, checked his papers, asked a few polite questions. He protested to a parliamentary privileges committee. Now there's an irony."

The phone rings. Ubul ambles over to answer it. As he takes the call, his face puckers into a frown. "Christ. What a line. It's an out of town call for you, Captain."

147

Kovacs listens hard. "Who is this?" A pause and a frown as puzzled as Ubul's. He shakes the handset and puts it to his ear again.

"Line's gone dead," he says.

"Could it have been Andrea?" I ask.

Kovacs suddenly takes off, hurling himself across the room.

"The note she left."

He finds it pinned to a board near the phone.

"I'd forgotten about this."

"Kozma found it under a glass paperweight last night," says Janza. "It was a bonus for him. The best way to distract you when you came in last night. You fell for it immediately."

Kovacs glares at this. But Ubul gets in before him.

"Yes, we need to talk a little more about your role in that little episode." He shoots Janza one of his poisonous looks.

"Do you remember what happened, Captain?" I ask.

"I remember running up the stairwell and seeing the door ajar. I stuck out a foot and pushed at it. I had my gun out by that time. I crashed into the room and swung it round in an arc. The lights were on. Andrea always leaves the lights on."

"But the door?"

"That's what bothered me. I closed it, letting the lock click into place. I went into the bedroom. No Andrea. And the bed was undisturbed."

"Then you saw the note pinned to the table," says Janza. "Janko was watching you from the kitchen."

"What does it say?" Ubul asks.

"Sweetheart. Sorry not to be here. Have been sent to Ozd of all places. Steelworks story. Bad accident. Workers killed. Charges of poor maintenance, negligence etc….."

"I heard that on the radio," I say. "That's not the sort of thing Andrea goes for."

The room is quiet. A radiator gurgles. Kovacs isn't looking at them. His eyes are glued to the piece of paper.

"Ozd," says Janza breaking the silence.

"What about it?"

"Kozma poked his nose into the official audit of a steelworks privatisation in Ozd."

"What's that got to do with us?"

"Two years ago the state assets agency offered to sell more than eleven billion forints worth of plant and machinery to a consortium of German companies and a bunch of ex-party cadres. But *their* price was only a billion. The Germans smelled a rat. The sale fell through. Since then, the assets have apparently been written off as worthless, while the finance ministry has poured four and half billion into Ozd just to keep it going. So the audit office wants to know where the money's gone. But when it's tried to question officials at the assets agency, guess who blocks the investigation?"

"How come Kozma can put a stop to an audit agency enquiry?" I ask. "He's got no authority there."

"Fingers and pies again," replies Janza. "You forget. This is a man who doesn't give a damn for demarcated jurisdiction. He might once have been a good communist, though I doubt it. But it taught him how to use the system. All he wants to do now is survive. And if he can't survive, he'll take a few down with him."

"And after this escapade," I interject, "he'll be desperate."

"Which puts the balance in our favour," says Janza.

"*Our* favour?" Ubul again tries to size up this man in the smart suit with a store of knowledge as big as the national archive. "You've decided, have you?"

A little light has switched itself on at the back of my eyes. "You said Ozd is in the north-east. And Petofi told us Kozma's Merc was last seen heading in that direction."

The phone rings again. Kovacs leaps out of chair and takes the call. Once more the puzzled frown. The frown changes to a look of disbelief. Kovacs mutters something into the mouthpiece, replaces the handset, and stares past us.

"Christ, Peter. What the hell is it?" Ubul has to ask him three times.

"They've found her car. Twenty clicks outside Ozd. In a ditch. Burnt out. No sign of her. Not a bloody trace."

Chapter 2

There is just enough time to tell Kovacs that in an hour from now I'm to discuss Hungarian political history with one of the country's greatest scholars.

"Use what you get out of Gyula Bokor for yourself," he tells me, "but remember, if we ever manage to prosecute Kozma, it'll be invaluable for any case we can bring against him. Then drive out to Ozd as fast as you can."

He yells at Ubul and Janza and scrambles down the stairwell at a speed which in my case would be conducive to an early heart attack. As I step out of the lobby into a surprisingly cheerful, sunlit day, I see Ubul's patrol car disappear round the corner on to Ulloi at an angle that seems to defy gravity. I contemplate the prospect of a crisis about to reach its climax. Apart from the political ramifications, Andrea's plight, whatever it is, adds a very personal dimension to the whole affair. I shall have to phone Fred again. But I know the role I have to play.

I shuffle my backside into a taxi and wonder how much I should tell the professor. Perhaps everything, or as much of Janza's analysis as I can recall.

"A remarkable young man," I mumble to myself as the taxi slides into the traffic. "Keep an eye on him, Kovacs. I'm glad you've got Ubul watching your back."

It's noon and I'm hungry. I tell the driver to drop me at Kalvin ter where I know a little *vendeglo* that'll satisfy my wants. I also need the papers. What are they saying about the Angyalfold riot? Will they carry so much as a hint of what was behind it?

At ten to one, I take a number 47 tram past the National Museum and hop off outside the grimy, neo-Baroque façade of Eotvos Lorand University. I don't think I've been followed. In any case, I've given over worrying about a hostile tail in broad daylight.

A guard with a beer gut takes no notice of me as I pass through the main gate and head for one of the teaching blocks. Following the professor's directions, I negotiate a warren of shabby corridors until I reach a door painted with white gloss bearing the occupant's nameplate. Gyula Bokor is thickset, with a grey crewcut and mischief in his eyes. He's perhaps in his early sixties.

"So, they've pushed shit through your letter box, Mr Barrow?"

This earthy reponse to the standard courtesies takes me aback.

"Me too," he goes on. "Twice in one day last week. I couldn't give a damn but it upsets my wife and that makes me angry."

He pours out the promised *palinka*.

"*Egeszsegunkre.* Good Health." I respond in kind and look round the room. It's comfortable but functional, with shelves of books and files, maps in the spaces on the walls, and a glass case displaying some faded military medals. It's a room for work and thought.

"So, what are you going to do about it, Mr Barrow?"

"I have my pen and my typewriter and my ability to give Szarka's party some bad publicity in the British press. Not a great deal, is it? But I can exploit a combination of my unpleasant experiences, the information I've gleaned from contacts in the police and the background you've already supplied in *The Circle of Hell*. It might get reprinted in a Hungarian newspaper. It's my job. I have to do it."

"That's not a bad start," says Bokor. "But you'd like to go further?"

I search his face for traces of approval.

"Yes."

He refills my glass and emits a dirty laugh, the one I'd heard over the phone.

"Go on," he says.

"Oh, I could knock up a couple of articles for my editor in London. But deep down I know there's more to be written about these people, something that will expose them for what they are, not just a bunch of mad pseudo-politicians, but a criminal gang with powerful connections. It's those links I want to report. And I need names in the political establishment in order to do any real damage."

"And you think I can give you those names?"

I cock my head on one side and give Bokor the look I'd often used during 'soft' interrogations in Belfast. You hold your mouth firm but let a hint of a smile play around the crow's feet of your tired eyes.

"Who are your police informants?" Again the direct approach. Cross the Rubicon, Charlie, or you'll get no further.

I spend the next ten minutes summarising the information supplied by Janza. I go the whole way with the material on crime and corruption, Department III/III's manipulation of the change of regime, Szarka's movement and its possible links to senior people in government.

"How come a British journalist found himself sitting at a table with a member of Hungarian intelligence and the officer in charge of the unit responsible for stopping illegal immigration?"

I protest that I've jumped ahead of myself, past the events that provide the context for these disclosures.

"I've known Kovacs for some time."

"So have I," says Bokor.

"Then you will know about Kozma's attempts to frame him."

He doesn't respond. So I pitch in with Kozma's hasty exit from the scene of the crime, the murdered Croat, and even the news about Andrea. I'm coming clean. There's no point in doing anything else.

"This is getting to be more serious than I imagined," says Bokor. "Your Mr Janza is obviously very clever and Kovacs is blessed with a rational mind that draws the right conclusions."

"You're one of his 'top people', aren't you? You've already told Kovacs what I want you to tell me."

"I wouldn't fret about that. Just because Kovacs hasn't passed on everything he knows doesn't mean he doesn't trust you."

"You'll fill in the gaps?"

He avoids a direct answer.

"Those of us who have come through the last fifty years of this country's history know all about Kozma and those like him. You remember that at the end of *The Circle of Hell* I write about the fish that got through the net and evolved into the frogs and toads of the new fascism. There's your Kozma. In your literature you have a poem about the Vicar of Bray, a cleric who boasts of his accommodation to the views of Catholic and Protestant monarchs and still keeps his job. Why shouldn't Hungary have the same? With the kind of violence we've had in the twentieth century, Hungary's Vicars of Bray have been very active."

He coughs and sips his brandy, warming to his theme.

"They too have accommodated to the views of politicians, from Bela Kun and the first soviets, to Horthy, Szalasi, the Stalinist Rakosi, and tragically in '56, to the avuncular communist, Imre Nagy, on to the more cunning version,

Mr Janos Kadar. I know Kozma because he tried to get *The Circle of Hell* banned. I know him inside out. I have sat in his office in Andrassy ut, in the 'House of Fidelity' where Cardinal Mindszenty was tortured in 1948."

He lets that sink in.

"I have listened to him hector me about patriotism and social responsibility. That man worked his way through the communist AVO, its successor the AVH, and wore his blue lapels with pride. He moved into Department III/III, Kadar's revamped intelligence network, and on to his present job in the interior ministry. And I know about his cosy relationship with old hands in the armed forces and a volatile politician who has had his nose pushed out."

"Who is…..?"

"Pal Konrad."

I try to sit as still as a corpse but the tension makes me shift uneasily in my chair. I ask if I can smoke. Bokor joins me, lighting up a small cigar.

"Pal Konrad badly wanted a senior post in the defence ministry. But prime minister Antall chose a rival from within the ranks of the Forum. So Konrad's right-wingers split from the coalition. Let me quote from an interview he gave."

He slides a piece of paper from a file on his desk.

"'*Some senior commanders have what I can only describe as the Muscovite spirit*'"

"The what?" I ask. But Bokor waves my snigger aside.

"'*They are always inviting former communists to address political education classes at the officers' training school. I wanted to expose these people but I was prevented from expressing my views, because they were too strong for the weak knees in the Forum*'"

"And what has Mr Konrad done since then?" Bokor asks pointedly.

"He has gone off in a huff and taken his faction into Szarka's People's Justice Party."

"I see you've kept up to date with your reading, Mr Barrow."

"I try," I say with as much conviction as I can summon. There's something about Bokor which makes me feel like a student inadequately prepared for a tutorial.

"Those inside the armed forces who think like Konrad, who want the 'Muscovites' out of the defence ministry, have been giving him tacit support and probably more than that."

"I thought you were a military *historian*, professor."

"I do not concentrate solely on the past," he replies. "Much of my research these days is on the reform of our armed forces and ways of integrating them into NATO. We keep pushing for membership. We've got as far as a Partnership for Peace. We'll get there in the end as long as the political process holds up. But given the state of our weaponry, it's hardly surprising we're seen as not quite fit enough to join the great club. But then you, Charlie Barrow, know all about this, don't you? Wasn't the study of the Warsaw Pact's conventional armoury one of your specialities when you were a British agent?"

He sees my momentary flicker of surprise. And laughs.

"Oh yes," he says. "Even Gyula Bokor served as a spy for Kadar. None of us here is untainted by the past. I know quite a lot about you."

"And you're going to tell me?"

"We were not unaware of the identities of those assigned to keep tabs on us in the old days. I think I know the exact date you left for your gruesome job in Northern Ireland. I lost track of you after that until you surfaced here as a journalist. I occasionally read a British newspaper especially if it's got something to say about Hungary."

He slips more liquid into our glasses, sits back and takes pleasure in my confusion.

"I have been sloppy, professor. I should have checked you out more thoroughly before coming here."

"Why bother? You know all about me. But consider this. I was a party member but I was never seduced by promises of a successful career. I never rejected the memory of '56."

"But your family had to eat."

"Exactly. And when those in power asked me to perform certain tasks for them, a bit of research here, some probing there, I had little choice in the matter. They needed my expertise. They showed me certain documents and yours was one of many names on those documents. Then I would be summarily dismissed until they needed the services of a military analyst yet again. My wife used to joke about it. She called me 'Weatherman'. You know, like those little figures that pop out when the sun shines and vanish when it rains. I must have gone in and out of defence ministry buildings more times than I've eaten hot dinners."

I hold up a hand. "I'm not here to judge you, professor. I just want you to tell me about Kozma."

He doesn't prevaricate.

"Kozma and Konrad have known one another for a long time. It's no secret that Konrad was once influential enough in the Forum to block any enquiries into Kozma's past, especially his role in the killings at Mosonmagyarovar in '56. He was 20 at the time, a keen AVO recruit, a little leaner and fitter. Any one who's been in and out of government service over the years knows these things."

He pauses while I bring my notes up to date.

"But when Janos Kadar, our last and seemingly everlasting communist overlord, was in power, he took great pains to keep the lid on scandal. He was so desperate for stability and a little prosperity. Run a quiet household and the Russians wouldn't interfere again. Not for nothing did the old fox say, 'he who is not against us is with us'. Before that, of course, he unleashed his own brand of discipline. Arrests, torture, executions. Poor old Imre Nagy wasn't the only victim. And people like Kozma were more than willing to play along."

Bokor looks away as if he's consulting some presence in the room whose shape and form I'm denied. Then he throws out his chest and resumes.

"Kadar's overthrow in '89, the reburial of Nagy, the fall of the Berlin Wall and the election of the Forum – and Kozma knows he's under threat at last. He can stave it off by virtue of influence and a knowledge of others' dirty deeds. But it won't last for ever."

"Do you think he's made his first big mistake, trying to frame Kovacs?"

"It could be. But he has access to sensitive files. He can still dish out the filth. Who's taking a cut from a government contract. Who's on drugs or running a mistress. Who's importing foreign goods without paying tax. He's not going to pass this on to the media. That's much too risky."

I lean forward.

"Instead, he's going to release it into the great whirlpool, the bureaucracy, parliament, the fashionable circuit, diplomatic cocktail parties and so forth. And he's decided he can win this game by building up Szarka's monsters into a private army."

"And how do I track down more of these people?"

"Hang around the right places, Mr Barrow. Restaurants and pubs. Get your ambassador to invite you to his receptions. What I can tell you is that Kozma and Szarka have been recruiting half-educated yobs and appealing to their worst instincts. Nationalism, racism and violence. They've studied Hitler, the abuse of the electoral process, debasing the coinage to wreck the economy, and they think they've got enough support to create a new Nazism here, 'Hungarianism' as Szalasi used to call it in the forties. They think the tide is running their way."

"Where do they get the cash for all this?"

"There's an awful lot of dirty money sloshing around. The tax authorities admit that the Black Economy accounts for a third of *all* economic activity in Hungary. They keep promising a crackdown but we've yet to see it. Even I have a hard currency account for earnings from books published abroad. I've been told there's as much as 20 billion dollars in these accounts. It isn't just private business stashing this money away. The state audit office says three billion forints is missing from the social insurance fund."

"And the black market?"

"Take something as mundane as domestic heating oil coupons. The crooks buy them at a good price. They use them to purchase cheap diesel and then sell it back as petrol."

"What about deals like the Ozd steelworks contracts Janza told us about?"

"Four and a half billion of state money invested in useless plant and machinery. Where's it gone? My morning paper says the director there has disappeared. The police can't find him and his wife says she doesn't know where he is. I bet I do. Vienna. Or Zurich."

"Which reminds me," I say, rising from my comfortable armchair. "I have to go. But before I do, answer this, please. You're saying the likes of Kozma can lay their hands on some of this cash to fund a political party or even a private army?"

"Couldn't be easier. My enquiries tell me it's found its way into Szarka's organization so that he can buy arms from our neighbours, maybe from within the armed forces. That's where Konrad's contacts come in."

"Your neighbours? Like Croatia for instance?"

"The murder of your Croat is more than a little intriguing. I had a report across my desk only last week that Croatia has been buying arms from Swiss dealers who in turn purchase them cheap from Slovenia."

"Like what?"

"Like automatic rifles, mortars, even anti-aircraft ammunition. Other stuff they get from the Serb underworld, happy to trade with the old enemy if the price is right.

Croats, Serbs, Bosnian Muslims, Slovenes, Albanians, Ukrainians, Russians. They'll sell you anything if you've got the wherewithal."

"But why would Kozma decide to get rid of Friend Janko, then?"

"I don't know. Maybe a double-cross. Maybe Kozma's Croat contacts asked for a favour. Get rid of someone who got too big for his boots."

Bokor reaches for another slip of paper. "Before you go, have a look at this."

It was a news agency report from Vienna.

"A gunman who shot and killed two Austrian border guards early Thursday during a baggage check used a Czech-made weapon of a type known to be favoured by a number of terrorist organisations, Austrian police said. The two guards, aged 22 and 24, were killed about 1 a.m. on board a night train from Graz, just before it crossed the border at Heiligenkreuz. The guards had asked the two men, said to be Hungarians, to follow them to a special police compartment. One of the men sprayed the guards with bullets from a Skorpion 7.65 calibre machine pistol fitted with a silencer. The man was later captured when police raided a trackside hut two kilometres from the border."

"You know," says Bokor, "when I began studying military history in my youth, I thought I would be able to hide myself away in a university, do some quiet research, publish the odd paper, take the salary, drink some of this stuff, and keep my wife happy. Instead, I find myself consorting with spies, politicians, journalists and policemen. And I receive threats from criminals."

"The fiery darts of the wicked, professor."

"Saint Paul also told the Ephesians to walk circumspectly, not as fools but as wise men redeeming the time. Good bye, Mr Barrow."

I have more gold for Fred. But Bokor has unnerved me. He's been almost too helpful. And I can't work out why.

PART 10

Chapter 1

For the first two days they shackle Coro to a breezeblock wall. He's forced to sleep on a concrete floor with a rough blanket for cover. The place is filthy and stinks of urine. His own toilet is a plastic bucket emptied every morning by another Roma captive. There's one meal a day. Bread, thin vegetable soup and water that's none too fresh. They're guarded by one of the skinheads who seized him on the road near Ketpo.

Then they move him across the yard to another hut. It gives him a chance to work out the geography. He sees three grey barrack blocks with wire netting over the windows and, beyond, an imposing house with cloisters and a bell-tower. To the right is a windowless wooden barn, smothered with pitch. Half a dozen vehicles are parked in front of the house, among them a white Suzuki, a large black Mercedes and the battered Niva used by his abductors.

He recalls the journey. It was long and painful, with every joint and limb pummelled by the Niva's unforgiving suspension. He feigned unconsciousness for as long as he could. The two men and their blousy leaderine were in no mood to do him any favours. He was sure that, if he moved, they'd take every chance to beat him up again. But the time spent travelling with Kalman had honed his ability to measure distance in his head. He calculated the Niva must have covered at least 150 kilometres by the time they turned into the compound and dropped him outside the hut. They hauled him through the door by the scruff of the neck and kicked him as they locked his shackle.

"Fucking Gypsy. I'd let you bloody well starve if the boss didn't want you for work."

The man called Gabi cuffed him behind an ear. He gasped, half blinded and fell forward. The chain wrenched his arm and Gabi spat as he left the hut.

Now Coro lies still. A hand touches his shoulder. For a moment he has premonitions of a glorious vision, an expectation that, if he turns his head, he'll see Judit. She'll take him in her arms and cradle him back to health.

"Easy. I've brought you water. Take your time."

Coro looks into the pockmarked face of an old Roma.

"Drink," says the man. Coro does as he's told and tries to focus.

"Thank you."

"You want to weep? So, weep."

"Tears are weakness. You won't see me weep."

"No one is weak who can survive in here. You'll find that out soon enough."

The old man introduces himself as Tomi. Coro replies in kind. The others in the hut gather round, moving in as far as their chains will allow.

"If it helps, tell us your story," says Tomi. "If not, go to sleep. We shall talk tomorrow."

"I should prefer to rest," Coro replies.

"As you wish. We'll be woken at dawn. And we'll be in the quarry soon after. Nothing but back-breaking work with a pick and a shovel."

"In any case," says another prisoner, "it's getting dark and it's bloody cold."

They withdraw like so many will-o'-the-wisps and Coro rolls into his blanket.

He's deeply asleep when the door is pushed open and two buckets are dumped in the middle of the floor. Gabi and his mate flash torches and kick the prostrate bodies.

"Up, you bastards. Time for work."

The prisoners rise as one and scurry to the buckets.

"Gypsy scum," Gabi sneers.

They keep their heads down and avoid eye contact. Tomi uses an iron bailer to pour water into beakers and bottles. The men drink quickly, then use the remains to sluice their hands and faces.

"Filthy bastards, aren't you?"

Coro watches them scramble into line like frightened sheep.

"You can piss and shit down in the quarry," he says.

The skinheads bring in a heavy chain with shackles. One by one, the captives hold out their arms and the metal bracelets click into place. They file out into the crisp morning air. Tomi brings up the rear.

Gabi leers at Coro. "You stay behind today. Big Gyuri wants a talk. I'm glad I'm not in your shoes."

He doles out what's left of the water, making sure a little slops on to the floor. Then he slams the door, cackling with laughter as he crosses the yard outside. Coro is left with two of his fellow inmates. One can't resist the temptation to speak.

"Your accent. Romanian?"

"Yes."

"My mother came from Romania," he sneers. "She said it stank."

"This place stinks," Coro counters. The man retreats into silence.

Coro lies with his back to the wall, stares ahead and tries to think.

"For all his double dealing, Tivadar will surely tell Kalman I'm missing. The alarm will be raised. But how will they find me? Kalman will know how. Won't he?"

The door is flung open and a huge man strides into the hut brandishing a riding crop. He wears highly polished black boots and a military uniform. The left sleeve of his jacket bears an armband with a star-like emblem. Coro has never seen the Arrow Cross insignia before. But Kalman has told him all about it.

"So you're the new boy. Stand up when I speak to you, Gypsy."

"I can't stand up," Coro answers. "The shackle won't let me."

The man bends and hits him hard on the mouth.

"Don't give me lip, Gypsy. Do as I say."

Another stinging blow. Coro somehow lifts himself to his feet.

"Now, do you understand?"

Coro reckons it's prudent to respond but with as few words as he can get away with.

"I understand." It works, for the time being.

"I am Gyuri. If you get clever with me, Gypsy, you will suffer, because I will make you suffer. We want our little slaves to work hard but we can just as easily dispose of you. Nobody will know."

Coro thinks of Kalman again. But Big Gyuri has more to say.

"The writ of the idiots in Budapest and their stupid police force doesn't run here. Those who break *our* law are punished by us. And punishment usually means….." He draws a hand across his throat. "What have you got to say for yourself, Gypsy?"

"I have nothing to say."

The big man whips another blow across Coro's swollen mouth.

"I warned you, you miserable little sod. You will answer my questions."

He spins round and shouts for Gabi who stumbles through the door like a drunk.

"Unfasten that shackle," orders Big Gyuri. "Drag him into the middle."

Despite the pain from his mouth, Coro is trying to make a fine calculation. How much to give away without compromising what's left of his dignity.

Under more questioning, he manages to avoid any mention of his Romanian origins.

"I have no family. I come from Ketpo, near Torokszentmiklos."

"Work?"

"Anything I can get. Labourer. Farm hand."

He's banking on the cowed silence of the other Roma in the room and on Gyuri's surprising failure to ask them what they know. The big man seems satisfied. He slaps Coro's face again, adds a string of insults, orders Gabi to fetter him to the wall, crosses to the others, spits at them and marches out as ludicrously as he entered.

The routine continues. Beatings, abuse, questioning and long hours of sitting and thinking. It becomes unbearable when his thoughts wander to Judit, to lovemaking and the sound of her voice, to warm summer evenings when they talked of the future. But he still won't weep. He gets no help from his fellow inmates. Tomi's initial interest has melted away into dumb insolence.

"He's been warned off by the others. I can smell it."

On the fifth morning he joins the chain gang. Again he takes in his wider surroundings. The four long huts, the house and the barn are set amid woods in the hollow of a hill. A late autumn wind is building up. The trees are almost bare and dead leaves cover the gravel in the yard.

Accompanied by four guards wearing Arrow Cross uniforms and armed with machine pistols, they trudge down a track for about a kilometer. They follow the line of a stream which opens out into a wider hollow. Here the trees have been felled, the topsoil eroded and the rock exposed. They hack at this with picks until they've broken enough to shovel it into metal buckets. It's a crude way of producing bedrock for the yard and the driveway to the house. They're kept at it until ten in the morning when they're allowed five minutes to drink water and eat a little bread. They're forbidden to speak and any slacking brings a bull-hide whip across the back.

They break again at two and are marched back to the hut at six.

On the second day Coro risks taking his blanket to cover his shirt. The guards don't object but revel in the chance to taunt him.

"Look at Mr Universe. Look at those muscles."

They screech with laughter, puffing out their barrel chests and bulging biceps. Coro notices they also have beer guts.

We're not chained when we work. I could make a run for it.

He's toying with the idea when one of the guards seizes him by the hair and pulls his head back until he thinks his spine will snap.

"I've been watching you. You thought I'd missed your little tricks, didn't you? Looking for way out, are we? There isn't one, Gypsy. No way out for scum like you. You're our slave. We do what we like with you. And we've got guns."

Coro doesn't react because he can't. Tightening his grip, the guard unlocks the shackle, drags his victim up a rocky slope and drops him. The hard surface draws blood.

"Dirty Gypsy blood."

His tormentor kicks him in the small of the back. He rolls down the slope, ending up spread-eagled and breathless. The guard takes aim.

"Get up, you little bastard. Or I'll kill you – now."

Coro pushes himself into a standing position and finds he can stay on his feet if he keeps his knees bent. He lifts his head and sees the muzzle in front of his nose. The guard lowers it to a point beneath Coro's chin and holds it there.

"I think we will have a little sport with you tonight."

Coro staggers into another guard who handcuffs him. For the rest of the day he tries to hide his growing fear that it will end in great pain.

Chapter 2

He's been left to eat his bread and gruel unchained and unmolested and he thinks perhaps the guard's threats have been no more than bluster. But at eight sharp they come for him and Tomi and drag them across to one of the other huts. Inside there are two rows of bunk-beds for about thirty men and, in the middle, a wood-burning stove surrounded by flimsy card-tables and an assortment of chairs. There's little sign of military order. Coro sees the remains of meals and cans of Dreher beer. The walls are covered with political posters and the lewdest pornography, the barking face of Szarka mingling with buttocks and oversize breasts photographed in ways that leave nothing to the imagination. Rock music blasts out of loudspeakers. The skins sit in a semi-circle, stamping and chanting in loose unison.

> "Flamethrower. Flamethrower.
> It's the only weapon we need.
> Flamethrower. Flamethrower.
> We'll burn the Gypsies, the Gypsies that breed like flies.
> Flamethrower. Flamethrower.
> We'll burn them,
> Till we get, till we get, till we get.........
> A Gypsy-free ZONE."

One of the skins throws logs and kindling through an opening in the stove. The fire inside leaps into life again. The guard who picked on Coro makes the two Roma stand face to face, no more than fifty centimetres from the quickening flames.

"Dance a Gypsy dance," Gabi hollers. "Dance, you bastards."

"Dance. Dance. Dance." The mob takes up the chant.

The heat is suffocating but Coro sees no reason to hesitate if the two of them are to survive. He puts his hands on Tomi's shoulders.

"My waist," he hisses. "Hold on to my waist."

Tomi's pleading eyes tell him the old man has no reserves to endure any of this. His limbs ache with rheumatism and his lungs are long since spent. Coro stares ahead trying not to blink, hoping against the odds to hypnotise him into action.

"Dance. Dance. Dance," comes the chant again.

Coro switches his mind to another time and another place. Now he is dancing with Judit, hearing Jenoe's fiddle and Kalman's wailing clarinet. He sees fields of sunflower and willow and leaps and cavorts like a kid goat on a day in early spring. His frenzy clicks Tomi's mind into memories of his own happier times. The old man forces his limbs to move to rhythms dredged from the subconscious, following the pattern of steps obliterated by age and hard labour. To the accelerating beat of the skins' booted feet, the two prance before the stove like souls possessed.

They keep it up for about ten minutes until Tomi lets go and collapses in a writhing heap, his gnomish head resting close to some heavy footwear. The skin kicks and Tomi's head jerks sideways. Coro springs at the skin and bites him. He howls and Coro bites again. When the others finally drag him off, blood is oozing from the man's nostrils.

The skin spits, hauls himself to his feet, puts his head down and charges. Coro takes the force of his bulk in the midriff. To jeers, chanting and manic laughter, skinhead and Roma roll across the floor, scattering chairs and beer-cans to the four corners of the hut.

"Pull that stupid bugger off."

It's Gabi, who's stayed in the background but now decides to take charge.

"I need that little tiger for the chain gang."

Three skins grab Coro's adversary just in time. He's already done considerable damage. The Roma's left eye is black and blue and closing. His rib cage aches with the beating he's taken. Gabi's intervention restores a measure of order. The skins, drunk on beer and sadism, amble back to their chairs. Tomi lies where he dropped.

"You want more fun?" Gabi's question provokes a raucous response. More stamping and chanting. He scoops Tomi into his arms, swings him round and dumps him on the lid of the stove. If the little man thinks the evening's agonies are over, the heat from the metal burning into his bony backside rids him of all delusion. Gabi seizes him again, hoists him high and plants him back on the stove. His shrivelled feet are scorched and scarred as this time he dances to no rhythm but his own. All he sees through watery eyes and a spinning head are braying faces and yellowing teeth, screaming and howling with lolling tongues and flared nostrils.

"Flamethrower. Flamethrower. Dance, Gypsy. Dance. Dance. Dance."

Coro is forced to watch Tomi's suffering through one good eye, gasping his own torment and despair until the old man topples headlong and lies like a rag doll at his feet.

Later, after Coro and an unconscious Tomi have been hauled back to the hut, the younger man steels his battered body and distraught mind into bathing his companion's face and binding his reeking flesh with strips of towel. The other prisoners feign sleep or turn their backs.

In the deep darkness, as Coro's one useful eye is finally closing with sleep, he hears Tomi stir and feels a frail hand on his arm. He reaches out and holds it gently, afraid of crushing the brittle bones. They lie together, their breathing soft and composed.

"Did I not tell you, Coro?" Tomi whispers. He coughs, almost apologetically. "Did I not tell you that he who survives this will have had a foretaste of Hell?"

"You said something like it."

The old man sighs and the skeletal hand stiffens. The breathing becomes uneven, energetic, then weaker. Coro stays quite still. All he can hear now is the night wind whining though gaps in the window frames. He bites a swollen lip against the pain, reaches for his blanket and spreads it awkwardly over Tomi's body and what he can see of his face.

"We shall need someone else to dole out the water in the morning," he says. No one moves.

PART 11

Chapter 1

I drive out of Budapest in the middle of the afternoon with the light already starting to fade. I turn off the motorway at Hatvan and head north along narrow roads, through drab little towns whose inhabitants have scurried into their houses, closed the shutters and locked the doors. The capital flaunts its new freedoms. Here in the provinces the ingrained habit of keeping yourself to yourself dies hard.

I have to sit behind slow-moving trucks. I take risks on bends, testing my judgement and the Opel's gearbox. I'm about twenty kilometres short of Ozd when I see blue lights and two patrol cars blocking the road. I pull in and wind the window down. A young uniform leans in. Before he can say a word, I hear Kovacs's voice giving orders.

He and Janza stand by the side of the road peering at the wreck of a Skoda saloon. Janza has a notebook in which he's writing with a silver propelling pencil.

"That's her car?" I ask.

"Steering wheel and column melted down into one mess of plastic," intones Janza. "All wrapped round what's left of the linkage. Seats reduced to frames and springs. Precious little fabric left. Some wiring dangling from the fascia. Front end one mass of charred components in amongst which we might still find an engine and transmission. Glass either broken or reduced to globules. Tyres gone. Nearside front door hanging loose on one hinge."

"Thank you, Janza," says Kovacs. "You sound as if you almost enjoyed that."

"If it brings you any comfort, Captain, I can tell you your lady did not die in this blaze. There are no traces......" Janza stops short of a lapse of taste.

"In any case," he goes on, "this car did not catch fire spontaneously. It was torched."

"How do you work that out?" I ask.

"Not enough in the average tank to do a thorough job like this."

"Which degree course taught you to recognise arson?"

Janza smiles. "Kozma tied me to a desk. But I did pass through one or two practical seminars before he purloined me. I can also exercise my common sense."

"Don't get tetchy," snaps Kovacs. "Despite your excellent examination of the evidence, I prefer to rely on Forensics' judgement."

Janza inclines his head to acknowledge the rebuke but continues to scrutinise what's left of Andrea's car with movements so graceful that I'm obliged to think the unthinkable......Could he be? No. Not in Department III/III. He'd never have made it through the selection procedure. And yet the finely wrought face, the feline walk, the expressive hands, the lift of the eyebrows, the short, well-groomed hair.

"Like a bloody gigolo," Ubul had whispered to me back in Budapest.

It's discomfiting. No wonder Ubul has misgivings about Janza. For Ubul is, I have to admit, about as heterosexual as you can get.

Kovacs beckons me over and we walk away from the scene.

"Do you trust this man?" I ask him.

"Trust, Charlie, is not a commodity I hand out too readily – as you well know."

"Then why give him the benefit of the doubt?"

"I haven't. To survive in this country, never take people at face value. In my father's day, they might inform on you for some perfectly innocent indiscretion. I haven't lost the habit of looking over my shoulder. Don't worry. I'll keep an eye on him."

"He's given you some priceless information. And he seems keen to break his links with Kozma and hitch a ride on your bandwagon."

"Look at it this way, Charlie. I must be getting bloody desperate or acquiring an exceptional faith in my own judgement. But where the hell's this taking me? I'm trying to focus on solving the possible murder of the woman I love on top of all my other problems and I get deflected by a kind of spurious psychoanalysis of everyone I come into contact with."

"Like Ubul says – you think too much."

"You mean – I think too much for a cop."

Two trucks edge through the roadblock. I can't delay much longer. Either on to Ozd or back to Budapest.

"I took a third call after you'd all left," says Kovacs. "From a colleague in Andrea's office. He said she'd failed to phone them from Ozd as pre-arranged, so he'd started to make some enquiries with contacts up here in Heves county. One of these called back with a story about a burned out Skoda. The police were alerted by a truck driver using the emergency number from a payphone. A sergeant in the local force had the wit to look at the rear number plate, still legible despite the inferno. That was how Andrea's colleague knew it was her car. I got in touch with the local force who passed me on to an officer called Rainer. He said the National Registration Bureau confirmed Andrea as the Skoda's owner."

A wicked wind sweeps off the surrounding hillside. Two uniforms stamp their feet. Janza is still pirouetting round the wreck making notes with his pencil.

"Where the hell is she, Charlie? Where the hell is she?"

I shrug knowing I can say nothing that will satisfy him.

"Where will you go now?" he asks.

I've decided. "On to Ozd. I want to make a few enquiries about that steelworks accident. And you?"

"I'll liaise with this bloke, Rainer. Might stay the night up here or return to Budapest. Not sure yet."

"See you." I march back to my car.

"Do like I do, Charlie," he calls. "Keep looking over your shoulder."

Chapter 2

It's dusk when I drop down into Ozd. The town lies fifteen kilometres from the Slovak border. It has no redeeming features. The stacks of its sprawling steelworks overwhelm a skyline silhouetted by the lingering daylight. I pull in at a *trafik* to buy some cigarettes. A heavy pall of polluted air hangs over workers' flats, shops and public buildings, the products of minds once besotted by notions of functionalism and a planned economy. Even in this gloom I can see the thick grime dappled and streaked by wind and rain.

My heart sinks at the prospect of having to spend the night here. Will Ozd have a decent hotel? I doubt it.

I head for the steelworks, hoping to buttonhole the relevant officials. I drive up and down until I find a building which bears two large plaques announcing that it doubles as executive offices and the local branch of the steelworkers' union. It'll take time before market forces sweep away these vestiges of communist management practice. But the interior is warm, even comfortable in the sparse manner of central European bureaucracies. A grey carpet, grey walls, fluorescent lighting and the odd scrap of living foliage countering the dehumanising effects of the world outside. Nor is the overpainted lady in Reception unhelpful.

"Yes. If you will just take a seat, I will call the director's office."

The call is put through. A secretary is on her way down. Here is courtesy and efficiency where I expect stony-faced obfuscation. They know I'm snooping. And yet they're co-operating. An elevator door slides open. Out steps another painted lady and a stocky man in clean overalls carrying two hard hats.

"I'm afraid the director - that is Doctor Oblath - cannot see you this evening, Mr Barrow. But he can manage tomorrow morning at nine. Mr Klein here is only too happy to answer any questions."

I accept, thank the secretary and shake hands with Klein.

He smiles lugubriously. "Let's go," he says.

"Go? Where?"

"You want to look the place over, don't you?"

"You're going to take me to where it happened?"

"Why not? Those are Oblath's orders. He says he's technically incompetent to explain it all. That's bullshit. But I am the plant engineer. So, come on. I don't want to spend all evening on this but at least you can buy me a drink when we've finished."

"Just a moment."

"I know, I know." The doleful smile never leaves his face. "You want to know why we're being so accommodating. Especially to a foreign journalist. You want to know why we haven't told you to go away and wait for the findings of an official enquiry, why we're so ready to give you a guided tour of a steelworks that should have been consigned to the scrap heap a long time ago – and why that should include a visit to the site of an accident in which eight poor souls, all of them known to me personally, died horrible deaths. All at short notice too."

We're walking across the street to the main gate. It's starting to rain.

"Now that we're out of there, I'll tell you why. Because some of us have grown up."

I haven't worked this out yet but he doesn't give me much time to speculate.

"Watch yourself on those flagstones. And wear this from now on."

I don the white hard hat and follow Klein into a cobbled yard where a diesel locomotive is doing a spirited shunt with two wagons. The screech of metal is outrageous. I look at my guide whose grin grows ever wider as he tries to lead me by routes that'll inflict the least damage to my shoes. I doubt they'll survive the mess of oil and clinker but it's too late to go back.

I've been in noisy factories before but this is a revelation. The mouths of furnaces belch smoke and flame. Blasts of hot air rip my breath away. Glowing beams and girders swing from gantries only metres above our heads. I choke on the fumes and recoil at the din and the casual regard for safety.

Klein opens a large steel door. When we've passed through, he slams it shut with such force that the clang of its locks hangs in the air. I adjust to a new acoustic. The tumult of the furnaces is muted. There's no need to shout. Klein's smile fades. He bears new worry lines and a deep, watery, sadness.

"I'll tell you a story," he says.

*** *** *** ***

"Rasko and Zsuzsa clock on just after 5.50 a.m. Rasko is forty-five, thick set, with a tuft of red curly hair above a broken nose and an honest face. Zsuzsa too is short, determined and serious. They've been married for twenty years. They have no children. They have dedicated themselves to the Party. And now they find it very hard to understand how the system they

have served as loyal workers and union officials should have disintegrated so swiftly.

"But they are undaunted. They will carry on as good communists in the belief that history goes in cycles and that socialism's day will return.

"Rasko supervises the shift that starts at six. Zsuzsa operates the controls of the continuous casting plant from a cabin built into the gantry high up in the rafters. They've been doing these jobs for five years.

"The huge ladle that hangs from the roof just below Zsuzsa's cabin contains molten metal. Beneath it is a refractory-lined reservoir into which the steel is poured at a rate measured by the instruments in front of her. From here it will flow through a mould that determines its shape and form – billet, bloom or slab. Then it glides into a long, vertical chamber where it cools and starts to solidify under spray from high-pressure water jets. As the strand of steel emerges, it's guided into the horizontal, to be straightened and cut to the required length.

"Rasko's team are proud that they can match the relentless demands the process imposes on them – the pace, the heat, the steam, the sweat and the pandemonium. They're all there, smoking, shuffling, pushing tin boxes into lockers – full of sausage, bread and pickle for the meal break. The youngsters are still dreaming about last night's girl or nursing a hangover after a noisy evening in the bar with European soccer on television.

"But they move quickly. Zsuzsa has already climbed to her console. She calls up Rasko on the radio link. He looks up and waves and she presses a button. Sirens wail, lights flash, the ladle shudders. The shift stand by, ready with gear and tackle to make sure the strand of steel isn't blocked as it leaves the cooling chamber.

"The new boy, Ignac, is the first spot that something's wrong. But he can't work it out."

Through the gloom I watch Klein brace himself for the climax to his tale.

"Ignac realises the ladle is out of true, askew in its mountings. He points and Rasko sees it too. He rasps into the radio. The ladle shudders again. There are more exchanges on the link. Rasko's men look at one another, confused. Except for Ignac, who's focusing all his attention on the ladle.

"But even Ignac is unprepared. He sees the ladle sway. Then like an object in a slow-motion space odyssey, it slips from its bearings and crashes through the mould and the cooling chamber. There's a blinding explosion. Ignac is torn apart by a bolt dislodged from one of the stanchions. More shrapnel rips into three of his mates. Zsuzsa sees Rasko and the others engulfed in a cocktail of gas and molten metal. She cannot shout. She cannot scream. But clings, witlessly, to the handrail of her cabin. How and why that cabin and the roof supports stay intact mystifies the committee of enquiry."

***   ***   ***   ***

I recall the wire copy.

"Budapest, 4th October. Eight people have died from injuries sustained in an explosion at a steelworks in northern Hungary. The state news agency said two were killed in the explosion early on Saturday morning. Six died later in hospital. The cause of the blast at the plant in Ozd is unknown. Fire-fighters were able to extinguish a blaze soon after the explosion but the plant was severely damaged."

From the catwalk half way up one of the walls, Klein stares down into the wreckage. It would be obscene to interrupt him. Salvage teams have started work but they've made little impression on the chaos wrought by the explosion.

I follow his gaze to the tangle of twisted metal and blackened brickwork.

"The grooves in the floor?" I ask at last.

"Just shows how hot the steel was when it hit them. If it did that to concrete, what would it do to flesh and bone?"

"What about the rescue services?"

"Actually, they were pretty quick. But they couldn't get near for at least an hour. The heat. The gases. The steam was so dense."

"Where you there?"

"It was early in the day. They called me at home. I rushed over as fast as I could. I tried to guide the fire crews. I knew the layout like the back of my hand. But even protective clothing didn't count for much."

"The explosion?"

"Officially, the cause is still unknown. But it must have been some sort of chemical reaction. I'm only an engineer."

I leave Klein to his thoughts and scribble some notes on to a pad. Then comes the outburst I didn't think he was capable of.

"Christ Almighty. They know what the cause was."

He fishes out a pack of cigarettes, lights one in haste and draws on it deeply.

"I inspected that ladle a month ago. I told them it wasn't safe. I found cracks in the bearings. Corrosion. Metal fatigue. It was rotting like old wood."

"Did Oblath listen to you?"

"I told him he should close the place down until we'd done proper repairs."

"And what did he say?"

"He said he couldn't afford to. They'd secured new orders. So it must be kept going. In any case, nothing had happened to justify an overhaul."

"It was an accident waiting to happen?"

"Oblath knows he can't keep this quiet. So he's all for passing the buck to the ministry of industry. Mix in a bit of 'more in sorrow than in anger' with a last minute show of unaccustomed integrity and he thinks he'll survive."

"What if I tell him this when I see him tomorrow?"

He ignores the question and ploughs on.

"This whole plant is falling apart. Did you see the state of those furnaces? Even you can tell they're clapped out. They should never have been built in the first place. How can you have a steelworks in a country that has no iron ore? It all goes back to Rakosi's time. Stalin wanted us to make steel. We made steel, whatever the cost. We have to have these things out in the open. Look at the town. You buy your kid a new coat and within a month it's falling apart, pitted with holes from the muck in the air. And we're breathing that stuff in."

"Mr Klein. Why don't I buy you that drink?"

"Bribed by a beer from a reporter?" His grin returns, but not before he's thrown a last, despairing glance at the devastation below us.

Chapter 3

The bar reeks of unwashed bodies and stale tobacco. We sit in a corner, as far away as possible from the blare of a television no one is watching. Klein looks into his beer. I run a finger round the rim of my glass.

"I told you we were ready to talk," he says.

"Who's 'we'?"

He can't look me in the eye.

"What you said was, 'we've grown up'. It's a good quote, Mr Klein. I might use it."

"Is that all you journalists think about? Whether it'll look good in print?"

"No, that's not what I meant."

I'm struggling to find a way out of this argument and get him back on side.

"The power of a free press," he declares. "It's something we're not used to."

"Look," I say. "You've given me a graphic account of the accident. I'm not going to quote you by name, unless you want me to."

"But everyone will know where you got it from. You see, in the end, I'm scared. I'm torn between seeing the truth about this rotten business out in the open and......"

"Losing your job."

"There's more to it than that."

The TV has changed from a soft-porn movie to the evening news.

"Look at that," he snaps. "It's not news. It's crap about politics in Budapest and things happening outside Hungary. No one understands. No one cares."

"Except when the Serbs start chucking Hungarians out of Vojvodina?"

"God. I hope it never comes to that. We'll have another war on our hands."

"You don't strike me as someone who just goes home at the end of the day and gawps at the box. You've been thinking this through, haven't you? When you do that, it can be disturbing."

He ignores the flattery and grins again.

"You're seeing Oblath tomorrow?"

"That's what the lady said. At nine."

Klein lights up again and blows the smoke towards the TV. He looks down at his weathered hands and then at me.

"Ask him. Ask him why I didn't get the money to repair that ladle."

"He'll tell me funds were tight. You said yourself the steelworks needs all the orders it can get. And he wants to push production as far as he can."

"It's been getting orders. Orders aren't the problem."

He drinks and pulls on the cigarette.

"Ask him why the price of anti-pollution filters for the stacks went up by ten per cent."

"How do you know that?"

"Rasko and Zsuzsa weren't the only husband and wife team working here. My wife's in Accounts. She processed the first order for filters from a firm in Austria. Then she saw the final invoices. Nothing tallied."

I sense he wants to say more while he feels strong enough.

"Ask Oblath what's happened to the workshop in the main yard, the first bit of private enterprise Ozd ever had."

"Explain."

"A year ago, six lads who'd been made redundant leased one of the old repair shops and started turning out pots and pans and other stuff from scrap."

"Was it a success?"

"You bet it was. They did well. For about nine months. Then, all at once, overnight, the place closed. There's been talk of protection money. Not enough profit going into so-called rent."

"OK. I'll ask him. What answers do you expect me to get?"

"That's the same question the other reporter put to me?"

"What other reporter?"

"The woman who came here yesterday."

"Her name? It's important."

"Tar. Andrea Tar. Worked for a magazine."

"Did you give her the guided tour, like me?"

"Exactly the same. And we came in here afterwards."

"Where did she go when you'd finished talking to her?"

"I don't know. A hotel maybe. Or back to Budapest. It was late when we finished. Why are you so interested in her?"

"She's a friend. Or at least a friend of a friend. And that friend is a police officer. She's disappeared. Her car's been found burned out on the road west of here."

"Christ," he whispers and pushes his chair aside. "I'm going. I'm glad we met. I'm glad I said what I said. But I must call it a day. Excuse me please."

"Wait. I want to thank you."

"You've already done that. And there isn't any more time."

He rushes out of the bar.

I gaze into the fug and noise. A group of youths in overalls stare at me then return to their conversation muttering prurient jokes.

I drain my glass, push my dog-eared notebook into my pocket, give the party at the counter a dirty look and step out into the night. I can smell the mixture of gas and cinders again. I cough as it catches my breath. I walk across the road and fumble for my keys. After a false start, the ignition fires. I abuse the clutch and drive smartly past a dimly-lit supermarket to a crossroads. There are signs to Eger. I follow them.

It's a forty-five minute drive. Eger is a pretty place, even in the dark. It has history and literary associations, baroque churches and a decent hotel. The room they give me is warm and homely. They even provide a late and tasty supper. I shouldn't have eaten it so fast. Indigestion keeps me awake until four in the morning. The sleep that follows is shallow and disturbed. I see furnaces and rivers of molten metal and hear the screams of locomotives and other shapes writhing behind a gauze of steam.

Ask him the right questions, Charlie. For Klein's sake.

Chapter 4

Ozd in the early morning is, if anything, worse than Ozd at night. I now see what Klein described so graphically. A population weighed down with dirt and dereliction, resignation stippled into their faces. They endure a kind of stabbing rain, rattling the car roof, spitting off pavements, a filthy, sibilant downpour, mocking those who hope it might just wash away some of the grime.

I turn into the long street leading to the steelworks. The winking lights of two police cars cut through the haze. They're parked directly outside the offices I visited yesterday.

"I'm sorry, Mr Barrow. Doctor Oblath cannot keep the appointment." The secretary looks at me with frightened eyes and bites her lower lip.

"Why not, for heaven's sake? He made a firm promise."

"Something terrible has happened, Mr Barrow. Something quite awful."

The woman can no longer hold my gaze.

"You don't know, do you?" she mumbles. "But you were the last person to see him alive."

I gape at her. The horror of what she's trying to say slowly dawns on me.

"You are Mr Charlie Barrow?" says a voice behind me.

I turn to face a tall man in a trench-coat, his black hair and sallow features wet from the rain.

"I am Lieutenant Rainer from Eger. I'm afraid I have to ask you some questions."

It's not a request or a threat, more a statement of the obvious.

"The body of Janos Klein was found on spare ground behind the Bar Corso. You were drinking with him last night, yes?"

"You make it sound very sordid, Lieutenant. Klein had a beer and so did I."

We proceed through a routine interrogation covering times of arrival and departure. I furnish details of our visit to the site of the accident. And I see no reason to hold back on Klein's subsequent fears and hasty leave-taking.

"He was scared?" asks Rainer.

"It came on suddenly, towards the end of our conversation. Up to then he'd been very forthright about wanting to have the truth told. He'd been indignant. Almost missionary in his zeal to tell me the how and why of it." I take a deep breath. "How did he die?"

"Do you really want to know the answer to that question?"

"That bad?"

"A patrolman saw a pack of town dogs howling and fighting over what he thought was a pile of old clothes among the weeds and rubble. That was about one in the morning. He went over to have a look. Even when he threatened them, the dogs were reluctant to back off. So he fired a shot in air. The dogs ran away but no one in the neighbourhood reacted. At that time of night they wouldn't want to know. Ozd is that kind of town, Mr Barrow."

"I'm beginning to get that impression, Lieutenant."

"The patrolman saw Klein's body, saved from mutilation by the thickness of the parka he was wearing, although it was badly shredded by the dogs. And they'd smelled blood."

"How?"

"His skull had been smashed. He was bludgeoned to death."

I can feel the colour draining from my face. Rainer goes to the water cooler by the lift.

"How soon after he left the bar did you follow him?" he asks, handing me a paper cup.

"I didn't follow him, Lieutenant. I stayed in the bar for about ten minutes. Then I drove straight out of Ozd to Eger. I stayed the night there."

"Yes, we know. We checked the hotels."

"Are you telling me I'm a suspect?"

Rainer is an old hand and second-guesses me.

"Thank you, Mr Barrow. There's no need for you to worry. Your *bona fides* has been vouched for. I am working with a certain Captain Kovacs on the disappearance of his partner, Miss Tar."

"Are you indeed? Than you should know that Klein told me he'd been talking to her the day before yesterday. He gave her the same tour of the steelworks and an account of the accident."

"Yes. His contacts with journalists seem to have attracted the wrong kind of attention."

"I suppose I ought to feel guilty," I say.

"Don't. If I were you, I'd go back to Budapest and file your story."

"What about my appointment with Oblath?"

"I think you'll find he's left, Mr Barrow."

"Left?"

"He rose early. His wife tells me he dashed out of his apartment with no explanation. Then he drove away in a hurry."

Rainer hopes I'll return to Ozd for the magistrate's hearing, shakes my hand and says good-bye. It's only later, recalling his vaguely archaic language, his courtesy and his luminous, green eyes, that I realise I've failed to detect the implied connection between the murder and Oblath's departure. I consider seeking out Klein's widow to offer my sympathy but baulk at the prospect. I'm overcome by a desire to get out of this miserable town as fast as possible. In any case, I've more than enough material to write something for Fred.

Depression dulls my concentration. I fill up at a petrol station just outside Ozd. It's only as I pull on to the main road that I notice a smart, white Suzuki jeep in my mirror. I watch it tuck itself in behind two cars and a pick-up that follow me into the traffic stream. I let the three vehicles overtake and afford others the same courtesy as I head for the motorway junction at Hatvan. But the Suzuki hangs back and keeps its distance.

The rain has stopped and the landscape is kinder. The trees have long since lost their leaves and the roadside grass has withered to a winter brown. But a line of hills to the south is pleasing and a brittle sunlight pierces gaps in the overhanging cloud.

The car radio tells me that the prime minister is now too ill to perform his official duties. He will continue to receive radiation therapy for his cancer. Then he will travel to Germany for further treatment. The government is now in the hands of his deputy, the interior minister. The news is followed by a prominent political commentator who makes no bones about his prejudices.

"Poor Doctor Antall. So well-meaning. So honest. Born in the era of Horthy, growing up through the war, the German invasion and the dark days of communism."

The man's voice drones on. I look in the mirror. The Suzuki is still there.

"And yet, despite all, he managed to gain a degree in history and turn himself into the country's leading authority

195

on anthropology and Islam. What a brain. In '56, he formed a Christian youth alliance and took part in talks with the great Imre Nagy. But for six long years after the Revolution, he was detained and questioned many times, by the Russians, by III/III, those despicable successors to the AVO, until, inevitably, he was fired from his teaching post. 'Unsuitable for instructing socialist youth'."

The commentator spits out his derision. The Suzuki has crept a little closer.

"Undeterred, he slowly edged himself back into academic life. In '89 communism dies. It seems Joszef Antall's chance has come. He founds the Forum and within a year has won an election. Now he is struck down by this dreadful disease. There is no justice for true democrats. His is the fate of all good men and women in Hungary. But it is not his physical frailty that matters. His political weakness has been to trust those around him. He has been tricked into appointing the wrong people to important posts. And he has been curiously unable to understand that a free press is not here simply to support his government. The Forum is not infallible. Above all, Joszef Antall has not noticed, or has studiously ignored, the tendency of extremists to manipulate him. The legacy of his quarrel with the leader of one of our Rightist parties will surely bring more trouble."

I laugh at what I've heard. Objectivity is absent even from the official media.

I take another long look in the mirror. The traffic has thinned and the highway is almost deserted. I'm on a stretch of road where drivers in a hurry would normally show a clean pair of heels to slower vehicles. The Suzuki has moved up and sits on my tail. It pulls out as if to overtake but holds its speed alongside.

The driver is a young male. He sports dark glasses and a wide grin. And he's vaguely familiar. I slow down, gesturing him to move ahead. But he stays where he is. I focus on the next bend. A truck coming towards us forces him to pull in behind, just a fraction from my bumper. The truck passes and the Suzuki moves alongside again. I wind the window down.

"What the fuck do you think….?"

He lurches to his right, grinding his near side into my bodywork. He bounces off and repeats the manoeuvre. I brake hard. He hares ahead, applies his brakes but slides into a skid he can't control.

A tyre bursts. The jeep heels over on to its right side. I watch it roll and bounce into the ditch. It smashes into a tree trunk. A door flies off together with the bonnet. It comes to rest on its roof in a patch of woodland on the other side of the ditch.

I wait behind the wheel gasping for air. The jeep shows no sign of life. I switch off, get out and walk round my own car. The off side is battered but intact. I climb back in. The engine restarts without a hiccup. I coast gently forward and stop again about ten metres back from the spot where the Suzuki left the road.

I'm about to walk forward and risk an inspection when I hear the blare of a siren. The patrol car crunches to a halt and out step Rainer and Kovacs.

"I had a hunch I should follow you," says the lieutenant.

"How did you guess?" I ask.

"That was the vehicle, or one like it," says Kovacs, "seen near Andrea's Skoda just after the truck driver watched it go up in flames."

Two uniforms are peering into the wreck.

"He's still alive," one of them shouts.

We climb off the road, push through the damp undergrowth. Rainer is using his radio to call for an ambulance. A bird sings somewhere high up above us. We smell oil and petrol and burned rubber. Kovacs is the first to see him.

"Christ," he says. "It's Janza."

197

PART 12

Chapter 1

The stench is of putrefaction and urine. Light comes from two bare bulbs swinging from wooden rafters. The floor of the barn is beaten earth and sawdust.

Coro leans on one arm and tries focusing with his good eye. After the beating he took from the skins, the other has stayed closed. But the pain is easing. He peers down the length of the barn and hears a woman coughing and spluttering. Then she retches. He reckons that if she doesn't move soon, she'll choke on her vomit. But before he can shift his aching body, stronger hands have grasped her shoulders and shaken her.

"Spit it out. Spit it out."

The woman obeys. In any other circumstances he'd say she was smartly turned out. She wears a leather jacket and a well-cut skirt. But the right arm of the jacket is badly torn. He can tell she's in agony. She holds a hand to her right ear, retches again and pulls a face as if she's disgusted with herself. She hasn't opened her eyes.

"Drink this," says a voice. The woman takes the tin mug, spits and coughs. Then opens her eyes and flies into a panic.

"I can't see. I can't see."

She tries to free herself from the hands gripping her shoulders. The grip relaxes. The woman turns and stares at shadows and movements slowly taking on shape and meaning. Coro meets her gaze and tries to send a tacit message of reassurance. Bending over her is another woman, the one who gave her water, an old Roma, with a heavily lined face and a firm chin framed by a scarf of indeterminate colour. She smiles. But the woman in the leather jacket recoils.

"What is this place?" she asks.

"It's a prison," says the Gypsy.

"Prison? But who keeps you here?"

"Some very nasty men and a slut of a girl. We are their slaves."

"Slaves?"

Another face appears. She hears the rustling of feet as more inmates gather round.

"She's all right then?" The question comes from a throat, rasping on years of tobacco smoke.

"She's as good as any of us in this foul hole."

The woman tries to move. She cries out.

"You're bruised and battered," says the Roma. "But as far as I can tell, there are no broken bones. You've got a black eye and some wicked scratches down one side. And your nice clothes are badly torn."

"What's your name?" asks Coro.

The woman hesitates. But his insistent stare demands an answer.

"Andrea. Andrea Tar. How long have you been here?"

"Who's to say?" The gruff tobacco voice sighs deeply. "Can't work it out any more."

"But who are these people who make you work for them."

"Fascists and thugs," says Coro. He introduces himself. "This is Mariska." As he nods towards the Roma, he flinches from the pain in his eye.

"I think I've been kidnapped," says Andrea. "I was in my car and they ran me off the road. I'd driven out of a place called Ozd. I must have been somewhere between there and Hatvan, where the motorway starts."

Coro nods and makes a mental note of the information.

She recalls his earlier answer. "Fascists and thugs? But who exactly?"

Coro edges nearer. "They have some sort of organisation. It's modelled on the Arrow Cross…"

"The Arrow Cross?" She looks at him with her mouth wide open. "God Almighty. Do you understand what that means?"

"I have been told," Coro replies. "They were the Hungarian Nazis in the Second World War." He holds up a hand. "Let me finish. Outside, there are four long huts, one for male prisoners. The others they use as barracks. They hold meetings and parade like soldiers. They drink heavily. The women and children here have to clean up after them. And some of the women have to do worse than that. They kick us and beat us and shout orders and call us 'scum'." Coro snorts his outrage.

"If the other men are held in one of those huts, what are you doing here with the women? What is *he* doing here?" She gestures to the man with the smoker's voice.

"He is too old," says Mariska. "He has weak lungs. He cannot breathe easily. He will die soon."

Andrea looks suitably appalled. But Mariska isn't apologising for telling the truth.

"And you, Coro?"

"If you have the patience, I'll tell you my story," he says.

Half an hour later he's describing Tomi's torture and death.

"The morning after, I collapsed under another beating. They tossed me in here. That was maybe two days ago."

Andrea says, "You will tell me all that again when we get out of here."

"You think we will?" He laughs quietly.

"Of course. We have to."

Coro shrugs. He neither enthuses over Andrea's optimism nor derides it

"Everything that's happened to me since I left Romania," he says, "tells me to resign myself to fate."

"If you do that, they'll defeat you."

The man on whom Mariska has pronounced a death sentence moves alongside.

"I have a story too," he says.

Before they can stop him, he's plunged into his tale of woe.

"I came long before Coro. I cannot remember the date. It was springtime. They entered our village one afternoon. They had guns and trucks. They rounded us up. Seven families. We lived in Borsod county. When we arrived, they prodded the women and kids into here but kept the men outside for hours. They made us stand in puddles. Then they ordered us to line up against the side of one of the trucks, raise our hands above our heads and spread our legs. They hit us with rifles, planks, rubber hoses, anything they could lay their hands on. I fainted and they poured cold water over me. After more beatings, they pushed us into one of the huts, threw in a bucket and told us to piss in it."

He pauses, savouring the effect he's having on his audience.

"Then they told us to drink it."

Coro and Mariska are for stopping the old man.

"Let him, finish," says Andrea.

"The next day I was taken away by a guard who put a gun in my mouth."

Suddenly he's coughing again. Mariska hands him a mug of water.

"He said I was done for. But another man, the one they call Gabi, told him to lay off. He said I was needed for work. Even so, he told me to lie down on my stomach. If I lifted my head, he stamped on me – on that part of the back where the kidneys are."

His chest heaves like a leaky bellows. Mariska leads him away.

A key turns in the lock. The Roma women drift back to the far corners of the barn as a powerful torchlight searches the gloom.

"Tar." The voice is female, rough and uncompromising. "I said 'Tar'. Where the hell are you?"

The torch finds Andrea and moves towards her.

"I am Tar, as you so politely put it."

"Oh, listen to her." The mockery turns sour. "I'll put it how I bloody well like, Tar."

She kneels in front of Andrea, thrusts her pouting face at her and spits. Andrea recoils, feels her wounds again, buckles and rolls over. The prostitute kicks, laughs and kicks again.

"Going to help the little lady, are we?" she says to the rest of them without turning round. "Just try it. Any one of you buggers moves…..You're on your own, darlin'. See? They're not going to lift a finger."

"I will," says a male voice.

The woman surveys the prisoners and sees Coro standing in front of them.

"Oh, you will, will you?" She marches up to him and prods at his chest. He hardly moves. "And what will you *do*?"

"You'll find out later." He smiles and says no more.

"I'll get Big Gyuri to deal with you, smart arse."

It's her parting shot and he knows he's confused her.

She turns her attention to Andrea again, grabs her hair and pulls her up on to her feet.

"You bastard," Andrea cries out. But her head has been jerked back so far that the tendons in her neck are taut, shooting pain through every nerve end.

"Walk, Tar. Walk. Towards that door. And keep your bloody mouth shut. Do you hear me?"

Too engrossed in her torment, Andrea fails to respond.

"I said, 'Do you hear me?'" There's another sharp tug of the hair.

"I hear you," she croaks. "I hear you. I hear you."

The whore barely relaxes her grip. "That's better. Now, move."

But the effort of putting one foot in front of another is too much for Andrea. A wave of nausea envelops her and she drops to the floor.

Chapter 2

She comes round to find herself slumped in a high-backed chair, its structure doing nothing for her aches and pains. The room is warm and yet she feels she must wrap herself as tightly as possible in her torn jacket. Somehow it helps to preserve her self-respect. As her eyes get used to her surroundings, she's aware of someone sitting a few feet away alongside her. She focuses and sees Coro. He's bound and gagged.

He can just move his head enough to indicate that she should say nothing.

In front of them, a table. For her there's bread, a bowl of hot soup and a mug of coffee. For Coro, nothing. His eyes say, "Eat and drink."

She leans in to spoon some of the soup into her battered mouth. She tries the coffee. As she lifts the mug to her lips, two powerful lights are switched on, casting a white and unrelenting glare on to the surface of the table. A figure on the other side seizes the black metal shade of one of the lamps and shines it directly into her face.

"Do you have to do that?" she hisses.

The figure doesn't respond. Somewhere beyond the walls she hears laughter. Then a scream and some muffled shouting. She waits. Coro watches, afraid that she won't have the resources to keep up a pretence of bravado.

The figure speaks. "Andrea Tar. Tough, investigative journalist. Fearless little body who won't crack easily. Am I right?"

The voice is cultured but harsh and nasal. She ignores the query and makes no effort to identify the speaker. The light is too strong and her eyes too sore.

"Learned those qualities from Peter Kovacs, did you?"

She catches her breath.

"I'm afraid Captain Kovacs can't help you now."

He moves round to her side of the table. She keeps her eyes shut but senses that he's bending to examine her.

"I presume you didn't relish the way Nora treated you. No one would, Miss Tar. She is a brute, a tart and a pervert. But she is useful and intelligent to a degree. You were unwise to call her names."

She opens her eyes, knowing that it's Kozma standing in front of her.

"I shall call *you* names," she says, "if you don't tell me where I am and why I am being held here with two dozen Gypsies in an evil-smelling barn with no ventilation, no sanitation and precious little food and water. And while you're at it, untie this man here."

"The Gypsies are nothing. They do as they are told. They are lucky. In the new Hungary they will have no place except, as the Bible puts it, as hewers of wood and drawers of water. They will have plenty of water then, I can assure you. Water to drown in and wood on which they will be impaled if they disobey us."

"Us? Who is 'Us'? "

"No, Miss Tar. I ask the questions. I might give you some answers later. But right now I need to hear one or two things from you. By the way, do finish your food and your coffee."

"Why can't Coro have some as well?"

"I've just told you. We don't treat Gypsies as human beings."

"Ah yes, I should have realised, Colonel Kozma. You pursue your own logic."

She turns and detects a faint smile in Coro's eyes. She smiles back.

"Look at me, Tar," Kozma orders. "It is very astute of you to recognise me. But I fear it will do you no good."

"You and I met over a drink once at a police function. And I don't forget faces."

"How clever of you."

"If you have decided I'm worth running off the public highway and kidnapping, then presumably you think someone will stump up ready money for me."

"We have no intention of asking a ransom for you," says Kozma. "You haven't been abducted. You have been captured. And you will be killed."

Coro shifts in his chair and splutters behind his gag.

"Oh dear," says Kozma. "I've upset your Gypsy friend. I think you should both understand that you will not leave here alive. But you won't die until I've extracted a little more information from you."

So far it hasn't occurred to Andrea that she may not get out of here. Coro watches the way she closes her eyes, tries to breathe regularly, feels more pain in her right side and resists the temptation to weep.

"We don't regard you as valuable, Tar. People like you, like Kovacs, are expendable in the new Hungary. We know you will never co-operate with us when we are in power. So there is no point in trying to persuade you. Hitler said, 'The broad mass of the nation will easily fall victim to a big lie.' But your kind are not of the broad mass. You think yourselves above them as you did when we had communism."

"And as you now think of yourselves," says Andrea. "The new elite."

"Very clever, Tar. Just know that this time we shall inaugurate a totalitarianism that doesn't make the mistake of letting people like you fester in the body politic."

"In other words, we shall be purged."

"Exactly."

"You admit then that what you are perpetrating is Hitler's 'big lie'?"

"I admit no such thing. Let me remind you of what another National Socialist said. 'The essence of propaganda consists in winning people over to an idea so sincerely, so vitally, that in the end, they succumb to it utterly and can never again escape from it.' "

"But Hitler and Goebbels failed."

"Yes, they failed. But we shall not. Not this time. We shall not make their mistakes."

He moves back behind the table but leaves the light shining into her eyes.

"How pathetic, Colonel."

Coro notices the sudden defiance but hides his surprise behind the gag.

"You act like a poor man's Doctor Strangelove," says Andrea. "I thought your rigorous Marxist training in the AVO made you think more subtly than that."

"My rigorous Marxist training, Tar, drove home one basic lesson. That the broad mass are fools. They have to be led and told what to do. Otherwise we bring upon ourselves the chaos of democracy, the kind of chaos we have now. And people like you make it more chaotic. And must be removed."

She watches his shaking hands. His chair scrapes the tiled floor as he drops his bulk on to it. He's physically spent but still pumping an excess of adrenaline.

Again she hears a distant guffaw and another scream. But before she has time to think about the remote possibility of escape, Kozma recovers some of his composure.

"What did the engineer, Klein, tell you about the accident at Ozd?"

"It wasn't an accident. You know that."

"Answer my question."

"The figures were falsified, weren't they, Kozma? Your friend, Oblath, was taking a rake-off."

She's trying to say as little as possible, groping for time to wring more out of Kozma before he flings them back into the barn.

"How did Klein know that?"

"He didn't know," she lies. "He's not the only person I talked to at the steelworks."

"He's dead," he tells her.

Coro sees her fight the urge to be sick.

"You had him murdered?" she asks.

"Not me personally. We have operational units who carry out orders."

"Operational units. Don't make me laugh, Colonel. You have gangs of thugs. The shock troops of your New Order, I suppose. Studying philosophy, are they? Reading Nietzsche and *Mein Kampf*?"

Coro is also watching Kozma. He's shaking again. Andrea is getting under his skin.

"Let me tell you something else, Tar. Take a few facts to the grave with you."

Kozma rises and stalks round the table, waving his hands in the air.

"You need to know these things. You and your Romany friend here."

He stops in front of Coro who braces himself for the blow. But Kozma simply stands, raises his head and looks down his nose.

"Every year in this country, about six thousand foreigners break the law. Theft, drunken driving, murder. Ukrainians, Chechens, Chinese…..and Gypsies."

"Croats too," says Andrea. "Like the one who killed Kovacs's corporal."

"That was very stupid. We have dealt with him."

"Have you indeed?"

Another pause. Kozma seems at a loss.

"Why didn't you have me bumped off in Ozd?" Andrea asks. "It would have saved a lot of time and trouble."

"If it gives you any satisfaction, we lost you. We were inefficient. But you made the mistake of going back to the steelworks. From then on you were a clear target. Like the other journalist who followed you."

"What other journalist?"

"He's British. His name is Barrow, I think. He won't get far. We'll deal with him."

Kozma presses on, looking almost messianic in his desire to explain the essentials of his own version of the truth.

"Almost anyone can come here and defile us," he says. "Western entrepreneurs who want to buy up our businesses and plaster our streets with adverts in English."

"What's wrong with that? We need the money. English is the universal language."

"It smacks of American and Jewish domination. We don't want it. The Jews already control our culture. They even own our best football club. And these bloody Gypsies. They call them 'economic migrants'. What hypocrisy."

Both Andrea and Coro know what's coming next. Kozma is thoroughly versed in the slogans of Hungarian nationalism, the calls for wrongs to be righted, treaties to be rewritten, the return of Erdely and Felvidek – Transylvania and southern Slovakia.

"All around us live millions of so-called foreign nationals who are not foreigners," he says, "because they are Hungarian. We want them back."

"That'll cause you problems," says Andrea. "They might not want to live under fascism. It didn't do them much good in the past."

He ignores this. "If those weaklings at the United Nations or the fools in Brussels refuse to let us change our frontiers, then we shall change them ourselves."

"And you will commit the same mistakes as Hitler," says Coro quietly. He's worked his gag free. Kozma grins like a predator about to devour its prey. But he doesn't faze Coro. "You will plunge us all into war, slaughter and destruction."

"A cleansing, Gypsy. A veritable cleansing, in which your people will be wiped out. After the cleansing, a wonderful purity, of race, creed and purpose. A cleansing of which you and Andrea Tar must now have a foretaste."

He presses a button. There is a long silence before Big Gyuri enters the room.

PART 13

Chapter 1

Janza lies unconscious in a hospital bed in Eger. He has a broken leg, three cracked ribs and a fissure in his skull. The doctor says he has a fifty-fifty chance of making it.

"I want a uniform posted outside this room at all times," Rainer orders. "No one except you and your nursing staff are to have access to him. Is that clear?"

The doctor doesn't like being addressed as if he's a police underling.

"Don't teach me my job. As it happens, isolating this patient will be the best thing for him."

"I'm glad we understand one another."

Kovacs tries to mollify the physician. "The patient is a key witness to several crimes, doctor. Please, do your best to save him."

I watch these exchanges with more questions buzzing in my head than I can cope with. Janza clearly slipped his leash at some point. But when and how?

"I made a bad mistake," says Kovacs, as we assemble in Rainer's office. "I sent him to do a second check on the Skoda."

"He's following Kozma's agenda," I proffer. "You should have taken Ubul's advice, Captain."

"I didn't realise he was ex-III/III," says Rainer. "If you'd told me, I'd have kept a tail on him."

"I know, I know," Kovacs protests.

We sit in silence. Rainer produces three bottles of beer.

"Did he have any papers on him?" I ask. "A bag? Anything at all?"

Rainer's face lights up. "The cloakroom," he says.

He returns brandishing a fistful of documents and an open briefcase.

"You're a genius, Mr Barrow."

"But he wasn't carrying that when we left Budapest," says Kovacs.

"You mean you didn't see him carrying it," I say. "You weren't meant to look."

"Maybe this will give us some answers," suggests Rainer.

"Before we plunge in," says Kovacs, "let's just determine one another's territory here. We must co-operate, Rainer. And I don't want to interfere in any way……"

"Captain, don't concern yourself. We both need to find out where your partner's being held….."

"If she's still alive, you mean."

"We must hope that she is. Janza himself said she wasn't in the Skoda when it went up in flames."

"I wonder if he meant to do the same to me?" I interject. "Run me off the road, torch the car and kidnap me."

"But someone else destroyed the Skoda. And abducted Andrea," says Kovacs.

Rainer stops this speculation by filling us in on his enquiry into Klein's murder.

"What I want from you, Captain, is any clue as to who in Budapest tipped off Andrea Tar – passed on rumours that the deaths at the steelworks were not simply a tragic accident. I won't beat about the bush. If anything you tell me leads to Klein's killer and, incidentally, produces an explanation for Oblath's swift departure from Ozd, never mind the burning of the car, then, for the first time in my career as a provincial policeman, I am leading an investigation into a case of national importance."

"Aiming for promotion and change, then?" I ask.

"Mr Barrow, I've been stuck out here for five years."

"You have my sympathies." I toast him with the beer bottle.

"We have already begun a search of the country round here," he says. "I can assure you that by the time my people have finished, they will have knocked on every door in three counties. I also have good relations with the military. They are sending up a helicopter at dusk in the hope of spotting lights in remoter areas, places where there may be dwellings we are not aware of."

"I admire your efficiency," says Kovacs.

"I am also certain that Oblath has not left the country. He has not gone to Vienna or Zurich with his ill-gotten gains. He hasn't got the courage or the imagination. He's with Kozma. Somewhere in this neck of the woods."

"Why are you so sure?" Kovacs is weary and ready for sleep. But I know he won't rest until he's tied up the loose ends.

"I've known for some time," Rainer replies, "that Oblath is a member of the People's Justice Party. He's never tried to hide it. There was talk in Ozd of his standing for parliament. He's probably worked it out that he won't have a steelworks to manage for much longer. He knows it's finished as a going concern, even if he wasn't milking it for party funds. My guess is that after you scuppered Kozma's plan to discredit you, Captain, he got word to Oblath to meet him. Oblath will now have told him about Klein's murder. Then he'll have been given orders to arrange for Andrea Tar's abduction. They want to know how much *she* knows. And since she is your partner, they're having to move fast."

"And me?" I ask tamely.

"You have eaten at the tree of dangerous knowledge as well, Mr Barrow. Kozma trusted Janza to play the double agent. Hence the attempt to trash your car. The difference being that this time he had to do the job himself."

"Let's have a look at those papers," says Kovacs. He hands them round.

The document he gives me describes a 'safe' house used by III/III in the past and Kozma's people under the new regime. There's a map highlighting a road that snakes up into the Matra hills west of Eger. After about ten kilometres, it shows a right turn along a track leading to a marked building on a contour line. Clearly high on a hill.

"He even wrote notes," says Kovacs handing more papers to me.

"House empty. Pick lock. Find main junction box. Throw switch, activate lights and telex. Transmit to ministry. Summarise conversations with Kovacs, Rainer and journalist, Barrow. Inform plan eliminate Barrow. No reply ex Budapest. Deactivate telex. Quit house. Intercepted by two man patrol. Car inspected. Lie low. No action. Return Eger."

"We've known about that place for a while," says Rainer. "But we left it alone. Not for the likes of run-of-the-mill policemen. Perhaps we should now take our courage in both hands."

"And question that patrol, if you can," says Kovacs.

Rainer gives him an old-fashioned look.

"Apologies, Lieutenant. None of my business, I know."

"Take a look at this." I push the document at Kovacs and Rainer reads over his shoulder.

"Reconstruction of Camps at Recsk and Szalajkahaz for Internment of Roma;

Provision of quarters for New Arrow Cross recruits;

Provision of vehicles for Transportation of recruits and Roma;

Provision of weapons and ammunition;
Provision of food and other supplies."

"And so it goes on," says Kovacs. He hands the papers to Rainer.

"Can I have another look?" I ask.

They leave me to peruse the contents in detail. I know about Recsk, a name rarely mentioned unless it's absolutely necessary. It's a small copper-mining town set in a valley in the Matra, once the site of Hungary's 'mini-Gulag', a forced labour camp built by Rakosi's communists in the early fifties. The AVO used it to torture and kill hundreds of 'class enemies'. The Budapest papers have been grinding out the gory details, ever since the new government unveiled plans to convert the site into a national memorial to the victims of totalitarian oppression.

I decide to pay Recsk a visit.

"Not before you've had a decent meal and a night's sleep," says Kovacs.

The phone on Rainer's desk croaks like a throttled frog. His face remains non-committal until he nods slowly and frowns.

"Janza's vanished," he says.

Chapter 2

My Opel suffered when Janza tried to run me off the road. Offside doors badly dented, steering out of true, not to mention two burst tyres. Rainer offers me a replacement, an unmarked police Lada of uncertain vintage. I rise early and after a swift breakfast of coffee and rolls, sort out its gearbox and head for Recsk. It's raining again. The car takes bends like a skateboard but I'm there in half an hour.

Recsk is strung out along Route 24, with hills on either side. The shops are shut. Apart from a couple of parked cars and an old woman wearing widow's weeds, the place is deserted. I wind down the window and holler through the hissing rain.

"Mother."

She peers at me through rheumy eyes, walking stick in one hand, plastic shopping bag in the other.

"I'm lost," I call. "Can you help?"

She stands her ground and says nothing.

"Well, can you?" I shout again.

She doesn't move. Forcing a smile, I get out of the car and walk across the road. She raises her stick and waves it vigorously.

"Get back," she snaps. "I don't talk to strangers, especially those with no manners. And I'm not waiting around to get soaked."

I lift my hands in mock surrender and resort to traditional courtesies.

"Adjon Isten jo napot. God give you a good day. I just want some directions, that's all."

"Directions? Where to? There's only one place to visit round here."

"And where would that be?"

"The Coach Museum at Parafurdo. Up the road there."

"I'm not interested in ancient modes of transport," I say. "Or beautiful horses."

She cocks her head and scrutinises me from top to toe.

"You're a foreigner."

I see no reason to deny this.

"English," I say. "Can you help me find the place I'm looking for?"

"You speak good Hungarian for a foreigner."

"I'll take that as a compliment. Now, can you tell me where the camp is?"

"The camp. What camp?"

"Where they kept the political prisoners."

"Why is everybody suddenly so interested in that hell hole?"

"What do you mean by 'everybody'?"

She retreats. "I don't talk to strangers. Don't talk to foreigners."

She turns to leave but I block her path.

"Neni. Mother. Look at me. I'm a journalist. Completely harmless. I'm not going to bash you over the head and steal your shopping. Now where's that camp?"

The rain is easing and a weak sunlight whitens the breaking cloud. I change tack.

"Suppose we go and have a coffee in that place over there," I suggest.

She opens her mouth but says nothing.

"I know, I know," I sigh. "You don't talk to strangers."

She looks me up and down again and grunts.

"Yes. Well then," she says. "Need a coffee. Come on. Haven't got all day."

She offers her shopping bag. I take it and she suddenly links her hand into my arm. We trundle down the road like mother and son.

The café sports the name *Hangulat* suggesting it has a convivial atmosphere. But I know that if I'd walked in by myself, I'd have met frigid hostility and perhaps a blank refusal to serve me. With the widow in tow, I am more or less acceptable.

"Another friend of yours, Klara?"

The stout woman behind the display of cakes and chocolate icing is already vetting me. Klara lifts her stick and bangs the handle on the counter.

"Yes. A friend, Marta. So how about two of those muddy '*duplas*' of yours. And don't take all day."

We choose a table by the steamed-up window. I hold a chair back for Klara. She smiles at me for the first time. Then shouts at Marta.

"And don't try eavesdropping, you nosy woman. It's private."

Marta sniffs but is suitably cowed. I put the shopping bag on the table and Klara grips it as if her life depends on what it contains. I fetch the coffees and pass her a sachet of sugar. Reluctantly, she releases her hold on the bag, tears at the little packet, pours the lot into her cup and stirs it with bird-like energy.

"Camp's down the road," she says abruptly. "The way you came in. Watch out for signs saying 'Kobanya' on your right. Then drive up the hill."

She clicks her tongue. "What do you want to go there for? Horrible place, Full of ghosts. Well it was. They're clearing it, you know. Planting trees."

Then she drops her bombshell.

"My man was in there."

She sits back and watches the effect this has on me.

"He was a miner. Good solid, no-nonsense working man with grit in the creases of his face. That was before his back killed him. And it wasn't all that killed him."

If I interrupt, I know I'll break the spell. I let the pauses, filled with Klara's slurping, work their magic. She places her tiny cup back on to its saucer.

"He led a strike in '47. Heard what was going on in Budapest. Rallied a few of his mates. Demanded higher wages and shorter shifts. They gave way at first, those bosses who never dirtied their suits digging in the earth for copper. Made life easier for a while."

She contemplates the empty cup as if it's the final answer to life's riddles.

"But the AVO got him. Put him away in '49. First jail in Miskolc. Then that camp. I was allowed to visit him twice a year. I remember the way they laid it out. Rough huts made out of tree trunks. I took him fruit and vegetables. I'd kept them for days so they weren't very fresh when he got them. But for a man stuck in Recsk they were luxuries. All *they* gave him was watery soup and stale bread."

"How long did he stay in there?" I ask.

"Came out in '53. Went back down the mine. Never said a word about the place. Kept going till '56. The Revolution raised his hopes. But not for long. Died soon after. Poor man. We never had children. I've been on my own thirty six years."

She looks up at me. "Haven't talked about it until now. Except to two Gypsy fellows asking where it was, like you."

"Gypsies?"

"Father and son. Big strapping lads. Came in here with them."

"I thought you didn't talk to strangers," I say with what I hope is a quizzical smile.

"They bribed me," she chuckles. "Like you. Bought me coffee and chocolate cake."

"How long ago was this?"

"Yesterday."

"Where are these Gypsies now?"

"Staying at my place. Want to meet them?"

There's an inevitability about all this which I don't resist.

"Not scared of Gypsies, are you? I live right at the end of town. You can give me a lift in that car of yours."

As we file out, the hubbub in the café dies and all eyes follow us. In the doorway Klara turns and meets their stares.

"Mind your own bloody business," she hollers, swinging the stick within a whisker of a red-faced man in overalls. I smile broadly at the assembled throng, nod farewell to Marta and follow my informant out into the street.

Chapter 3

Kalman and Jenoe are housed in the loft of Klara's cottage. It has a dormer window, from which, sitting in two high backed chairs, they're scanning the road outside.

"Visitor," says Klara bursting into their eyrie. "English journalist, he says. Wants to meet you. Wants to visit that camp."

They turn, scrutinise me cautiously and are as disconcerted as I am by Klara's artlessness.

"Whatever you say, Klara," says Jenoe who has clearly come to the conclusion that when Klara springs surprises there's no point in raising objections. We do the introductions.

"Well, go on," she says. "Ask them why they're so interested in the Recsk camp."

I raise an apologetic eyebrow.

"Why are *you* interested in it?" asks Kalman.

"I've seen evidence," I say, "suggesting that a bunch of neo-fascists want to turn it back into what it was – and use it to incarcerate their enemies."

"Who happen to include us," observes Kalman.

"So it seems."

They sit down again. Kalman picks up his pipe from a large glass ashtray and applies a match. The flame throws shadows on to whitewashed walls. Klara descends to make coffee and we hear the rattle of cups and the gurgle of water as she fills a kettle.

Jenoe peers out of the window.

"Quiet as the grave," he says.

I push on with my explanation.

"I want to write about it for my newspaper in London. It's part of an investigation into corruption in high places and some nasty business involving officials with extreme right wing views."

The two Roma nod at me.

"Now, why are you so interested in Recsk?" I ask.

"We're looking for one of our kind who's vanished into thin air," Kalman answers.

He tells me Coro's story.

"We went to the Ketpo settlement to fetch him home," he says, "and he wasn't there. We were told he just walked out one day. I got angry with the official who was supposed to keep an eye on him. Coro had crossed him over some money he was owed. Then he got angry with me - told me about raids on the settlement, with truckloads of skinheads demanding payment. Not cash. People. And if they don't get them, they threaten to burn the place down. He said these aren't ordinary thugs letting off a bit a steam. These bastards wear uniforms with Arrow Cross armbands. They carry guns. When he reported all this to the police, they just laughed in his face."

"So what do they do with the Roma they kidnap?"

"An old man there told us they were used as slave labour. He said as far as they're concerned, we Roma are racially inferior. They've got big ideas about what they're going to do to us when they take over. It's called ethnic cleansing. Then he told me to follow my nose."

"What did he mean by that?"

"That was when he mentioned Recsk. He said he was survivor from the old days. He lived on bread and soup for twelve months – ate beetles and spiders and tree bark "

"Just like my husband," mutters Klara returning with a tray of cups and a packet of biscuits.

"He said they worked in a quarry from dawn till dusk, winter and summer. If they fell ill, they were taken to the camp quack. He made sure they recovered just enough to be put back to work. They cleaned latrines. The guards used newsprint to wipe their arses. One day in '53 they found a scrap of paper telling them Stalin was dead and Rakosi had been kicked out. They were released soon after. But they were also sworn to secrecy. That's why people clam up when anybody mentions the place."

"It gets better," says Jenoe. "Or worse, depending on your point of view."

"Go on," I say.

He takes up the story, while Kalman puffs on his pipe.

"The old fellow said Recsk was where the Arrow Cross were taking their Roma prisoners. Not to the old AVO camp but somewhere nearby. There'd been others around here and they hadn't been dismantled. Someone has enough money to do a bit of renovation, buy arms and vehicles and bribe the local police. And someone has the power to pull the wool over the eyes of top people in Budapest."

"Look out of the window," says Klara.

I see the road and houses on the other side and look bewildered.

"Every now and then," she goes on, "we see two or three of those old East German trucks bringing in bits and pieces – prefabricated huts, concrete posts. And sometimes young men in uniform. I know they're not army. *They* haven't been round here for ages. I know where those trucks are going."

"Where?" all three of us say at once.

"To the old copper mines where the kids play on the slag heaps."

"Can we get up there?" I ask.

"You can follow the road but you can't get inside the compound."

"We can have a bloody good try, *Neni*," says Kalman.

"All right," she counters. "What are we waiting for? Let's go now."

We break into nervous laughter. But Klara's dead serious.

"Finding your young man is my revenge, Mr Kalman. Revenge for what they did to my husband. And revenge for the way these villains are giving this miserable little town a bad name again."

Her feeble eyes twinkle in the half light of a winter's day. Then as if she's pronouncing an oath, she says it again.

"I want revenge."

We've stopped laughing.

"And I think you do too. All three of you."

Chapter 4

Klara says we should take a look at the original camp first. And what Klara says we should do, we have a mind to do.

We pack ourselves into Kalman Olah's Mercedes and she guides us up the hill to the site of what a shiny new notice-board declares is 'The Annihilation Camp of the Bolshevik Red Dictatorship, secretly founded and operated between 1950 and 1953'. The authorities have started to clear the ground and turn it into a memorial to the victims and survivors of the Rakosi regime. They're rebuilding one of the barracks, a crude log cabin in which prisoners eked out a spartan existence or died from hard labour and bad food. Other reminders of the past have been left intact - an old watchtower and a stretch of barbed wire. Otherwise it's an open space where saplings are sprouting from the sand and gravel.

But this theme park is not where the IFA trucks are going.

"They head west towards Parafurdo," says Klara. "Nice little place. Pretty houses and restaurants." Her hands tremble as she strains for the irony she's trying to convey. "But they don't go as far as that. They turn right about a kilometre from here."

We climb into hilly country past mounds of shale and abandoned pit gear and reach a gateway of rusting iron surmounted by an emblem of crossed hammers.

"That's where the workers of the people's democracy were urged to find fulfilment," she says. "Those mines are lethal. Hundreds died digging out the ore and the slurry ruined the countryside. Look around."

We're about to get out of the car when a fearsome German Shepherd, snarling like a hound from Hell, appears out of nowhere and hurls itself towards us.

"Stay where you are," Jenoe orders. "Keep the doors shut and the windows up."

I see a figure move across the gateway.

"He's got a gun," says Klara. "And he's in uniform."

Kalman lifts his binoculars. "And he's wearing an Arrow Cross armband."

I watch the guard raise his weapon and take aim. Jenoe sees him too, spins the Merc round and guns the accelerator. I look back to see the dog in pursuit. If the guard fired, he missed. And we don't hear a shot. The dog soon decides it's not worth the effort. We race on down the road.

"Stop," shouts Kalman suddenly.

"Are you crazy, Father?"

"We've come this far. We've got to take a proper look. That bugger won't follow us."

"How do you know?" asks Jenoe as the Merc bounces over a pothole.

"Your father's right," says Klara. "Otherwise this has been a wasted journey."

Jenoe sighs. But even he is curious enough to slow down as we approach a turning on our left. There's another road, a narrow embankment, leading to more derelict buildings with wooded slopes beyond. The land is only now recovering from the abuse it's suffered. Coarse grass and small oaks struggle to survive among the slag and slate. To the right stretches an old quarry full of stagnant water. We don't get far. A weather-beaten sign warns, 'Danger – Explosives – Keep Out'.

"Look," says Klara. "Trucks coming up the hill."

We see three IFA's on the road below, heading slowly towards us.

Jenoe reverses to the turning and drives on sedately, as if we're an old folks' outing.

"If he stops and flags us down, smile sweetly," I say. I'm relying on Kalman and Klara to exercise their gift of the gab and talk us out of this.

But the IFA's don't stop. They grind past in low gear. Jenoe waits ten seconds.

"Hang on," he says. We speed away again, down the hill to the main road.

"Not much doubt about that," says Kalman back at the house, as we steady our nerves with shots of *palinka*. Even Klara has succumbed to the offer of a cigarette.

"But they weren't carrying young men in Arrow Cross uniforms," I say.

"How do you know?" asks Jenoe. "There could have been anything – anyone – under those canvas drapes."

"I'll tell you what I think," says Klara. We wait for her latest words of wisdom. "It was just after two when those trucks passed us."

"So?" says Kalman.

"What we have to do," she goes on, "is keep watch, see what time they come back down the hill. Did you notice how clean they were? Well, they're not clean when they leave. So they must drive them along some rough roads up there."

"We ought to give it another go." Kalman puffs at his pipe again. "See if we can get inside."

"No," says Jenoe. "If you want to do that, you're on your own, Father."

"You're not using your head, Kalman Olah." Klara wags her finger and peers at him over her half-moons. "Your Coro isn't inside there. He's kept somewhere else. Like I told you, those trucks carry equipment and armed guards. No prisoners. No Gypsies."

"You're saying we should follow them when they come back?"

"Exactly," says Klara. "That way, you'll find your boy. They'll lead you to him."

She surveys us triumphantly. "They'll be leaving soon. Now's your chance."

"In which case, I'll go and fill up in the village," says Jenoe who looks as if he's glad of a chance to do something mundane.

Klara goes back down to her kitchen with a promise of soup and sandwiches.

"She's a splendid woman," observes Kalman.

"A brave one," I answer. "Has she told you her story?"

"Yes. And I've told her ours. Not just Coro and why we're desperate to find him. I told her about the Roma, what they have to put up with in this country. I told her there are saints and sinners among us, just like everybody else. There are rogues and thieves, the idle, the scroungers and the drunks. They give us a bad name. But there are good people too. Honest, generous and hardworking."

"Will you tell me more when we have time?"

"We do have time. Aren't you coming with us? To find Coro? Leave that clapped out Lada here and we can all go in the Mercedes."

"I'm flattered," I say.

"Has nobody ever told you, Englishman, you have a face that doesn't lie."

Jenoe is back. We eat Klara's food and hear the revving of engines. The IFA's are rumbling back into Recsk. We give them five minutes. Farewells are brief. As the Merc bumps away from her door, Klara turns her back on us. Kalman closes his eyes. Jenoe glances at his father and allows himself a ghost of a smile. We bounce over a level crossing and see the tailboard of an IFA up ahead.

The rain has returned and the day is dying. It takes skilful driving to maintain the right distance behind the trucks.

This time there are two of them, slow, cumbersome, hardy survivors of an East German vehicle industry killed off after the fall of the Berlin Wall. They look like troop carriers with green tarpaulin covering a steel framework. The instincts of the Merc are inclined to something faster. Jenoe has to stop, wait a couple of minutes and then push on, hoping he hasn't lost them or given the game away.

From Recsk we go east to the junction at Sirok. The trucks turn left, following the Tarna valley up to Petervasara. The rain sweeps across open country hardly visible in the gloom beyond the beam of our headlights. No one speaks until Jenoe sees the IFA's pull off the road into a wooded clearing.

"Damn," he grunts. "I'll have to pass them."

"Park up ahead," says Kalman. "Round that bend. We'll wait."

Time drags. Kalman's losing patience.

"Let's walk back," I say. "Just far enough to see what they're up to."

We do everything in slow motion, closing doors as quietly as we can, treading stealthily, tired eyes straining to see through the drizzle.

"We're in the right place at the right time," whispers Kalman.

"I hope that's true," his son answers.

The trucks are parked a hundred metres back from us. Not a light, not a sound from either of them. We crouch under the long bough of an old sycamore. The rain slackens.

We hear an engine, the groan of something heavy as it crawls up the road from Sirok.

"Look. Lights," whispers Jenoe.

"It's a bus," I say. "An old Ikarus bus."

The note changes as the driver double-declutches and labours for an even lower gear. It stops. The engine ticks over. Three men jump from the back of the second IFA, run towards the bus and bang on the bodywork.

"They're armed," says Kalman.

"Quiet. Just watch," I hiss.

The bus driver moves from his seat and opens the nearside door. There's a scuffle and shouts, screams and curses. And shots.

"What the hell do we do, Father?"

"Stay where we are. We've no weapons. Just keep your eyes skinned."

The bus disgorges its contents. First out, one of the thugs waving what looks like an automatic rifle. Then a group of terrified women and children, followed by another of the gang bawling at them to shut up. After that, two men, passengers, and the third attacker dragging a body.

"Christ, they've killed the driver." I move out beyond the verge but Kalman pulls me back.

"Let's get to the car," he says, "move it off the road, out of sight. We need to be behind them."

The armed men are too busy to pick up the sound of the Merc as we head off towards Petervasara looking for a suitable turning. We hit the centre of the town and a T-junction.

"Which way?" asks Jenoe breathing heavily.

"Don't know," says Kalman. "Spin her round and park by that shop. Cut the lights."

The trucks go past. We watch them turn left and disappear behind a row of houses.

"Now," shouts Kalman. We pick out the IFA's as they roll round another bend.

"Where the hell are we going?" asks Jenoe. The trucks swing off to the right. He whips the wheel over and swears again. The Merc bucks and yaws over twisted tarmac.

"Did you see the road sign?"

"Bugger the road sign," laughs Kalman. "Just follow them. I know where we're going. We're going to get Coro."

PART 14

Chapter 1

A doorway spews out a column of young men in Arrow Cross uniforms. They drag Coro into the centre of a courtyard. He hears the voice of Big Gyuri.

"Watch, Tar. Watch how sub-humans get what they deserve."

He looks across the yard and sees Gyuri and Andrea standing on a wooden tribune. Gyuri grips her wrists in one enormous hand. He jerks an arm up into the small of her back. With the other hand he wields a Skorpion machine pistol.

"Pay attention," he barks, "or I'll break it."

Floodlights are switched on. Martial music blares from loudspeakers. Kozma appears from a doorway and mounts the platform. He wears his suit and topcoat. From a third exit comes another column of young men, goose-stepping in something like unison. They line up. The music stops. Kozma raises his right hand. They respond with the same salute. He speaks through a poor quality microphone which distorts his words as they bounce back off the walls.

"Men of the Arrow Cross. Be ready for the first stage of our battle, the first battle of a war. A war to sweep us to power, crush our enemies, the Jews, the soft-bellied politicians in Budapest, homosexuals, atheists, communists and freemasons."

The young men fix their eyes on Kozma as if he's their messiah. Then, as abruptly as he arrived, he steps down and walks back the way he came. The columns stay intact.

"Take a good look, Tar. And you too," he shouts. "Gypsy boy."

And Coro knows that both of them have been very foolish to suppose that their captors will ease up on them.

"It's a pity, Tar, that you won't get a chance to write this up for that rag of yours. 'I was there…..at a secret Arrow Cross parade…..deep in the forests of the Matra…..the young men of Hungary are on the march'. Isn't that what you would have written?"

"No," says Andrea trying desperately to muster some defiance. "I work for a financial journal."

"Did work," gloats Gyuri. "Don't work for it now. And won't - ever again. But Kozma wants you to take a lasting impression with you. To show you what we'll do when we take over."

"You mean you're the new SS, the new AVO."

Gyuri preens himself.

"Both of them had a weakness for documenting atrocities," she says, "as if their brutality had an insatiable need to justify itself to future generations."

"Don't be so fucking pompous, woman."

But Andrea knows that for a split second Gyuri is confused.

"How come you got into all this?" she asks.

"You are taking a big risk asking me that," says Gyuri.

"Since I'm going to die, there's no risk at all."

Again he's fazed. "Why should I tell you anything about myself?"

"Because you can't help yourself," says Andrea. "You are a thug. But you have brains. More brains than any of these idiots." She waves a free hand at the parade.

"Shut up. Don't insult them. Or me. I come from where they come from – from miserable, bloody, tower blocks in Debrecen or wherever. My father couldn't keep a job even when being out of work was a crime."

Gyuri spits.

"A communist crime," he sniggers. "You remember that? Kadar's mob made unemployment an offence without telling my old man's generation that if the local factory had no work, there was no work. So he got drunk instead, on handouts from the state, which thoughtfully supplied the beer and the liquor. He was so pissed most of the time, he didn't recognise me. Neither did my mother who still lives in fear of him."

Gyuri flashes a triumphant smile.

"I joined because this gives me a purpose in life."

The smile fades. He grimaces as if dredging for memories that bring real pain and the ghosts of things he wishes hadn't happened.

"After school – oh yes, I went to school – I can read. So can some of those boys down there. After school, I got a job in a bakery. I met others who saw what I saw. As soon as the Reds lost power, more fucking foreigners arrived. Not just all those freeloading niggers on grants and the like. Romanians, Slovaks, Ukrainians and more bloody Gypsies. And Jews crawling all over Budapest."

His chest heaves as he pours out his venom.

"I joined the skins. We had a good time. Drinking and getting into fights with punks and gays. And with the police. We picked our moment with them. Made sure we had proper weapons."

"But this is different, isn't it?" says Andrea. "This isn't just lads out for a good time."

"This, Tar, is it. This is money talking. This is real. There are men with brains behind this. Even intellectuals, university types who can organise and get things done."

Triumph returns, joining scorn and menace.

"I love violence," he says. "I really love it. And I love a man like Kozma who can use it, exploit it and put his ideas into practice. He will win, Tar. Because he loves violence too. With him, it's the violence of words. With me, it's these."

She steps back as he lifts a fist and shakes it like a prize-fighter.

He gives a signal and the serried ranks break free. A group seizes Coro. They beat and kick him until he lies on the ground motionless. They throw the blanket over him and kick again. Then they stand back, muttering and pointing. Somehow, Coro finds the strength, does what he did on the night old Tomi was tortured to death, leaps to his feet, hurls himself at the nearest Arrow Cross uniform. It's the guard, Gabi. Coro grabs his head and bites. The man howls. The others laugh hysterically. Yelling and screaming, they pull Coro off his victim and hold him by his hair.

"What shall we do with him, Gabi?"

Gabi doesn't answer. Wiping blood from his savaged nose with the back of his gloved hand, he raises his automatic high above his head, holds it for a split second, secures a two-handed grip on the barrel and brings it down hard.

But they've relaxed their hold. The weapon misses Coro's skull. He takes the blow on his left shoulder, spins round and falls heavily. Andrea throws up. Gyuri gets the full force of her vomit in the midriff and hits her across the face. Gabi steps forward and pushes the muzzle of his gun into Coro's mouth.

And freezes.

The recruits look up. Gyuri pulls Andrea into the lee of a wall. The chopper is clattering away above their heads.

"Run," shouts Gyuri. "Get out of his line of sight. Back inside. All of you. Go, you stupid buggers. Gabi. Grab the Gypsy."

The courtyard empties. Gyuri hauls Andrea round the side of the house. Gabi struggles behind him with a half conscious Coro draped over his shoulders. His breathing comes hard through mangled nose and a mouth full of blood. The helicopter hovers low. If they make for the barn where the Roma prisoners are kept, they'll be spotted again. They have no choice but to wait under cover.

Kozma runs out of the main house.

"What the hell's going on?" He looks up but doesn't see the chopper which has skewed over to the other side of the building. A rising wind deadens the noise of its rotors. Even so, Gyuri pulls him back.

"What the hell do you think you're doing?" snarls Kozma. "Get your hands off me."

"Shut up and get out of sight," Gyuri shouts. "Do you want to be picked off by that thing?"

"Picked off?" Kozma is still unaware of the danger.

"By a gun or a camera with a bloody good lens. For Christ's sake, keep in against the wall."

The pilot swings his machine back over the huts and the barn. There's no way they can make a run for it.

"We have to get out of here fast." Kozma's eyes are wide with panic. "Come on."

"What do we do with these two?" Gyuri gestures to Andrea and the prone body of Coro. Before Gyuri can stop him, Gabi decides to leg it across the yard to his mates. He doesn't get far.

There's a burst of gunfire. Gabi's back arches and Andrea sees him suspended in mid-air before his bulk crashes on to the pounded quarry stone. Kozma seizes the big man's parka.

"Have you gone even more insane than you are? He's there. Out there. In full view. You asshole."

Gyuri is paralyzed. Andrea guesses that for all his brutality, it's the first time he's killed anyone.

"Leave these two where they are." Still Gyuri doesn't move. "Now, you fool. Back to the house."

They're gone. The helicopter stays overhead for another half minute then banks away into the winter sun. Coro is showing signs of life. He sits up and sees the Arrow Cross piling out of the huts, making for vehicles parked in the yard. He holds out a hand. Andrea grabs it and leans against his bruised shoulder.

"Keep still," he says. "Wait till they've left."

"But they'll see us."

"They're too busy trying to get out of here. Just hold on."

The Arrow Cross fight like ferrets in a sack until every single one has clambered aboard a pickup or an IFA truck. They reverse wildly and head off into the forest. Gabi's body lies where it dropped. The wind whips round a corner of the big house, catches the baseball hat he was wearing and blows it into nearby undergrowth.

"So, what do we do now?" Andrea asks. "Sit and wait to be bumped off? Or hope that those nice young men in their helicopter will come and rescue us?"

"You do nothing, Tar."

They turn. Gyuri and the whore, Nora, are standing side by side. Gyuri waves his Skorpion.

"Back to the barn. Both of you."

Andrea risks a question. "And what will you do, now that your little chicks have flown the nest?"

Big Gyuri's had no time to clean himself up and still smells of vomit. He grins.

"Still being nosy, Tar? Old habits die hard, don't they? And you will die with them."

He comes close and Coro thinks he is going to shoot. Instead the big man prods him in the chest.

"Walk."

For all his accumulated pain, Coro lets Andrea lean on him as they stumble past Gabi's corpse.

246

Chapter 2

Andrea slumps to the floor, calling through her tears. "Peter, Peter, Peter Kovacs. Where are you?"

Coro touches her shoulder but she withdraws. He lets her settle.

"Listen to me, Andrea Tar."

She wipes her eyes on the sleeve of her ragged jacket and looks at Coro in despair.

"I know what he will do," Coro whispers. "I know precisely what Big Gyuri will do."

She doesn't answer.

"He will try to burn this place down."

"God Almighty, Coro. What are you saying?"

"Think about it. The barn's built of wood."

"And the wood has been coated with pitch or creosote."

"Exactly. Smell it. It keeps our own stink in check."

She lifts her head and sniffs. "You're right. It's a tinder box. How can you be so calm about it? He'll roast us alive."

"He'll try," says Coro. "And if he does, it gives us our chance."

"A chance to escape? How? We're not going to be digging a tunnel or climbing through a hole in the roof." In the faint light she sees him smile. "Have you told the others?"

"Not yet. But I shall have to very soon. We must be ready. I faked unconsciousness when they held me and heard them talking about torching the barn if the authorities caught up with them. And not just the barn. House, barracks, huts, the lot."

"But a fire will be seen for miles around. It'll give them away completely."

"They're past thinking about that. Gyuri, the tart and Kozma are the only ones left. The question is – will they do it while there's still daylight or wait until it goes dark?"

He assembles the captives and tells them about the helicopter, about Kozma, Gyuri and Nora, and how the skinheads panicked and fled. But he's reluctant to tell them what he knows of Kozma's plan to destroy the barn with them inside.

"I know that some of the men in the huts are your fathers and brothers. But there's no point in worrying about them now. We have to get ourselves out of here first."

They huddle round him, feeding off his confidence.

"I can promise you nothing," he says. "Breaking out looks impossible. But I want the strong ones among you to chip away at that door. We may be able to weaken it. I don't think it's as stout as it looks."

"What do we use?" asks one of the women.

"We have no tools," says another.

"No but we have pots and pans. Cracked cups and plates. Use them."

They need to be kept busy. It will occupy the time before the real crisis comes. He looks at Andrea who senses he wants her to take the lead. When she tells them about the plan to burn the barn, there's a collective shudder of terror. One of the girls begins screaming. Others weep and moan in chorus.

"Shut up. All of you." It's Mariska standing with hands on hips. "Do you fools not see what Coro and the lady are telling you?"

Coro moves to intervene but Mariska waves him away.

"You think the fire will give us our chance, don't you?"

Coro acknowledges her understanding of the way his mind is working.

"But we cannot know which part of this building he will torch first," she points out.

"Which is why we have to steel ourselves, why we have to be ready and alert."

"And brave," adds Mariska. "Your thinking is good. But you know and I know that some of us may die."

This time there is no weeping and wailing, just a silence pregnant with expectation and the will to obey any instructions they're given.

Coro organises a team to attack the door. They hack at it with anything they can lay their hands on but the thick, tarred wood holds out against their frenzy. They stand there, lungs bursting and heads spinning with the effort.

Then one of the younger boys yelps with delight from a corner where he's been searching for a tool.

"Look what I've found." He holds up a spade, handle and blade intact.

"It was under the straw over there."

"I wish we'd known about that before," croaks the old man with the rasping voice. "We could have hit one of them. We could have killed him."

"You would have killed nobody," scoffs Mariska. "You are too weak."

"Give it to me," Coro shouts to the boy. He stabs at the doorframe with all the force he can muster. When he tires, the boy takes over and repeats the process under Coro's instructions.

"Take care not to split the shaft," Coro warns.

Nothing gives. Andrea watches their frustration and feels a growing mood of challenge among the women. When the boy gives up, she steps forward.

"Let me try." She takes the spade and strikes three times. At a fourth, the wood splinters and a sliver of timber drops to the floor. There are cheers and ribald comments at the feebleness of men. But the wiser ones hold back and look sadly at the meagre fruits of so much effort.

Coro is trying to guess the time. Is it late? Is it dark outside? If it is, that brings the prospect of action from Kozma and Gyuri.

"Wait," Andrea calls. "Let's take another look."

She runs her hands up and down the door moving one of them over the scar they've inflicted on the wood. She puts her finger to her lips, holds her breath and feels cold air. She turns and grins.

"It may not be much. But we're through."

They're about to repeat their jubilation but she waves them away.

"Keep chipping away at that hole, Coro."

He tries the spade again. Andrea raises her hand. Coro understands.

"We must listen for any sounds outside," she says. "We must try not to give ourselves away."

The boy takes over. Another piece of timber falls from the door. Again a pause. Again only the wind wafting through the small aperture. They keep at it until they've made enough of an impression on both door and frame to produce a hole at waist height. A little more hard work and it's big enough for a child to squeeze through.

Then they smell it. The creeping odour of burning wood. And the smoke. They hear it too. The crackle and spit of fire. Where though? Where is it? Near the door? Or at the other end of the barn?

"Use that spade again, Coro. Try to make it wider."

"Some of the kids could get through now," he says.

"No, wait. We don't know who's outside. They may have guns. It would be just like Big Gyuri to pick us off one by one."

Coro wields the spade again while the boy kicks at the cracking timber. Some of the children start to cough and retch.

"Get towels, cloths, anything. Soak them in water if we still have some. Go on, all of you. Quickly."

The women scatter then run back to the door like wraiths in a nightmare, faces covered except for frightened eyes. The two old men haven't moved. They're staring at the first flames licking at the walls.

Coro hears a crash. The doorframe and surrounding timbers shatter.

"We shall have to risk it," he shouts. "As soon as you're outside, lie flat. Then crawl away from the barn."

He too has seen the flames and is gasping as the building fills with smoke. The children line up to leave. Coro pushes them through, then grabs the smaller of the two men. He lifts him high and hurls him through the gap like a sack of garbage. There are ten of them left. All women. The far end of the barn is burning fiercely, the stench and fumes leaving them precious little air.

"Andrea, you go now," Coro orders.

"No. I must be the last," she retorts. "Mariska and the others next."

"No heroics, Andrea. Go. The kids need rounding up."

She waits a fraction of a second. Blazing timber drops from the roof at the far end. Andrea pushes through the splintered doorway.

Coro marshals the women. None of them is large but thickening hips have made the likes of Mariska slow and clumsy. It's an age before the last backside vanishes into the night. He steadies himself for his own escape just as another beam smashes down in a shower of sparks and debris.

He checks. The other man? The one who told his tale of torture. Where is he?

The heat courses towards him. If he delays, he'll faint.

Then he sees him. The old man has wandered to the centre of the barn. Coro's way is barred by blazing timber. He knows he cannot reach him. Then like some angel of death, the man lifts his arms above his head. Coro hears his scream, a long ejaculation of pain and self-sacrifice. The flames wrap him in a gaseous shroud. And Coro sees him no more.

He hears a voice. Andrea's face, smeared with ash and tears, is yelling at him out of the darkness. Coro stares ahead, rigid with fear and loathing. Andrea yells again. She pulls herself back into the barn, shakes him viciously, spins him round and pitches him on to the earth outside.

As she scrambles after him, the barn gives one massive heave. Andrea grabs his arms and hauls him clear. Enveloped in smoke and flame, the building collapses in slow motion.

"I'm sorry," Coro wheezes. "I saw him die. I could not move."

"You must move now. Come on. Join the others." Andrea points to a patch of ground about fifty metres away. He can make out the figures huddled under trees, their branches lit up by the blazing barn.

"But he will see them. He will shoot," says Coro nursing visions of Gyuri lurking in the shadows with a Skorpion. "We must hide before he fires."

"No one has fired," Andrea replies. "They have gone. They've convinced themselves that they've fried us to death.

A reflection of the pyrotechnics dances across their faces.

"Let's get away," says Coro.

They stumble across the muddy ground to where the others are standing transfixed by the destruction of what for so long has been their foul and filthy jail.

"What happened to old Karcsi then?" asks Mariska, hard and solemn in the flickering light.

"He turned back," says Coro. "He walked into the fire. There was nothing I could do." He gazes at Mariska and stops himself from weeping at the memory of what he's seen.

"He was mad," she says. "Turned mad by what they did to him. He is best forgotten."

Coro hasn't the energy to protest. Mariska has been a prisoner for so long, there is no point in reprimand.

"The fire will die," says Coro, "and the night will be cold. We have thin clothes and some of the children are barefoot. We must follow the tracks."

"What about the chain gang – the men in the hut where you were held?" asks Andrea.

"They will have to wait. It's best for us to skirt the big house. When we get to the covered way where we saw Gabi shot down, we'll take stock."

They shuffle forward.

"Stay close together," shouts Coro.

They look at him stoically, uncomplaining. He and the woman got them out of the barn. They will do whatever they ask.

As they reach the house, Andrea spots lights.

"Down," she urges.

They crouch by the wall and watch as trucks swing into the yard. The tailgates are dropped before the drivers have braked. They can't see much. But even at this distance, Coro knows that the men who jump down are armed.

PART 15

Chapter 1

I did see the signpost. It said *Szalajkahaz – 8 kms.* But Kalman is acting on instinct. Only one name is important now.

Three kilometres after the Petervasara T-junction, we pass rows of small houses, all in darkness, shutters up, families in bunkers, watching the box or in bed. The road forks.

"Right," shouts Kalman. But Jenoe doesn't need telling. He's seen the faint tail-light of the IFA up ahead.

We slew over a bridge, twist through a chicane, dipped headlights picking out undergrowth and the overhanging branches of tall trees.

And then the trucks are gone.

"Where the hell…..?"

We push on, hoping this is an illusion. Rounding the next bend, we pass another sign for Szalajkahaz and chance upon a different convoy, three vehicles parked in a semi-circle, lights on full beam, and a village square, bounded on three sides by a small church and poky houses of rough stone. We see police in riot gear, some bearing weapons with telescopic sights, others straining to hold back a variety of savage dogs. Jenoe brakes in time to avoid hitting a uniform with arm outstretched. Kalman winds the window down.

257

"And where do you think you're going?"

The true answer to this will confuse the man.

"A hunting lodge," Kalman lies. "A bit of weekend shooting. What's all the fuss?"

Before the uniform can tell us to push off, I catch my breath. There's Kovacs, some twenty metres away, in deep conversation with a man resembling Father Time.

"We know the officer in charge," I say. "I'd like to speak to him, please."

"Why would he be interested in your spot of weekend shooting?" asks the uniform.

"None of your bloody business," says Kalman. "Come on Charlie Barrow."

He pushes at his door but the uniform leans in with all his weight. I grab my chance, slipping out from the back seat on the driver's side. Before the officer can stop me, I run towards to Kovacs and tap him on the shoulder. He whirls round, annoyed by the interruption, then runs a hand through his rumpled hair.

"Good God. Where the hell did you spring from?"

"Picked up some interesting characters in Recsk, Kovacs. You should meet them."

"After I have spoken to this gentleman," he says turning back to Father Time who seems to be some sort of village elder.

The man wears patched trousers and a moth-eaten jacket. Behind him, peering round half-open doors, I see pale, thin faces, men, women and children scared out of their wits by uniforms and paraphernalia. The dogs sniff the ground and growl their menace.

Then I spot another line of trucks, IFAs like the ones we thought we were following, parked under trees at the very edge of the square. Plus a rather smart white Suzuki.

"They were in those when they quit their camp," says the man.

Other figures approach, among them Rainer and a police sergeant.

"Confirmed by the man in the chopper, sir," says the sergeant. "He found the camp during daylight and saw them pile into trucks. He says they abandoned them and took to the woods. Best guess is, they're lying low till morning."

"Thank you, Sergeant, I was beginning to work that out for myself," says Rainer.

"Did the helicopter crew see anyone else?" asks Kovacs. "Anybody not in uniform?"

"We put that to him, sir," says the sergeant. "But he says, not as far as he can tell. And he got pretty close."

Kovacs bites his lip. That's not the answer he wants to hear.

Rainer walks over to the village elder, reassuring him that he and his men haven't come all this way to throw their weight around.

"So I should hope," is the response. "Are you after those buggers wearing the Arrow Cross? I hope you get 'em. Made our lives miserable. Always demanding food and cheap labour. We hadn't got any to give. So they roughed up some of the young ones and raped two of the women."

"Arrow Cross?" asks Kovacs. "Are you sure that's what they were?"

"We've put up with them for the past six months," says Father Time. "Their camp is two or three kilometres inside the woods to the east. You follow a stream. You can see where their trucks used the shallow riverbed as a road. Then there's a left turn. They pushed a track through the forest. Wrecked some good timber."

We hear shouting and cursing. I recognise Kalman Olah's voice.

"What the hell's that?" asks Rainer.

"My Roma contacts, Lieutenant. From Recsk. The father is a stubborn old man but he has a heart of gold. He and his son are looking for a young man they call Coro."

I tell the story as briefly as I can.

"Let them through," says Kovacs.

The sergeant goes off to sort things out with the uniform holding on to Kalman.

The Roma walks up to us, panting his indignation.

"You have some funny friends, Charlie Barrow," he huffs.

I do more introductions and explain that we have been following two IFA trucks which suddenly disappeared for no obvious reason.

"They swerved off further down," says the village elder to Kovacs. "There's more than one way into the camp. Someone told them you were here already."

"That's an interesting statement," says Rainer. "Would you care to elaborate?"

"The helicopter," he says crustily. "You've not exactly disguised your presence. They've got radios and such like."

Kovacs looks at Father Time with new respect.

"The ones we were following have women and children on board," I say. "And their intentions aren't honourable."

"There's not much we can do for them now," sighs Rainer. "We must press on."

"Sir." The sergeant is clearly wondering whether he dare make another contribution. "The guy in the chopper says this road peters out after about twelve kilometres. But he can talk us in to where they spotted the house."

Kovacs has anticipated my request.

"Yes, you can tag along, Charlie. You've been involved in this since the start and you're an old soldier. But I can't risk taking your friends."

Kalman is about to protest but Jenoe lays a hand on his arm.

"If and when I meet Coro, Kalman, I'll send word back down. I promise."

He accepts my offer but insists that he and Jenoe will stay in the village.

"Klara gave us plenty of food and drink. We'll live off that until you get back."

The rest of us, dogs included, clamber into the trucks. We climb into the forest. The metalled road gets steadily worse until we're pitching and rolling along dirt tracks. It must be nearly midnight.

"Got a weapon, Charlie?" Kovacs asks.

"No. In this job, I don't carry one. Against the rules."

"Well at least wear a waistcoat." Rainer hands me a bullet-proof vest. I promise to put it on once we're stationary.

We meet the stream in its wide rocky bed. Recent rains have made it livelier and deeper but we can still use the narrow valley as an access to the woods. Rainer has been blessed by the latest departmental purchasing policies. Our trucks are German four-wheel vehicles with a high clearance, just right for rugged country. But they don't give a smooth ride. I think I'm going to throw up at the next jolt.

"Cut your engines and your lights," shouts Rainer.

"What is it?" asks Kovacs. The only sound I can hear is the swollen stream.

"Listen."

Mingling with the rush of water we hear the comforting rattle of the helicopter. Its pilot picks us out with his spotlight.

"Tell him to douse that thing," snaps Rainer.

His sergeant speaks sharply into a microphone.

"Lieutenant says he greatly appreciates your gesture of solidarity but doesn't want us turned into sitting ducks for any villains hiding in the woodwork."

The light goes off. There is no apology from the chopper. The pilot simply confirms that our convoy is in the right position to move on. We should take the obvious route.

"Proceeding to recce camp again," he barks from above.

"Typical special forces," mumbles the sergeant.

"Maybe," says Kovacs. "But I admire the way you've summoned them up."

"Even I can pull a few strings when I have to," says Rainer testily.

"The chopper passed on a message for you, Captain," adds the sergeant. "The officer known as Janza has been killed in a road accident."

Kovacs stands stock still. Rainer takes him to one side but I can still hear what he says.

"I think your friend was doing a little moonlighting, Kovacs. After he vanished, we picked up his tail. Despite his injuries, he was able to drive. One of my bike patrols spotted him heading for the hills. He followed him to what he thinks was that old AVO safe house. We'll get more details later."

The trucks start up again and turn into a tunnel of foliage. Kovacs withdraws into his own world, taking no notice of the rest of us and unmoved by the jolting and the noise. The route veers neither to right nor left. All we see in the glare of headlights are the branches of conifers and small oaks and flashes from the eyes of frightened animals. But the track is dry and firmer than the river bed.

Then we see the camp gates. They've been left open. The driver accelerates into the compound. He pulls up sharply, transfixed by the flames.

"Christ, Lieutenant. Look at that fire."

Rainer doesn't wait to reply. With the rest of his men, he's racing across open ground past the huts, heading for the blazing barn. Kovacs yells at the half dozen uniforms closest to him.

"Spread out. Look for survivors."

I move towards the big house with an officer on either side of me. One of the dog handlers follows, his charge barking furiously at nothing in particular. But he's the first to reach the cloistered wall. He and the dog freeze as shapes rise up before them.

"God Almighty," he breathes. "We're seeing ghosts."

I see them too. Kovacs has caught up. He flashes a torch just as the chopper swoops in low and switches on his spot again. There are perhaps a dozen of them, women and children. At their head, a man in his twenties and a wizened old boy bringing up the rear. They're clad in rags and scared out of their wits. All except one of the women, wearing a tracksuit and a ragged jacket.

She runs towards us shouting, "Peter. Peter." On and on until she has almost fallen into his arms.

There's gunfire out of the darkness. We all hit the ground.

Andrea too. Her legs thrash at empty air as the bullets bowl her over.

Another burst. This time the uniforms have seen the spurt of flame and fire back. And fire again, until the shapes of a heavily built man and a woman dressed in blouse and skirt break cover and run towards the compound gate. I don't know whether to look at them or at Andrea lying on the gravel, motionless and exposed.

Gyuri and Nora never make it. Gunned down in quick succession, the man sprawls with his head in a pool of water, the woman on top as if reaching to embrace him. The chopper hangs low, swirling smoke from the blaze that consumed the barn. Kovacs kneels at Andrea's side.

"They are Gypsies, Peter. Used as slaves."

She coughs away blood and saliva.

"Don't talk," he says. "We'll get you out of here."

I see her lips form the words. "I don't think so."

The pilot has deftly landed the helicopter in the confined space of the compound. Its rotors chunter in the raw night air. A crew member runs over with a stretcher. The two men who killed Gyuri and Nora are lifting the bodies into a truck.

Coro steps forward. He squats next to Kovacs.

I see Andrea open her eyes. "Let me introduce you….."

Her smile is as gentle as it was on the evening she and Kovacs gave me supper and helped to lay my own ghosts to rest.

Chapter 2

Kovacs does not accompany Andrea's body to Eger.

"She'd dead," he says. "Dead and gone. I have a job to do. I'll mourn when the time comes."

In the artificial twilight of headlamps and the smouldering barn, I look into his face. No grief or shock. Simply clear eyed determination. No one is going to argue with him.

"Right now, we must look after this young man."

A paramedic from Rainer's team drapes a blanket over Coro's shoulders, bathes his swollen eye and examines the damage inflicted by the Arrow Cross.

"He ought to go to hospital, Lieutenant. I think he may have some broken ribs."

"There are others in the huts," says Coro. "The men they used in their chain gang."

With only two trucks Rainer knows he can't transport the Roma victims and a full complement of police back to Szalajkahaz all at once. He details four men to escort them in relays and orders the others to make thorough searches of the camp, not least the big house. Kovacs says he will stay with them. I ask to do the same.

"There's hard evidence in there," says Kovacs. "I want to have a look at it."

We swivel at the sound of a car squealing into reverse from under a clump of trees.

"Kozma," says Kovacs. "Damn him."

Rainer draws his gun as the big, black Mercedes races down the track into the forest.

He runs to the lead truck. "Radio ahead," he yells. "They must stop him."

Later, a chastened young officer in Szalajkahaz will tell how a car, lights ablaze and siren at full blast, plunged through the village, scattering police and curious locals like so many autumn leaves.

"We never had a chance, sir. He was driving like a mad man."

But Kovacs knows where Kozma is going.

"Ozd," he says with a slightly mystical smile. "He's running out of options."

Rainer takes off for Szalajkahaz. Kovacs asks Coro if he feels fit enough to help with a search of the house. Stunned by Andrea's death and Kovacs's apparent indifference, the Roma hesitates.

"I know what you're thinking," says Kovacs. "You've sized me up as not much better than the callous bastards who flogged you and damn near killed you."

"That is not what I think." Coro bridles in spite of his pain and the bitter night wind. The paramedic has patched him up as best he can and withdrawn. "I think that you and I have a mission, Captain."

"And so have I," I interject.

Kovacs explains my status and role.

"Then let's get on with it," says the Roma.

Some of Rainer's boys have broken into the house. They've found the room where Kozma interrogated Coro and Andrea. Kovacs switches on every light he can find and gazes at the walls. I gawp at the Arrow Cross emblems, the flags and the posters.

"A dangerous delusion, Charlie." Kovacs turns to Coro. "Tell me your story."

I sense that Coro cuts his narrative to the bone but he makes sure we all understand the importance to him of Kalman Olah.

"Then I have good news for you," says Kovacs "Kalman and his son are waiting for you in the village."

"I knew he would try to find me."

"I met him in Recsk," I explain. I too pare the story down. "He said he'd been to the Ketpo settlement only to be told you'd left. He got angry at the pack of lies he was getting from the official there, someone called Tivadar."

"I know Tivadar," says Coro. "A creep and a crook."

"But Tivadar put him right on how the Arrow Cross were abducting Roma and bringing them here."

A sergeant wanders in and tells us they've found a well stocked armoury, a sophisticated communications room, comfortable quarters for senior Arrow Cross members and enough food in a bank of freezers to last for months, not to mention the booze.

"Any documents?" Kovacs asks.

"Not just documents, Captain. There's a room full of computers, disks, videos, files. You name it. They had it."

"Keep looking," Kovacs orders . "Collect as much as you can. Bag it. Seal the place, switch off the lights and keep a guard on the house. You'll be relieved at daybreak."

The sergeant smiles nervously. "I'm glad about that. This place scares me."

Standing in the middle of the compound, we take a last look round. Kovacs moves to the spot where Andrea died. We leave him to his thoughts. When he joins us in the truck, I see his mouth quiver and lines of misery gouged into his face. No one speaks. We keep our heads down and the truck bounces towards the riverbed again. Rounding the bend into Szalajkahaz, our lights pick out another of Rainer's men, frantically trying to wave us down. We brake and cut the engine. We hear shots. Kovacs hops out.

"What's happening, officer?"

"A fire-fight in the village, sir. We were taking a breather before moving on down to Eger when these two IFA's arrive. The bastards got out and opened up on us."

There's more gunfire.

"Anyone hurt?"

" 'Fraid so, sir. Two of ours and a couple of Gypsies. A boy and a woman, one badly."

He hesitates and draws breath.

"And the lieutenant, sir."

"What happened to him?"

"Got one in the leg, sir. Last I saw, he was taking cover behind the wheel of a truck, trying to bandage his shin with a scarf."

More firing and an explosion. Kovacs tells Coro and me to stay in the truck. But he doesn't object when we disobey. We move through the undergrowth towards the village and take cover behind the trunk of a beech tree. One of the IFA's is ablaze. I see mangled bodies strewn around the square. But the blast has given Rainer's men the initiative. They have the second IFA covered from all angles. Two uniforms wrench fire extinguishers from their own vehicles. They do their best with the first truck. But they know by now that anyone inside hasn't a hope.

Someone from the other IFA jumps down with his hands up. But he still has a gun.

"Drop it or you're dead," yells an officer. The weapon smacks to the ground.

"How many more of you in that thing?"

"Wouldn't you like to know?"

Rainer's voice wafts out of the trees soft and clear.

"If you hurt anyone else in that truck, I'll put a bullet through you."

Ignoring his wound, he's crept up on the Arrow Cross and stuck a handgun in his neck.

"Let them out, Pisa," the man shouts. "And you too. Come out with your hands up or they'll waste you."

Someone throws back the flap and leaps off the tailboard. He brandishes a machine pistol through forty-five degrees. There's another burst of gunfire. The man writhes and falls. The burning truck spits flames. Rainer's men stand statuesque in the light of the blaze, every weapon trained on the second IFA. The flap is pushed back again.

"Hold it," shouts Rainer. The hand on the tarpaulin quivers, then stays still.

"Now, come out slowly, very slowly, one by one."

Two small boys, faces white with terror, jump out and turn to help the others, three young women and an old couple.

"Walk into the shadow," Rainer calls gently. A uniform steps aside and leads them to the cover of our beech tree. Coro shepherds them further back into the brush. I keep my eye on Rainer. I can tell from his body language he isn't convinced the IFA is empty.

"You've got another friend in there haven't you?" He nudges his gun into the nape of his prisoner's neck. "Tell him to come out with his hands up or we rake the truck."

A long half minute slides by. An arm flicks at the flap. The gunman hurls himself from the IFA. Firing wildly, he hits the ground and rolls towards Rainer, trying to give his companion a chance to break free. But Kovacs has timed his own move. Cowering in the half light, he fires twice. The man twitches and lies still.

I look at the chaos of bodies, scattered belongings, uniforms and frightened survivors. Then beyond to where Kalman and Jenoe are emerging from behind their old Mercedes.

"Kalman Olah."

Coro steps forward. The blaze from the truck is dying but there's enough light to watch him run towards them. The three men embrace. Kovacs walks over, his right hand extended.

"You are, I think, the son of Kalman Olah," he says to Jenoe.

"I have that honour, sir."

The handshake is swift and firm. The uniforms relax. One of them relieves Rainer of his prisoner. Another catches the lieutenant as he collapses, faint with pain from his leg.

"And that is my good friend, Charlie Barrow." says Jenoe.

All four turn round and beckon me.

Kalman's face has melted into a grin. Kovacs almost falls on him, grasping his arms and resting his head on the old man's shoulder. Taken aback, Kalman feels the captain's convulsions. He looks at me and his eyes say he understands. He holds Kovacs in a bear hug. Jenoe leads Coro away. I stand and stare and think of Andrea. And then, for no reason at all, I think of Janza.

PART 16

Chapter 1

Having run out of cars, I'm forced to take the train back to Budapest. The time has come to re-establish contact with Fred and do some serious writing. Kovacs and Rainer have given me permission to report everything I've witnessed. I worry about Kovacs but Rainer assures me he'll keep an eye on him.

"Work won't cure him," he says. "But it'll keep the ghosts at bay."

I have my doubts. But I also sense that Kovacs wants me out of the way. I'm a constant reminder of what he's lost. I annoy him just by being there.

As the train rolls into Keleti station, I see uniforms in abundance. Heading for the exit, I'm accosted by one of them who wants to see my I.D.

"What's this about?" I ask.

He registers the suspicion on my face and grins.

"My sergeant wishes to speak to you, Mr Barrow."

Before I can ask any more questions, I spy the battered countenance of Ubul.

"Is this the worthy sergeant you're referring to?"

"The very same, Charlie Barrow," says Ubul dismissing the uniform with a curt nod.

We get into step, negotiating the Chinese takeaways and the Arab traders cluttering up the concourse of a terminal sardonically dubbed Budapest's Gateway to the East. The crowds are too raucous for conversation. I'm assuming Kovacs has sent word ahead. Doubtless Ubul will explain all in the back of a patrol car.

"Fear not," he says as we join the traffic. "You're not under arrest."

"Now, why should I think that, Sergeant?"

Ubul sniffs the fetid air. For once he isn't smoking. He wears an expression, which suggests he's having private fun at my expense.

"All right," I say. "I'm blinking first. What's all the mystery about?"

"I have been ordered by Captain Kovacs to let you in on all our material. I have nothing against you personally, Charlie, as you well know. But I do question whether investing this much confidence in a journalist, and a foreign journalist at that, is setting a good precedent."

I do not respond. He drives on.

"Where are we going, Ubul?"

"All in good time. Let me just say that events have clearly taken on a life and a momentum of their own. If you are to be the means whereby the world gets to know about one of the hottest political scandals in the history of my country, why should I stand in your way?"

"I don't know," I say. "Why should you?"

"Even I, Sandor Ubul, have started to throw caution to the winds."

"You did that when you had your little brush with Kozma. Remember?"

"Yes, I enjoyed that."

"So?"

I'm getting the impression that this conversation is designed as much to fill time as enlighten me about his intentions.

"Charlie. Has it occurred to you that Kozma will now have the big battalions out, police units whose loyalty he can count on to make our lives complete misery?"

Now it's my turn to bring him up to date and tell him what happened at Salajkahaz.

"Fuck me," he says reverting to type. "This is getting exciting."

I suddenly realise that we're back at the hospital where the Ethiopians were being treated.

"They're still here for their own safety," Ubul explains. "We have to question them again. I'm told the talkative one has more to tell. Should be just up your street."

For once there is a brighter side to life. The two Africans who were put in intensive care are now out of danger. Yohanes is still bubbling over, anxious to show Ubul what he's remembered and written down. There are lengthy descriptions of Kozma, the People's Justice Party leader, Szarka, and several skinheads who are clearly regular members of his bodyguard. Yohanes has also recalled enough of Szarka's speeches to add spice to these pen portraits, which can perhaps form the basis of a prosecution for criminal defamation. He's also added a few salient dates on which rallies and other neo-fascist get-togethers have taken place in and around the housing estates of Budapest.

"And I can use this?" I ask.

"Help yourself," Ubul proffers. "Only, you know Peter's conditions. You have to exercise a little patience. Curb your natural instincts and all that. Don't spill all the beans at once."

"Patience is my natural instinct, Sergeant. In any case, it'll take time to get this translated. And I want it to be absolutely accurate."

"I've never heard a reporter say that before."

"Give over, Ubul. If we come out of this smelling of roses, I'll buy you as many beers as you like. I'll be more than simply grateful – to you, to Kovacs, to Yohanes here, even to Janza. I suppose you know he's dead."

"I can't say I'm grieving, Charlie. Kovacs was too naïve about that bugger."

"Stole a Wartburg patrol car and ran off a mountain road."

"What for?"

I explain the so-called safe house and the messages transmitted to an unknown party in Budapest.

"We must pursue that. But right now I propose a vote of thanks to Yohanes. You've done us proud, my friend."

Yohanes is beaming. Then drops his lower lip and wears a worried look. "Do you think the hospital will let me stay until I know for sure that Michael and Efram are OK? I don't fancy going back to our place on my own."

"I think that's the least you deserve."

As Ubul extends his gruff smile, the glass behind us shatters like a windscreen caught by a stone. Almost simultaneously comes the crump of an explosion.

"Hell's bloody teeth," I shout in English.

The flying debris misses us but as cheap cotton curtains flutter vigorously in the sudden wind, I muse on what might come next. It could go one better and blast us all to Kingdom Come. I spring at Yohanes, pitch him into a firemen's lift and yell at Ubul to get through the door into the corridor. As we clatter out of the ward, a second shell hits the back wall, splits it in two, demolishes the iron bedstead and brings down the light fittings in a shower of dust and thick shards of plastic.

The three of us land in an undignified heap by a water dispenser. I take the full weight of Yohanes on what I already consider to be an overloaded collarbone. It holds. Doctors, nurses and assorted orderlies rush towards us.

"Out," bawls Ubul. "Get the hell out of here before there's another one."

They stagger into one other like characters in a Keystone cops movie, stare at Ubul for a fraction of a second and flee. All except the medic who's been treating Yohanes.

"You stay and check the patient."

For once, Ubul doesn't baulk at my order. I run down the corridor, heading for the emergency staircase. I have three flights to descend and know as soon as I emerge into the vehicle compound that my search for the artillery has been futile.

"I saw 'em in a pick-up. I saw 'em in a pick-up. I did." The cry comes from a maintenance man in dirty blue overalls.

"What did you see, for God's sake?"

Ubul has joined me. "Sweet Jesus, why does this keep happening to us?" His despair completely disconcerts our would-be informant.

"I thought you cops were rough and tough," he sniggers.

Ubul's snarl abruptly changes Dirty Overall's opinion about the fundamental nature of policemen. "I am rough and tough, especially with clever sods who get in my way."

"I didn't get in your way. I said I saw 'em. And their truck."

"Where?" I ask.

"Other side of the road. Opposite the tram stop."

"Make?"

"Ford. Said Ford on the tailgate."

"Colour?"

"Bit o' this and a bit o' that."

"What's that supposed to mean?"

"Scruffy job. White mostly. But patched up with red lead paint. And filthy."

"Number?"

"You must be bloody joking. I wasn't going to rush out and get that close. Anyway, they drove off like Batman and Robin."

"I see you've been watching some enlightening television then?"

"What?"

"Forget it," says Ubul. "And thanks."

"That's all right. If you want me again, I'm on….."

But Dirty Overall's efforts to impart his departmental number are lost in the wind as Ubul and I limp back to the hospital lobby. Smoke billows from a jagged hole where the rockets hit the third floor. A fire truck has arrived, plus patrol cars and a posse of uniforms.

"Yohanes is OK," says Ubul. "That young doctor took charge again."

"What about that lot?"

"Let 'em get on with it."

Ubul offers a cigarette. I don't refuse despite the *No Smoking* signs stencilled on the walls.

"Come on, Charlie. To the office. We need to get a few things sorted. If this goes on there'll be civil war by tomorrow."

Chapter 2

Several hours later, I bang the phone down in triumph.

"We're through to the Top, Sergeant Ubul. Minister's office at ten in the morning."

"Charlie Barrow, you're a genius."

My grin reflects thanks for Ubul's appreciation of certain skills I have exercised, as well as Ubul's own strategy, not to mention his uncharacteristic patience.

"I need to get as high as I can," he explained. "But I'm only a humble cop with a very low rank. I have no clout. I speak my language well but not quite as an educated Hungarian should. There is no way I can persuade those clever dicks in the ministry to listen to me personally."

And so with a rush of blood to the head born of a refusal to be beaten, we contrive the wording and style of an assault on bureaucracy. It involves a series of telephone calls which I put through to a list of names drawn up by Ubul – requests for interviews in the name of Captain Peter Kovacs, head of the Special Squad Charged With Counteracting Illegal Immigration. Posing as Ubul, with my slightly accented but very correct Hungarian, I cajole and persuade. It's hard graft. It involves the consumption of too many cigarettes and not a few cans of Dreher and it takes us until two in the morning to pull it off. The outcome is that both of us are invited to attend a briefing to be given by the Minister of the Interior.

Ubul, being Ubul, oversleeps and is slightly late. I am already sitting on an uncomfortable chair at the back of the ministry's press and information room. In the circumstances, the minister's aides and even the assembled reporters feel he is being decidedly restrained.

"I am a peasant by birth," he pronounces. "My father is 97 and my mother 88."

He looks up and rubs his nose. The journalists are puzzled.

"Both are in good health. I think I have durability in my genes."

The aides stay silent while the minister surveys them with narrowed eyes.

"It is true that the workload I carry is not sensible for a man in his sixties. But I sleep well. It runs in the family. I can usually manage to tie things up before I go to bed. Or I can leave them as question marks for the following day. Of course there are times when my colleagues ring me up with important information in the middle of the night. And sometimes I snap awake in the small hours."

One of the aides steps forward.

"Minister."

"Quiet, Kupa. I haven't finished this little monologue, the purport of which I should like you all to take on board."

He gazes round the room again.

"I want you to know that I am a reasonable and fair-minded person, as are all the members of this government. We do not seek to overwork our staff. We do not ask for more than is necessary to the good running of our ministries and departments. Now I am well aware that there are political roots to the degree of disorder in our society, disorder which has grown out of the initial euphoria and freedom we all enjoyed when the regime changed and the country moved from totalitarianism to civil democracy virtually overnight. Since when, the courts and the law enforcement agencies have been extremely careful to avoid restricting the people's civil rights."

He pauses, rearranges papers and moves a pen from one side of the desk to the other.

The pen is closely followed by a paper knife.

"And this, even in cases where the government has thought that perhaps a modicum of restriction was called for. We all know, do we not, that the legal and judicial systems inherited from the communists were, to put it mildly, defective and unsuitable? And yet, and yet….."

The paper knife moves back to its original position.

"The cumulative effect of all this," the minister goes on, "is clearly apparent in a lack of public discipline and the inability of our wonderful police force to cope with it."

A door behind me opens just enough to let Ubul slip in behind a minor official. The minister looks up but is not deflected from his final flurry.

"Which is why what might have been a succession of routine working days has seemingly degenerated into a period of chaos. Riots in the streets. Fifty arrests. Three African students the victims of a racist attack, detained in the intensive care unit of a major hospital, itself subsequently rocketed – rocketed, dear God – in broad daylight."

There is a further collective effort to make sure that the right files are in the right hands and that, when the minister calls for a particular piece of intelligence, as assuredly he will, nobody is going to be caught napping.

"Then I learn that the chief official in charge of important investigations – investigations, that is, with a distinct bearing on national security – I learn that he has disappeared. He cannot be traced. By phone, by fax, by radio, at his office in this ministry, or indeed at his home. He has, in short, vanished into thin air."

The minister surveys the room again, fixing on each and every aide in turn. This time no one moves. Feet stay unshuffled and the air-conditioning purrs contentedly.

Outside, the sun breaks through a cloud and lights up the white drapes hanging from gilded poles high above our heads.

"And finally," he sighs, "I hear that a police officer was shot three days ago in a café just off Rakoczi, while the body of a man, a Croatian, now lies in the main morgue, after being removed by members of a special squad in charge of enquiries into illegal immigration from the apartment of another senior police officer, namely the head of this squad."

Ubul stays where he is, looking down at the parquet floor and trying hard not to ogle the trim ankles of a young female official. We all await the Big Bang.

It doesn't come in quite the way we expect. The minister merely utters a sibilant plea.

"Will someone, for pity's sake, please tell me what is going on? Or do I have to divine by myself, unilaterally, solitary and cut off from reality, that the state, the Republic of Hungary and the civil order are collapsing around us, with the presumption that the government of which I am a senior member is being left to fiddle while Rome burns?"

Kupa, the aide, judges his moment has arrived. He rises and with a skill that I cannot but admire, offers the minister assurances that reports on these incidents have been prepared but that, owing to the swiftness of events, they are even now incomplete.

"In which case, Kupa, I am distinctly unwilling to wade through a mass of outdated paperwork. It may be admirably drafted and full of sound advice." He sits up and waves his arms. "But there isn't time, is there?"

The journalists titter at this put-down. Kupa isn't fazed.

"No, minister," he says. "But you may wish to have these documents to hand once you have had a briefing from one of the officers dealing with these cases."

I sit up like startled rabbit. My notepad drops to the floor along with a collection of pens. Eyes turn on me.

"And who might that be?" the minister asks.

I watch Ubul summon the kind of courage he'd shown when, trawling the very depths of his soul, he faced up to Kozma. He moves out from behind the official and walks through the mass of reporters up to the minister's desk.

"It might be me," he says quietly. "Sergeant Sandor Ubul from the Illegal Immigration Squad of the Budapest City Police."

The minister looks at Ubul over the top of his half-moons. Nothing surprises him any longer, not even the presence of junior police officers in the inner sanctum of government.

"Sergeant Ubul," says the minister. "You will forgive me if I ask Mr Kupa exactly why you are here, fresh from the streets, so to speak."

Ubul peers down at his badly creased slacks, his soiled jacket and a pair of shoes still bearing the marks of the Angyalfold riot. But Kupa is an honourable man. He explains that after the RPG raid on the hospital, Sergeant Ubul, who was nearly killed in the attack himself, decided that urgency demanded the extraordinary step of a phone call or two to the ministry.

"The officer's reasoning was that, in the absence of Colonel Kozma, of whom you will hear more anon, minister, and that of the head of the Illegal Immigration Squad, Captain Peter Kovacs, you and your advisers were badly misinformed."

"Misinformed?"

"Perhaps not misinformed so much as not informed at all."

All the journalists are now leaning forward on the edge of their seats.

"Sergeant Ubul's case," Kupa goes on, "is that the whole affair has taken a critical turn which does indeed threaten state security. Captain Kovacs is even now checking out various serious and fast-moving developments within and outside Budapest."

Ubul has swivelled through forty five degrees and catches my eye.

"The sergeant was brilliantly persuasive, minister, I have to say." Kupa allows himself the ghost of a smile. Ubul winks and I gulp. The journalists eye me again but turn back when they hear Ubul's voice.

"I was damned…..sorry sir…, *very* lucky." Ubul coughs, keeping a straight face at the obvious memory of the deception we pulled off in the early hours of the morning. But he feels bold enough to add a rider. "You have in Mr Kupa, sir, perhaps the most reasonable official I have ever come across…."

"Sergeant Ubul," the minister interjects quietly. "I still don't know what the hell's going on."

Ubul steps back from the desk allowing Kupa to tell the crux of the story to the growing astonishment of officials and reporters alike. With effortless cohesion, clarity and economy, he repeats Ubul's account of the past week.

"Sergeant Ubul was clearly determined to impart his information to someone of influence before Colonel Kozma had time to strike back."

The journalists don't wait to ask questions. There is a mad flurry for the exit. Aides bob and weave to get out of the way.

The minister is not annoyed by the exodus but clearly confused when he notices that I have not followed suit. As the rumpus dies down, I see Ubul murmur into Kupa's ear.

He in turn bends towards the minister. I stay in my seat. Kupa approaches.

"Mr Barrow. His Excellency would like you to join us."

Ubul and I are quizzed for another half hour. We're then asked to wait while the minister looks through the reports Kupa has given him.

Kupa takes us to lunch – a little place on Nador utca not far from parliament. As we slurp our soup he adopts a slightly conspiratorial air.

"You might be interested to know," he says, "that I have received reports telling me that Captain Kovacs has teamed up with the local police in Heves county on three related enquiries – three murders."

"Three Mr Kupa? We know of two. Andrea Tar and an engineer called Klein. Who's the third?"

"An official called Janza."

"But he died in a road accident." I look at Ubul who's warning me not to say any more.

"The accident was staged, Mr Barrow. He was driving an official car but failed to negotiate a bend on a steep hill. A patrolman found him hanging out of a broken windscreen. The brakes and steering had been tampered with."

"By whom?"

"We aren't sure."

"Kozma needed to get rid of him," says Ubul.

I cast my mind back to the print-outs I'd read of Janza's messages to Budapest.

"Inform plan to eliminate Barrow……Reconstruction of Camps at Recsk and Szalajkahaz for Internment of Roma….. Provision of quarters for New Arrow Cross recruits".

We look at Kupa but we don't get a response until he says, "One report told us that Kovacs was – I'm sorry to say – at the end of his emotional tether. I think those were the words used. It said he was no longer capable of making rational judgements about evidence and circumstances. Sick leave seems to be in the offing."

"And was that from Janza?" This time I'm not in a mood to take bullshit.

"I can't say," says Kupa.

"Won't say," snaps Ubul. "It's bloody ridiculous anyway. Kovacs has his obsessions. I know that more than anyone. I also know the pressure he's under. But I don't question his sanity or his professionalism. In any case, might I remind you that Kozma tried to kill him?"

"That is, if I may say so, *your* version of events, Sergeant."

"And mine too," I add. "Do you really think, Mr Kupa, that we would invent the serious allegations we've laid before your minister? Do you?"

Kupa concentrates on the food on his plate.

"Listen," says Ubul. "Kovacs isn't sick. He's grieving because Andrea Tar was his partner. And he's overworked. But there's nothing wrong with his judgement. And since you're not able or willing to tell us who filed this report……"

"I might add," says Kupa, "that it's only one of several we have had. I'm sure you can leave the minister to assess its worth."

A waiter sidles up to us. There is a message from Kupa's office.

The minister wants the three of us back and quickly.

"You realise," he says, "that this material on Colonel Kozma is extremely damaging. Not only for him of course but for the government, this ministry, the security forces and the police, of which you are a member, Sergeant. God knows how far this cancer has spread. It obliges me to make an awful confession. That the Forum government – we – have been singularly naïve and incompetent. I would remind you all by the way that you are in a classified and confidential briefing."

"Not this morning, we weren't," I say. "This morning was on the record. It's gone too far, minister. Read the evening papers."

He riffles irritably through the tabloids in front of him.

"Do you or do you not accept the allegations against Kozma?" I ask. Kupa looks at Ubul who looks at me.

"I accept nothing, so far," the minister answers.

But we're not bottling out. And he knows it.

"Very well," he says. "Given Kozma's extraordinary behaviour, given the week's events, given Sergeant Ubul's tenacity in bringing this to my attention, given, Kupa, your own obvious concern that we should examine this stuff thoroughly, I admit it. I think Kozma has a case to answer. Is there any news of him?"

The winter daylight is fading. An aide turns on the discreet lighting which casts comfortable shadows down walls, across desks and tables and on to the choice carpeting and the burnished woodwork.

"We saw him drive at high speed and very recklessly out of the compound at the Arrow Cross camp," I say.

"In an official car?" the minister asks.

"Just so. The police in Szalajhaz said he raced through the village heading for the main road to Eger. Kovacs thinks he's gone to Ozd to rally his troops or tie up some loose ends before slipping across the Slovak border."

"And what will you two do now?" The minister scribbles a note as Ubul gives his reply.

"Wait for Kovacs to return to Budapest, I think." Ubul shrugs. "Or join him in Ozd if he thinks that's a better bet. But first we have to sift through evidence from the hospital and examine the remnants of ordnance used by the terrorists. I'm glad to say we have at least found the pick-up truck. Unfortunately, though it's hardly surprising, their weaponry had been dismantled and removed. The vehicle was left on a patch of ground in Angyalfold."

Ubul takes a breather and stares at me. "Mr Barrow will doubtless be filing to his papers in Britain and Australia."

"I hope you will not paint too unflattering a picture of my country and its government, Mr Barrow."

The minister smiles ruefully and rises from the comfortable depths of his armchair. He shakes my hand and then Ubul's.

"I am more than grateful for what you have done, sergeant. But I must have everything checked before I can act. I promise you, I shall see that the work is completed quickly. In any case, the future may, so to speak, overtake us."

I frown at this. He smiles again.

"You have honest faces. Please remember where you have been today."

"And what did he mean by that?" I ask as Ubul drives into the afternoon rush hour.

"The bit about honest faces or the hint that the future could overtake us?"

Ubul swings in and out of the traffic stream annoying taxis and trams alike. It's the fag end of the day. I can't get Kupa's reports out of my mind.

"Which bastard in Kozma's wide circle of friends and acquaintances is doing his best to discredit Kovacs?"

"They're all out there, Charlie, loitering in the shadows and waiting to pounce."

I taste my furred-up tongue. I want another beer and a change of clothes. We turn off Rakoczi and head for my apartment. It's nearly six o'clock. Ubul switches on the radio expecting the early evening news.

This is Radio Budapest.

He leans forward and turns up the volume.

"Here is a special announcement. Jozsef Antall, prime minister and chairman of the Hungarian Democratic Forum, died this

afternoon at 5-15 in Sote Medical University Hospital. He was 62. His death followed a prolonged and serious illness....."

Ubul pulls into the kerb. I notice other motorists doing the same. The radio continues with a short biography and a list of the prime minister's academic achievements and publications. The announcer tells us there'll be a statement from the president.

"I'm sure that'll be enlightening," Ubul mutters.

We hear Hungary's melancholy national anthem. I am wafted back to 1956 and memories of listening to the same melody from the last free radio station before the Soviet invasion finally crushed the Revolution.

The president speaks.

"Although we were prepared for this, the news has shaken us all and fills our hearts with pain. As the first elected prime minister of the new Hungary, Jozsef Antall took on an extremely difficult task – to lead the country to the threshold of democracy after almost uninterrupted centuries of authoritarianism. I say 'to the threshold' because the border between dictatorship and democracy is not one that can be crossed with a single step. It is more like a frontier zone, full of political and economic obstacles. A country becomes democratic only when the overwhelming majority of its people have struggled through this zone, trying to adopt new values, a new way of thinking and new ways of behaving.....

There is more of the same plus a fervent call for 'spotlessly clean elections' next year. Then the president tells us what we need to know; that the man we have spent most of the day with will continue as acting prime minister until further notice; and that when he said goodbye to us, he already knew that Jozsef Antall was dead.

Chapter 3

After a quick beer and a wash and brush-up at my place, we drive towards the river. We park the car near the taxi stand in Bathory utca. For this is where the crowds begin. Silent citizens. Only footsteps echo from walls and pavements as they make their way in Kossuth Lajos Square.

The radio says tens of thousands have gathered in the heart of Budapest to mourn Jozsef Antall. It's a vague, non-committal estimate but conveys the right impression. At first, Ubul and I can get no further than the metro entrance on the south side of the square but his I.D. and some deft manoeuvring eventually bring us closer to the parliament building. Here candles and night lights flicker and dance round the monument to victims of the AVO, a swathe of flame cutting through the gloom and stretching across to the statue of Kossuth – leader of the 1848 Revolution against the Hapsburgs.

Silence gives way to subdued singing, to hymns and prayers and tributes. Some hold small black flags, others wear rose-shaped *kokarda* badges showing the national colours of red, white and green. They listen as our minister intones his own eulogy from a distant microphone.

"Jozsef Antall," he says, "set our country on the road to democracy *and* happiness."

Ubul throws me the glance of an old cynic. I smile sadly in return.

"Keep hoping, sergeant. In spite of all you've seen and all you know."

"The man said 'happiness', Charlie. 'Happiness' for God's sake."

He gestures that we should move away but I hold up a hand. A young man, his dark, straight hair ruffled by the breeze blowing off the river, is reading from a piece of paper.

There are murmurs that he should be silent, that he's desecrating a solemn occasion. But others urge us to listen.

".....where there is tyranny
all is in vain,
even the song, however fine,
is false in every line,
for he stands over you
at your grave,
and tells you who you were,
even your dust serves tyranny."

There's some polite clapping but subdued voices continue to protest.

"This is not the right place for words like those," says one woman. "*Our* singing is not in vain."

"Jozsef Antall deserves a better epitaph," says another. "He of all people never served tyranny."

The young man says no more, folds his crumpled paper and walks away.

"What was all that about?" Ubul asks.

"You don't know one of the greatest poems in the Hungarian language?"

"I don't know any poetry, Charlie. When have I had time for it?"

"You ought to know that one. It was written by Gyula Illyes, a staunch communist but one who saw through the hypocrisy and tried to get things changed. It's called *A*

Sentence About Tyranny, a hundred and eighty three lines on the terrible reality of totalitarianism. The sort that killed your uncle."

"You have a good memory, Charlie Barrow."

"Illyes penned it in 1950. But it stayed unpublished until a few days after the '56 Revolution. The Kadar communists always said it was aimed at them."

"And was it?"

"When he first wrote it, Illyes was having a crack at Rakosi and Stalinism. I suppose it was meant for all the bastards who like to push us around, keep us quiet, lock us up, or murder us, just for being what we are. It's also about you and me and what we've got ourselves into."

Ubul looks out over the square, at the sea of candlelight and at the huge bulk of the much abused neo-Gothic parliament house, just about a century old, stripped only recently of the red star the communists stuck on top of it. He peers at the extended arm of Kossuth, a journalist and lawyer who thought he'd led his country to freedom and independence.

Then he turns and stands quite still.

"Charlie," he hisses. "Stay close to me. Don't say a word."

I do as I'm told, trying to work out what's happening. Shoulder to shoulder, like two bouncers in a night club, we ease our way round the back of the crowd, its attention still fixed on the portals of parliament.

Ubul lunges, grabs an arm and holds his victim in a half-nelson. The man cries out. The crowd parts, appalled that violence should mar their vigil.

"My apologies, ladies and gentlemen. I am a police officer and this man is under arrest."

I keep the man's other arm in a hold learned on some half forgotten training course.

"Who the hell do you think.....?"

"Shut up," says Ubul. "And keep moving. Or I snap this arm into little pieces."

We frog-march our captive through a hostile crowd. He kicks out and yells abuse at us. I'm sure some idiot will intervene and give him a chance to escape. But it doesn't happen, not even when a bunch of uniforms approaches us and asks Ubul what he thinks he's playing at. Ubul manages to fish out his I.D. and wave it in their faces.

"Well, don't just stand there," he shouts. "Help us get this piece of work into one of your nice blue vans."

At which point I suggest I deserve an answer to some pertinent questions.

"Sorry, Charlie. And thanks."

"But who is he?"

"Don't you recognise him? He's the second of the two bastards who gave us the slip at the Troika. He's the other Croat. I still don't know which of them killed Lajos. Maybe it was the one picked off by Kozma in Kovacs's apartment. But this one is still alive. And I'm going to roast him."

Ubul has his Croat in an interview room, walls of dark green tile, bare light bulbs, concrete floor, and two utilitarian tables and chairs. The only relatively modern items are a microphone and a cassette recorder. A young uniform stands by the door. I sit outside, watching through a small window and listening via an ancient loudspeaker. Ubul thumbs through the detainee's papers.

"That's not very bright, is it?" he ventures.

"What isn't?"

He's trapped the man into speech and passable Hungarian.

"It's not very bright to use the same name in your second passport as the one in your travelling companion's. 'Janko – Dobroslav'. Who was, in case you didn't know, shot dead by his protector, about forty eight hours ago."

"He was shot by Kovacs. In the back. He was murdered."

The Croat looks up and sneers.

"Oh, he was murdered all right. But not by Captain Kovacs."

The man's expression never changes. Ubul draws on a cigarette and blows the smoke straight at him.

"He was murdered by Kovacs," says the man, "in revenge for the death of the officer at the café." He sits back and looks at Ubul down his nose.

"Now that is a very interesting statement, Mr.….Janko, or whoever you are. But I am telling you again. It was not Kovacs who did the deed."

Ubul pauses and scratches the skin above his upper lip. His gaze never leaves the Croat.

"Then who? Who, for Christ's sake?"

The man has risen from his chair. The young uniform steps across and puts a hand on his shoulder. He brushes it aside but sits down again.

"In a word – Kozma. Or three words. Colonel Mihaly Kozma."

The Croat's jaw drops. He stares vacantly ahead, at the wall behind Ubul. Then he leaps out of his chair again and stretches across the table, trying hard to grab the lapel on Ubul's parka. Ubul thumps him hard in the chest. He falls back. The chair topples. The man lies spread-eagled on the concrete. Ubul is kneeling on him, pinning his arms and spitting new information into his ear.

"Before my young colleague reminds me that I have committed an assault on someone in detention who has yet to be charged with any offence, let me tell you this, Sunshine. I don't know which of you pulled the gun that killed officer Lajos….."

The man squirms under Ubul's grip.

"But since you are the only one left, I am going to make sure you go down for a long stretch in a very uncomfortable Hungarian jail."

He grabs a handful of greasy hair and pulls the Croat upright.

"I didn't kill him," the man gasps.

"Mr Janko, I am going to give you an hour. In that time you will prepare a statement on what you have been up to since you crossed the border on or about October the 16th. You can write it in that funny language of yours if that will make it easier for you. But write it you will. And when you have written it, you will read it out so that we can tape it. And then we shall translate it."

I watch Ubul relishing the prospect of firing his last salvo.

"Then I shall charge you with a long list of criminal offences and you will be held until such time as one of our nice new democratically constituted courts sees fit to try you."

"Sarge?"

The uniform's soft voice drifts in from somewhere behind Ubul who is still holding the Croat by his hair. Ubul turns and the uniform nods towards the detainee. Ubul turns back. The Croat has closed his eyes and is breathing heavily. Ubul lets go. The man slumps to the floor.

"Oh dear," says Ubul. "It's all been a little too much for him."

Then he looks at the young officer.

"Are you reporting me?"

Swallowing hard, the uniform deftly explains that if Ubul wants a statement out of the Croat, they had better revive him and give him some nourishment.

"You are right," Ubul responds. "Food and drink, plus a biro and a few sheets of paper, to induce conditions suitable for thought and reflection."

The officer stoops to haul the Croat to his feet.

"You will go a long way, young man." Ubul gives him his most winning smile.

Chapter 4

At one in the morning over assorted cups of coffee, bottles of beer and ashtrays full of evil-smelling stubs, Ubul and, with his permission, I, Charles Barrow, assisted by officer Petofi, sit in the office at the Western Rail Terminal reading through the Croat's statement.

"I entered Hungary from Croatia several times in the past twelve months. The last occasion was on October 16th via the border crossing at Letenye. I was accompanied by the man known to the Hungarian police as Dobroslav Janko, but whose real name was Mate Paraga. I insist that I am Dobroslav Janko and that it is my passport, a second passport with a substitute photograph, which was found on Paraga's body after he was shot dead in the apartment of Captain Peter Kovacs of the Budapest City Police. For the record, our other passports, which were forged documents, were given to Captain Kovacs during the raid on the Café Troika. He did not have time to hand them back before Paraga shot Officer Lajos."

"We'll have to put a date and time on that, Petofi."

Ubul rubs the stubble on his chin and ponders this opening paragraph.

"I'm still worried about this mix-up with the names. Why go to the trouble?"

"Precisely that," I answer. "To worry you, confuse you. They did it in Ireland all the time. The IRA had a lot of fun with aliases and name-swapping."

I am anxious to get on with this. I have loads to write and not a lot of time to do it.

"We worked as freelance middlemen cutting deals for the supply of equipment both to the Croatian armed forces and to factions and illegal paramilitary groups in the former Yugoslavia and Hungary. These included the Arrow Cross.

This has been revived and reorganised by right wing politicians with the help of senior police and military officers and officials in various ministries. Among them, Colonel Mihaly Kozma of the Central Directorate for the Prosecution of Crime."

"Well, there we have it, in black and white," says Ubul. "That's good enough, given the rest of the evidence" He looks enquiringly at Petofi and me.

"There is no shortage of arms on the black market in central Europe, as long as people are prepared to pay the price. The end of communism has opened up a trade in all types of weapons. Senior officers in the old Soviet republics and in the former satellite states, including Hungary, are only too willing to do deals, buying and selling ammunition, uniforms, plastic explosives, small arms, artillery, even tanks and missiles.

"In any case, arms manufacturers and governments alike are keen to do business in this part of the world. Last month the Hungarian Defence Ministry put on an exhibition in Budapest showing military equipment made by more than 150 companies from 20 countries, including Lockheed, Bell Helicopter, Thyssen and Saab-Scania. Even Mikhail Kalashnikov was there. But it wasn't open to the public or the media.

"Two days later, a senior official in the Hungarian Ministry of Industry and Commerce said the country's ability to defend itself was being undermined by obsolete equipment. So they were

going to produce cheap weapons by privatising all arms factories. Some of these would go for export. This is on the record."

"Knows his stuff," I interject. "Reminds me of Janza."

Ubul scowls.

"He's dead. Forget him."

I let it drop. I don't want Ubul turning cantankerous again.

"The Russians are also going to deliver to Hungary at least $50 million worth of military hardware to help pay off their debts. I have been told this will include armoured vehicles and turbines for MIG 29's.

"I can tell you for certain that if that happens, it will be even easier for freelance operators to make a killing. The region will be swamped with weapons and it won't just be conscripted soldiers who'll be using them. Yugoslavia is full of private armies who have all done their little bit of ethnic cleansing. The Arrow Cross is trying to copy them.

"Paraga and I did several deals with Hungarian officers for the sale of Russian-made arms and equipment held at the former Soviet base of Taszar, near Kaposvar. Everything from fatigues to rifles and IFA trucks from East Germany. I am prepared to give more details and dates."

"I saw some of those trucks up at Salajkahaz," I tell them.

"The weapons sold to Kozma's outfit have been transported in army vehicles and stored at various locations, mainly in the north east at abandoned copper mines near the former Recsk concentration camp and derelict warehouses attached to the big steelworks at Ozd. There are others but these are the ones Paraga and I dealt with. The director of the Ozd works, one Oblath, is also involved. He has received substantial payments from Kozma."

Ubul blows smoke at the ceiling. "What a bunch of bastards."

"The cash for these arms comes mainly from drugs and illegal immigration. Asia is the main source and Hungary the major transit route for this traffic. But many of the immigrants get no further than a Hungarian police station."

"Looks like you and Kovacs got something right."

"Not quite," says Petofi. "Read on."

Millions of forints worth of heroin and cannabis are smuggled in every year, mainly from Romania. The individual amounts are usually small, say 20 to 25 kilos. They're hidden in petrol tanks and bodywork. The Hungarian police are getting better at catching the smugglers but they are not targeting the suppliers.

"As for illegal immigrants, they are just being ripped off and even dying in the attempt. Once the middlemen are paid off, nobody cares what happens to them. Last summer 20 people from Bangladesh were found sleeping on top of corpses in a container lorry near the Austrian border. The temperature inside was 40 Celsius. Those who died had been suffocated. They had paid something like $5,000 each to agents at home and another thousand to so-called fixers at this end."

"I remember that," says Petofi. "Our boys up at Gyor had to empty the truck. One of them couldn't take it. He ended up on the shrink's couch."

The phone buzzes. Ubul takes the call. Apart from the odd grunt and a shake of the head, he says nothing for five minutes.

"Who was that?" I ask as he replaces the receiver.

"A Lieutenant Rainer calling from Eger. They took Kovacs to hospital. He was worn out. Couldn't think. Couldn't function. They left him to sleep it off, to rest for a few days. But he's checked himself out. Disappeared. Rainer thinks he's back in Budapest."

Ubul looks at the sheets of paper containing Janko's written statements.

"Let's finish reading this lot. Then we'd better get round to Peter's apartment."

"Can't this stuff wait?" Petofi asks.

"No. I don't want any loose ends. Then we can look forward to some action."

"Mihaly Kozma is in this up to his neck, as are several highly placed officials in at least five ministries and government departments. Not only has he revived the Arrow Cross and seen to it that his thugs are well armed. He has put the money into two right wing groups and a magazine called Szent Istvan, *a perverted patriotic reference to Hungary's first king. It has a circulation of about five thousand. Its editor was an important member of the anti-communist underground in the '70's and '80's.*

"Kozma has also paid into the coffers of some in the ruling party who have been trying to get the government to abandon its more liberal policies. And he is a leading member of a mafia that's trading in drugs, forged passports and other documents and spiking criminal cases and official enquiries that might embarrass him."

"Now comes the pay-off," growls Ubul.

"I admit that it was Paraga and I who shot our way out of the Troika. We were sent there to hand over forged papers to some of the illegal immigrants your men had tracked down. One was a drugs courier. We gave your men the slip and believed Kozma would protect us because he needed us for other operations. In any case we were to return to Croatia with his proposals for a deal with certain people in the army there.

"I also admit to organising the supply of RPG's for the attack on the hospital and the attempt to kill the Ethiopian students who witnessed the violence in Angyalfold. But I deny taking part in that attack which was the amateurish work of Arrow Cross recruits resident in Budapest. I have names and addresses which I am ready to pass on. Given this confession and the information it contains, I am prepared to come to an arrangement under which I am afforded immunity from prosecution.

"I wish to enter into negotiations to this end at the earliest opportunity. Signed……Dobroslav Janko….."

"Swine," snorts Petofi.

"Too true officer," says Ubul. "But he's our best source. I notice he admits to being at the Troika but accuses Paraga of furing the shot that killed Lajos." He runs a finger over the text again.

I am impatient to leave. "Can I keep my copy of this?"

The phone again. Ubul rolls his eyes.

"I am summoned," he announces. "Back to the ministry. The acting prime minister is very interested in the arrest I made and already has this confession on his desk."

Ubul grins and can't resist the temptation to think aloud.

"Now I wonder who passed it on without bothering to tell me?"

PART 17

Chapter 1

"Requiem aeternam dona ei, Domine,
Et lux perpetua luceat ei.
Requiescat in pace…..
De profundis clamavi ad te, Domine.
Exaudi vocem meam….."

I find Kovacs standing at the side of her grave listening to the priest intoning his blessing. It should have been a cold winter's morning with a biting wind, ruffling the floral tributes and the coarse cemetery grass. Instead the sun shines and the air is still. Birds sing in the leafless trees. The city buzzes in the background.

He catches my eye and smiles.

"I am burying Andrea Tar. The people are burying Joszef Antall. Lajos's widow is burying a good cop. Kalman Olah is holding ceremonies for all the Roma killed by the Arrow Cross. And Pal Janza's parents are taking the body of their son back to Szombathely. A hell of a week, Charlie."

"And who will bury Big Gyuri, Nora, Gabi, Mate Paraga, or any of the thugs killed in the shoot-out at Szalajkahaz?" I ask.

I know the answer. Bodies sometimes disappear and officialdom turns a blind eye. Nobody even bothers to ask the question.

"You were the only one here?" I ask.

"No. Her parents came. But they never spoke to me. It was all my fault, you see."

We walk away from the newly dug earth.

"I spent thirty six hours in that hospital," says Kovacs.

"Not long enough, Captain."

"I couldn't stand it. I came out of a deep sleep and felt every fold of the bedclothes and every crick in my neck. I lay with my eyes closed. But I saw many things, the dead and the living. Andrea's face drifting in and out of a vision of twisted bodies, Lajos, Roma and Arrow Cross. They were yelling at me. Only I couldn't hear them. Then she would smile and vanish."

I don't interrupt. He wants to let it all out but he doesn't want to discuss it.

"I dreamed I was walking in a warm wind along the ridge of a green hill. In the valley below, a mist rolled violently towards the source of a stream. It swept up the hillside and wrapped itself round me. I saw nothing but a white veil of vapour. I daren't move and I couldn't speak. And still I felt the warm wind. Then I saw the same images again, the quick and the dead. Andrea with Kozma and Ubul, Janza, Rainer and Coro."

He turns to me.

"Why the enemy partnered with my lover, Charlie? Why our chief suspect and a trusted colleague standing side by side?"

"You've lost the thing you loved most, Kovacs. Don't be surprised at the consequences."

"I'm supposed to be a tough cop. I'm not supposed to have nightmares. I'm supposed to think, analyse and perform. And what do I do? I screw up. And the villains stay free."

"But you said it yourself. You've got Kozma cornered – in Ozd."

"So I thought. But someone's helping him. Rainer can't find him."

He changes tack, gets angry, kicks at the gravel path leading us back to the main road.

"And what about Ubul? I left him to sink or swim in this tank of piranhas."

"Ubul's doing fine," I tell him.

"I hear he's arrested the other Croat, that he's been called to the ministry, for God's sake. It's unthinkable. Ubul at the ministry. They must have fried him alive."

"They did nothing of the sort. He's nailed the Croat and got a confession out of him. It's invaluable evidence. And the minister loves him."

"I don't believe you."

"Let me buy you a drink and I'll explain." Even though I could use the time to do more writing, Kovacs needs company. Perhaps the reports on his mental condition were right after all. Perhaps he has cracked.

"I want to go back to the flat, Charlie."

***   ***   ***   ***

I watch him wandering aimlessly from room to room, picking up photographs and ornaments like the glass paperweight that held her message down.

"How many days is it since the three of us sat in here and talked about the winter in Balaton? How many nights since I made love to her? How many more since I was hit over the head and woke up to the sight of Kozma standing over me with that gun in his unsteady hand? How long since you and me and Janza and Ubul chewed the fat and absorbed all that information? How long since the phone calls that summoned us to Ozd and Eger?"

"Days, Kovacs. Just days. They've flashed past and we haven't noticed."

He finds the *palinka*, the half empty bottle from which we all derived much sustenance during our council of war. He treks to the kitchen, tidy again after harbouring Kozma's dead Croat.

"Who cleaned up in here, I wonder?"

I don't know the answer and I'm not speculating. Kovacs returns with two glasses.

"What time is it now?" he asks. "Too early for this? Is that what you're thinking, Charlie?" He almost shouts at me.

"I'm not passing judgement. You should know that."

He sits at the big dining table, throws his head back, closes his eyes and waits for his visions to return.

The bell rings. I walk to the door and swing it open. A glowering Ubul stands before me, hands thrust into the pockets of his parka, cigarette protruding from tight lips. He does a little soccer player's shuffle and brushes past me.

"Thought I'd find you here."

He sees the bottle and the glasses.

"Solitary drinking was never your thing, Peter."

"Charlie's here, isn't he? But he didn't want to join me."

"Well, I do. Get another glass."

Kovacs does as he's told, lurches off, returns and slumps into an armchair.

"I know what you're going to say. You're going to tell me to stop feeling sorry for myself."

"Has Charlie said that?" Ubul squints at me.

"No."

"Then neither will I. Satisfied?"

Ubul pulls up a dining chair, spins it round and sits with arms folded across the back.

"You're entitled to feel all that and more. But I just thought I'd come and remind you that we have a job to do. A job you started. A job you gave us to do."

"Did I?" says Kovacs, eyes closed again.

"The job you spelled out in such agonising detail in Mitzi's. It was called 'Catching Kozma' or 'Saving the Country', or something like that. And by the way, the prime minister would like us to get on with it."

Kovacs shoots him an anxious glance.

"Since you abandoned me to my fate, Captain, I have moved into high circles."

Kovacs wants to interrupt.

"No. Shut up and listen. Before you tell me I'm out of my depth, let me tell you that I have specific orders to get you back to Eger, team up again with your good friend, Rainer, and his merry men, who, it is thought with good reason, have prevented Kozma from legging it across the border into Czechoslovakia. Or is it just Slovakia these days? I can't remember."

"How can they be so sure?" I ask.

"They can't," Ubul replies. "But Kozma hasn't been seen at any of the regular border crossings and the area's still more or less as it was in the old days. Plenty of razor wire and not a few landmines. Since the word went out, it's been heavily patrolled again. You have no idea, Captain, how resources suddenly become available when a minister gives the order. Men, choppers, weapons, vehicles. You name it. We get it."

Ubul smirks from over the top of his nicotine-stained moustache.

"You're getting cheeky, sergeant. I know when you're trying to needle me."

I'm watching this like a spectator at a tennis match.

"If you've got him cornered," adds Kovacs, "why have you waited, you and Rainer, or whoever's in charge up there?"

Ubul fishes another cigarette out of the pack in his jacket, taps it tight and lights up.

"Because our acting head of government, with whom I have had several interesting conversations of late, is persuaded that this is your show – that, if we are going in for the kill, you must lead us."

"So this is all your doing, is it?" Kovacs snaps his fingers. "And I get tossed the scraps from the table?"

"Listen, you idiot. I may have had access to the very top for which, incidentally, I have to thank Charlie here. But I still had to worm my way round one or two well-heeled sods in the ministry who tried anything and everything to muddy the waters, delay orders and keep me waiting with well timed cups of coffee in outer offices. For a start, they tried to get you taken off the case."

Kovacs pricks up his ears.

"I can vouch for that," I say. "I hope it's dawned on you, Kovacs, just how far Ubul's got with this thing. You can have the P.M.'s signature on a piece of paper, safe and sound in your pocket. You can shake his hand on the deal. But walk out of his office, and you still have to burrow your way through a labyrinth where Kozma and his protectors have their friends. You can never be sure who's minding whose back. You should know that."

Ubul tells him about Kupa, the ministerial aide.

"An ally perhaps but with a tendency to procrastination and character-assassination. He's got other fish to fry. I can smell 'em. He told us about certain messages he'd had from agents in the field, Kovacs. Messages slagging you off, questioning your sanity and judgement."

"Janza?"

"Playing both ends against the middle. Told you I didn't trust him."

"But he wasn't the only one," I add. "I phoned Rainer to find out where you'd got to. Among other things, he told me it had been established, as he put it, that the car Janza was driving at the time of his death had *not* been tampered with. He said it was a pure accident. He stole the wrong vehicle."

"Do you believe that?" asks Kovacs.

"No. But we can't prove anything. Perhaps your friend Rainer's more of a mystery than you suppose."

"Meaning....?"

"Meaning, Peter, that there are all sorts out there giving orders and taking them, conducting private wars, and not averse to dirty tricks."

"Rainer? You've got to be kidding. He's as straight as a die."

"He may be. But I'd like to take a look at the personal files of some of his staff."

Kovacs tosses off his brandy. "How's the journalism going?"

"I've been lucky. The British papers have picked up on my original exclusive. As have the wires, Reuters and the rest. TV crews are swarming all over the camp at Szalajkahaz. They've interviewed Coro and Kalman Olah and were right behind Rainer's men when they burst into one of the disused mines at Recsk."

"What about the old girl whose husband spent time in the camp?"

"Klara? Yes, she's had a ball. Told them all about sinister convoys."

"Take a look at the papers." Ubul extracts a couple of Budapest dailies from inside his parka. "Editors are asking questions about the government's competence and complacency. And the comment columns are agonizing over the rebirth of fascism and the Arrow Cross. You're missing it all. Andrea would not have been pleased….."

"That's cheap, Sergeant Ubul. Bloody cheap."

They're back at the taxi rank. Tight and tense. I think they might even come to blows. But Ubul makes amends in double quick time, gets up and does his little shuffle.

"I'm sorry, Captain. You're right."

Kovacs subsides.

"But we've got to move soon." It's half an apology. Ubul knows he has to goad Kovacs out of his lethargy.

"There's a car outside ready to take us north to rejoin Rainer. Petofi will be there, Yohanes and some of the Gypsies. They've been giving statements. A quick cup of coffee, Captain, a shower and a shave. Then get off your ass and do it."

Kovacs shoots out a hand to pick up his glass. Ubul grabs his wrist.

"You don't need that, Peter."

Tired eyes take in Ubul's strength and his authority.

"We're all changed men, Peter. We're all drained."

"And more mature," I add.

"But the difference, Charlie, the difference is….."

"I know. Ubul still has Rozsi."

Chapter 2

Three hours later, after a swift dash up the motorway and beyond, we are back in Rainer's office in Eger. The lieutenant sports a plaster cast on his left leg.

"I'm immobile for the next few weeks," he says. "Confined to desk work. Doctor's orders."

He's trying to make light of it but his face shows he's annoyed. We make the appropriate sympathetic noises. He's keen to get down to business.

"Oblath is the key to everything for the time being," he says. "He disappeared on the day you arranged to see him, Mr Barrow. But he's been found again. He was foolish enough to return to his apartment on foot in the early hours of this morning. He must have gambled on sneaking back unnoticed under cover of darkness. We apprehended him on his doorstep."

Rainer's predilection for the formal phrase has not deserted him despite the rough and tumble at Szalajkahaz.

"Oblath didn't take long to capitulate. He was scared stiff." Rainer laughs. "He was actually more afraid of his wife than of anything we could do to him. She let him have it with both barrels, said she would never forgive him for countenancing fraud and bribery, misusing state funds, siphoning them off to finance the Arrow Cross. The

Arrow Cross, I ask you. Her indignation knew no bounds. How could he, a respectable official, get mixed up in such things?"

"She has a good bourgeois conscience," I observe.

Rainer looks down at his notes.

"But he insisted he did not order Klein's murder."

"No," says Kovacs. "Kozma did that."

"Why are you so certain?" I ask.

"Because Oblath is terrified of Kozma," says Rainer. "He's admitted telling him that Klein had given you and Andrea tours of the steelworks and was overheard spelling out the details of what went on there."

"Who overheard him?"

"Someone in that seedy bar where you had a drink with him. Now he wonders what Kozma will do to *him*. Coro also has a version of this, based on the interrogations Kozma conducted at the Arrow Cross camp. He questioned both the Gypsy and Andrea."

Rainer stops short, fearful that he's said too much. We look at Kovacs who shrugs.

"It's all right. I can handle it." He clears his throat, embarrassed by his own candour. "Ubul has rehabilitated me."

"I am glad," says Rainer.

"Lieutenant. Where's the money Oblath took?" I feel the need to move on.

"In various bank accounts and in strongboxes and safes in Oblath's apartment. We even found wads of cash in cupboards in the office at the steelworks."

"We also found computers and disks and a load of documents in the big house at the camp," says Kovacs. "I'm always intrigued by how people who want to hide their crimes also keep meticulous records."

"Yes," says Rainer. "All the money can be traced except for a few million forints which may be stashed away in corners where we haven't looked or in accounts we haven't had time to examine."

For some reason we never subsequently fathom, Kovacs suddenly asks if he can go and look at the site of the accident in the casting plant at Ozd.

"Don't punish yourself, Captain," says Rainer.

"No. It has nothing to do with Andrea," Kovacs replies. "It's my sixth sense returning."

Ubul looks at me and raises his eyebrows.

"In fact," Kovacs goes on. "I want my own conducted tour of the whole place, furnaces, workshops, railyards – the lot."

"At this time of day? It'll be dark by the time you get to Ozd."

"Even so," says Kovacs. "Ubul, Charlie and I will go….. and Petofi."

"Then take radios with you. And weapons," Rainer insists. Ubul is beaming at the prospect of action.

The squad car gets us to Ozd within half an hour.

"You're on a high, Captain," I tell him.

"I have a premonition, Charlie, that we are on the last lap."

We arrive at the main gate of the steelworks in a flurry of blaring sirens and flashing lights. The citizens of Ozd, who know by now that their nasty little town has become the focus of national, even international, attention, give us a quick glance and trudge on. They've read all about it in the papers and seen the pictures on television but most of them have decided that, as of old, it's better to steer clear of busy policemen.

Waiting to meet us are two men in overalls, holding a collection of hard hats.

"Drossler's the name," says the first, a thin little man in his fifties with a distinct snivel. "Got the message from Eger. Funny time to be taking a stroll round this place."

Ubul takes his cue from Kovacs. "You are about to help in a murder enquiry, Mr Drossler and friend. Or isn't it convenient right now?" His sarcasm passes them by.

"Murder? Klein's murder?"

"His and a few others."

"Now, look…," stammers Drossler.

"That is precisely what we want to do," says Ubul. "And we need you to show us where to look. You will be invaluable."

I can sense that Ubul isn't quite sure what we searching for. We all assume Kovacs has something in mind which will reveal itself in due course. In any case, the sergeant is more than happy to see his boss absorbed in work again.

Drossler swallows hard but his companion, a strapping lad with a face like a contented cow, seems more sanguine. They both take in Ubul's no-nonsense countenance, Kovacs's hard stare and the patient smiles worn by Petofi and me.

"You'd better put these on," says Drossler without much enthusiasm. He hands out the hard hats.

"What a good idea."

Ubul signals them to lead the way.

Our itinerary is virtually a carbon copy of the one I followed with Klein. It takes in the same clanking locos and hopper wagons, the same bank of roaring furnaces, the same deafening row and the same pungent smells of coke and fumes. We reach the big steel door leading to the wrecked casting plant. The light is dim, supplied by an emergency rig of bare bulbs, swinging in a wind blowing through smashed window panes. When the access door clangs shut, the sudden peace and quiet unnerve me.

We peer down from the gallery into the debris of the explosion that killed Rasko and his team and sent his wife, Zsuzsa, into a hospital for the mentally disturbed. We see the twisted metal and gouges in the concrete floor. The control cabin high above us is curiously intact.

"Why has nobody cleaned this up?"

My enquiry produces looks of indifference.

"No one's giving any orders, "says Drossler. "You've got Oblath under arrest and poor old Klein is dead. Management has collapsed. We're doing what we can but we're only going through the motions."

"And you've been told not to touch the evidence until the big boys in Budapest give the word. That's if they haven't already forgotten about it?"

"How did you guess?" Drossler looks at his watch. He's not enjoying any of this.

"I want to climb down there," says Kovacs. "I want to look around."

"Are you following one of your famously inspired hunches?" Ubul asks. "Or are we looking for something specific?"

Kovacs pokes about among the jungle of wreckage.

"Don't pull anything free," warns Drossler. "The whole lot might collapse on top of us."

Kovacs heeds his advice and spends his time staring at different combinations of distorted girders and useless components.

"What do you make of it, Charlie?"

"I keep looking up at that control cabin," I reply. "And the gantries right at the top."

They follow my gaze.

"And I think we're being watched," I add.

Kovacs turns to Drossler. "I want to go back to the railyard. I want to see more."

The guide looks at Ubul in despair but decides it's not worth arguing. We return to the railyard. Ubul's attention is drawn to a series of wooden doors in the high outer wall of the main works, giving access to what look like large lock-up garages.

"Those were repair shops," Drossler explains. "Or sheds for vehicles."

"And now?"

"A year ago some lads who'd been made redundant got permission to use that one."

He points to the second set of doors. "They started a private workshop making tools, pots and pans, spades and hoes, that sort of thing. All out of scrap. Paid rent to Oblath. Bloody hard work. But they made a go of it."

"But they're not here now, are they?" I say. "I heard all about this from Klein."

"They were thrown out," says Drossler. "Their faces didn't fit any more."

"I heard the same story from Coro," says Kovacs. "Andrea told him how Klein had talked about all sorts of scandals and stitch-ups."

"I'll bet that cost him his life," Ubul observes.

"And hers too." Kovacs stands in contemplation. It brings the worry lines back to Ubul's face.

Kovacs snaps out of it.

"I want to look inside that shed," he says.

Drossler protests that he hasn't got the keys. Ubul pulls his gun and shoots the locks off. The door swings outwards on creaking hinges. We walk forwards. I find a battery of switches on the left hand wall. A row of neon lights flickers into life.

"Holy shit," breathes Petofi who can't contain himself at the sight of computer terminals with all the attendant bits and pieces, printers, filing cabinets, wall maps and charts and one, just one, Arrow Cross emblem fixed to the innermost wall.

"You wanted to know where the rest of Kozma's loot was hidden, Ubul? Feast your eyes."

"What clever people you are."

318

The voice resonates from the depths of the railyard. We haven't noticed how uncannily quiet it's gone. There's a whisper of steam and a tiny tornado of dust dances its way into the shed.

Ubul leaps for the switches. But the bullet finds its target. Sparks fly and we're plunged into a darkness relieved only by faint rays from wall lights out in the yard.

"You all right, Ubul?"

"Who the hell is it, Kovacs?"

"I don't care who it is," Drossler whimpers. "We're getting out of here."

"Get to the back, as far back as you can," Ubul rasps. "And stay there"

"Where's Charlie?" asks Kovacs.

"Over here," I call. "Behind a filing cabinet." Then I let my small cat out of its bag. "And I've got a gun." I produce my service revolver.

"Naughty boy," says Kovacs. "But then you were a soldier. I suppose you know how to use it."

"It's Kozma," whispers Ubul. "Got to be."

"Oh, I'd recognise that voice anywhere." Kovacs laughs softly. "Told you we were on the last lap."

"But is he alone? And if he isn't, how many of the bastards has he got with him?" Ubul's trying to do some quick reckoning. "And what are they carrying? We've no cover and even if Charlie's armed, we haven't got the most powerful artillery in the world."

"You have found my final secret," Kozma calls from the gloom of the railyard. He has the actor's gift of projecting his voice out of thin air. "But you won't live to relish the discovery."

Another bullet shatters something once fixed to the shed's ceiling. Glass and plastic drop on to my shoulders. Petofi fires back, aiming for the spot from which Kozma dispatched his first salvo. On the evidence of moving shadows and the sound of feet on clinker, Petofi has succeeded.

"You've flushed him out," Ubul chuckles.

But Kozna is quick. He runs across the yard and scurries towards the huge furnaces. We follow. Again it's Petofi who's the first to catch sight of him. For all his unhealthy bulk, Kozma ducks and weaves, turning twice to use his gun with astonishing accuracy.

"He's on the catwalk, Boss."

Another missile bounces off the metal trunking and whines away over our heads. We huddle behind a pile of timber. Kovacs says he'll take the obvious route into the casting plant. Petofi is to work his way round the back and get inside at ground level.

"Ubul, give me cover."

"He'll pick you off, Peter."

"He can try. But he's running out of clips. And he's no great shakes with a gun."

"His performance so far," I point out wearily, "seems to undermine that theory."

But Kovacs isn't listening to me. He's making for the catwalk. Ubul looks up and sees Kozma take aim some twenty-five metres ahead of us.

I use my gun for the first time and miss.

"Never mind, Charlie," says Kovacs. "You've made him have second thoughts about a shoot-out among the furnaces."

Kozma hobbles his way through the hatch into the casting plant.

Drossler has caught up with us.

"The lads say they can't just abandon the furnaces even if there is a gunman on the loose. The whole place will go up."

Our collective knowledge of metallurgy is too rudimentary to contradict him.

"Just keep them out of sight for another ten minutes," says Kovacs.

Drossler beats a retreat.

"Before we go after him, let's call for some back-up," Ubul suggests.

"You call. If I don't go in there now, I'll lose him. Charlie, stay here."

"Oh no, Kovacs. I've come this far. And if I've got a gun, I'm going all the way."

I hear Ubul bawling into his radio. "He's in full flow, Lieutenant. For God's sake, get someone across here fast. And some paramedics."

Kovacs works his way through the hatch to be met by another shot pinging off the metal of the catwalk. He knows he's exposed but Kozma has moved on.

He's climbing furiously, hand over hand, making for the control cabin. Kovacs fires but the shadows and the half light botch his aim. Kozma presses on like a demented spider. Ubul has followed us through the hatch and tries his luck. The shot echoes round the concrete cavern and the slug bounces away into a corner.

"What the hell's he going to do up there?" shouts Ubul.

There's another shot but not from up above. And a second. Ubul clutches his shoulder and loses his grip on the catwalk rail. His gun clatters into the wreckage.

"Where the fuck did that come from?" he spits.

I hang on, holding my service revolver behind my back. I look down into the pit of the wreckage. Standing in a dark corner is a figure clad in an overcoat. I can't see the face but I can make out the grey crew-cut and a weapon held in a steady hand pointing straight at me.

Kovacs too has seen the silhouette and the gun.

"Dear God." The words come as a sharp whisper penetrating the background noise of plant and machinery.

"Good evening, Captain. And to you, Mr Barrow."

The deep voice rises from below.

"I think Colonel Kozma and I have all three of you covered. Stay where you are."

He moves just enough to let a beam of light reveal his features.

"But why?" asks Kovacs. "Gyula Bokor. In God's name, why?"

"Put not your trust in scholars, Kovacs. As I told Charlie Barrow, I once thought I could lead a quiet life in Academe but found myself in the company of rogues and charlatans. So I accepted the consequences. I joined in, with the intention of manipulating them."

"I don't believe you," says Kovacs.

"You have to. Unfortunately, our enterprise to forge a better Hungary out of the scrap metal of its history has gone badly wrong."

"How right you are," I say under my breath.

"Of course, Colonel Kozma doesn't agree with me. He thinks we can still get away with it. But we shall settle our internecine differences later. Meanwhile we shall have the satisfaction of killing you."

"Who is this bastard?" Ubul asks through clenched teeth.

"I am someone Kovacs and Charlie Barrow thought they could confide in. I am the teacher who led them astray, handing them precious tit-bits of information which they believed were valuable. And they were right. But they did not get the full story. Because I, Gyula Bokor, professor of military history, servant of many masters, am a consummate liar, one of the fishes who swam with communists and climbed out of the slime as a neo-fascist toad."

"I think I'm going mad," says Ubul. The sleeve of his jacket is soaked in blood. He's trying not to faint.

I see Kovacs easing himself up the ladder towards the control cabin. I expect Kozma to fire from above but for now he's out of sight. I'm assuming the only way out is to gain time by getting underneath Bokor's skin.

"Tell me one thing before I die," I shout. "Why were you so eager to give me such a generous briefing? You knew that much of what you told me was true and damaged your cause. If I delved further, I was bound to stumble across your part in all this."

"You are naïve beyond belief, Charlie Barrow. Knowing the game was up after what you told me about Kozma, I needed you and Kovacs to deflect suspicion away from me."

"Why?"

"I was researching new weapons for a citizens' army."

"You were telling the Arrow Cross where to get their guns, which ones to buy and how to pay for them?"

"Just so." Bokor preens himself.

"And you call them a citizens' army? That bunch of morons who got caught in the fire fight at Szalajkahaz?"

Bokor shifts to his right. He's impatient now. Ubul has spotted Kovacs's deft progress up the ladder. He risks a glance at the control cabin. Bokor takes note.

"It's time to end this meaningless dialogue," he says. His hold on the gun stays firm. "My colleague, the man I so shamelessly abused in my effort to divert your attention, Colonel Mihaly Kozma, is up aloft and will fire on a signal from me."

Out of the corner of my eye, I see Petofi, who's followed his orders to the letter. He's found a second doorway into the casting plant in time to see Bokor readying for the kill. Petofi fires. Bokor pitches forward into a pile of debris and loses his grip on the gun as the slug finds his shoulder. His fall dislodges a twisted metal strut which pins him to scarred concrete. Petofi retreats.

There's more gunfire from on high. Ubul gapes at the sight of Kovacs shinning up the ladder like a schoolboy in a gymnasium. He braces himself for the shot that will send Kovacs hurtling down to skewer himself on a sharp piece of metal.

But Kozma is preoccupied.

Kovacs reaches the final rungs. I hear another shot as he clambers into the cabin. It shifts on its moorings. A siren wails. A warning light in the gantry suffuses the whole place with an intermittent red glow.

I see Kozma pressing buttons and pulling levers. Then I hear him roar with laughter. The siren is silent.

"You and I will go together," he shouts. "We'll join the good professor, Kovacs. The prosecutor and the prosecuted will perish as one."

It's my turn to climb up to the cabin.

"Charlie. No," shouts Ubul. But I press on wondering where the energy is coming from. The cabin sways, its supports groaning with the strain.

"Very precarious, Kovacs. The more I move it, the more precarious it becomes. Just like the Hungarian state, wouldn't you say? In a few minutes, it will break loose and fall into that disgusting mess. And we shall die such horrible, such wonderful deaths."

I have reached the hatch. Kozma laughs again, waves his gun but I fire first. His white shirt front blazes bright crimson. His face wears the agony of final understanding. He falls forward, his fish eyes staring out from over a squat nose and a mouth streaked with blood.

Kovacs kneels in front of him.

"I should have killed you a long time ago," croaks Kozma.

"Your problem was you thought yourself infallible, Colonel. But you were second rate. Clever to a point but ultimately a failure."

A sudden, terrible anger twists the face out of recognition. Kovacs bends low again, funneling all his loathing into one last unforgiving remark.

"You killed my lady, Kozma. Remember that."

Ubul cries out. The cabin sways again.

"Peter. Charlie. Get out now. For Christ's sake."

I stagger back to the hatch and slither down the cold steel of the ladder. Ubul grabs me with his one good arm and pulls me back into the furnace shop. The siren howls a final lament to Rasko and the others. Its baying is drowned in the splintering of wood and the clang of metal as the cabin tears itself from its moorings and, in a cloud of concrete and dust, joins the wreckage in the pit below. There is no sign of Kovacs.

Chapter 3

I lift my glass, drink deeply and wipe my mouth with the back of my hand.

"Cheers," I say in English.

Ubul laughs. "That was not the gesture of an English gentleman, Charlie."

"I went native a long time ago." I produce a large white handkerchief and dab my lips with deliberate care. "Anyway, what's so funny apart from my body language?"

"The way you credit me with current trends in Hungarian politics."

I shake my head. "Hardly that. I mean I don't exactly blame you for bringing the communists back into power."

"Reformed communists, Charlie. Repackaged as Socialists. There is a difference."

"I'll believe it when I see it."

Time has moved on. And here is Ubul, now Captain Ubul, pulling in villains as only he knows how and fending off awkward questions from ignorant politicians who think the police can wave a magic wand and solve all crime at a stroke. But these days, he knows the vocabulary, knows how to deal with the huffing and puffing and the blandishments of those trying to impress him. His contacts are wide-ranging, ministers, ex-ministers, senior officials, villains and a bunch of Roma musicians who've become very famous.

And he has time to share a drink with me.

"And so, Charlie Barrow, what are you up to?" he asks, scrutinising me over the rim of his beer glass.

"I am a mere visitor from London," I say.

"I believe that, of course," he snorts.

I explain that after months of wrestling with myself, I gave in to the persuasive powers of Fred.

"I left my beloved Hungary for a senior post on a paper offering its wares to the British public from a high-tech operation in Canary Wharf. Then I got bored. A TV station in Berlin offered me a job as a newscaster. And off I went."

"They must have been desperate."

I ignore this insult and explain that the Germans wanted experience.

"They were fed up with blond bimbos and wanted the wizened face of wisdom, Ubul. *Ein Mensch*, in their own language."

"Women?"

"There is a lady in Berlin who gives me board and lodging."

He laughs again and we subside into a bout of reflection.

I pick up the threads. "I am assuming that the dismal performance of the neo-fascists in '94, and that of a few of their more respectable allies, must have had some connection with your success in bringing Kozma to a sticky end."

"Perhaps, Charlie. But it's all gone sour since then." Ubul is rarely encouraged by my hopeful view of his country's achievements in post-communist Europe. He retains the basic pessimism in which Hungarians love to wallow.

"Look in the papers. You won't find much to lift to spirits." He tosses me a copy.

"A businessman in Szeged has been killed outside his home. He was shot eight times in what police describe as a settling of scores by local criminals. They said a Yugoslav-made M75 hand grenade also exploded at the site as the shots were being fired."

"Read the next page, Charlie."

"Police in Budapest have detained more than a hundred people after raids on bars and nightclubs. The police said officers had visited every club in the capital after a series of shootings and bombings, all part of gang warfare which the authorities say has got to the stage a civilized European city cannot tolerate.

"One gangland leader, Jozsef P., had been shot at point blank range with a 9mm. handgun. He was sitting in his jeep at the time. Four hand grenades exploded nearby causing damage to property but no injuries. Police said the grenades came from a consignment that disappeared from a military arsenal. There were of a type used during the wars in former Yugoslavia."

Before us on a low table lie more tabloids and broadsheets, with headlines proclaiming victory for FIDESZ, the Federation of Young Democrats, nationalist and bourgeois and tinged with not a little anti-Semitism, and not quite so young any more.

"A bit different from '94, Charlie, when the press welcomed success for the Socialists. The Forum, Jozsef Antall's legacy, was swept away and reduced to a rump in parliament while the Far Right scraped together less than two per cent of the vote. 'Let the experts govern,' the reformed communists proclaimed. It was a good slogan. We were seduced by their flawless television performances. They didn't deny serving the old regime. Some of them helped to put down the '56 Revolution. But one of their leaders made much of the fact that his father had been executed by the Gestapo."

"Brownie points," I say.

Ubul's brow puckers. I don't think it's worth the effort explaining a dated cliché.

328

"Credit in the bank for Gyula Horn," he says, "the man who opened the gates for all those East Germans and their Trabis in '89."

"As I recall," I say, "Horn was adept at projecting good-natured and long-suffering weariness."

"After four years of incompetent non-communist government, he was spot on. It wasn't just corruption that let Kozma and his ilk play their games. It was woolly thinking. After all, how could we allow Hungary to be run by a bunch of historians and writers?"

"But the worm's turned?" I ask.

"For all their so-called expertise," Kovacs goes on, "the Socialists were just as bad. Corruption is as rife as ever. Inflation's rising. So the inevitable happens. A new breed of conservative has come to power. Taxes and public spending will be cut, they say. But the country must grow. All good Hungarian couples must have three children. On top of which, the neo-fascists have gained enough support to win seats in parliament. They won't get a post in the new government but the interior minister is a former police officer who is no lover of civil liberties."

He's smoking again, inhaling deeply, vehemently stubbing out half-finished cigarillos.

"We've already had the purge," he says "Two of my mates have been given the push because they refused to massage crime statistics. What were they supposed to do? Then we had this car bomb in the centre of town. It killed a valuable source – a restaurant owner who had clubs and other joints down near Balaton. He gave us gold-plated information on fraud involving thefts of oil and petrol. We wait for the backlash. The villains are as thick with the politicians as they used to be."

"What's all this about a trial?" I ask.

Ubul leans back and stretches his legs.

He has given evidence in court against some of Szarka's thugs. The charges referred to 'incitement against Jews and Roma, the use of outlawed symbols, and circulating neo-Nazi propaganda'.

"One of my more successful operations," he says.

"Go on."

"The courtroom was packed with skins wearing a watered down version of the Arrow Cross uniform. They hurled abuse at all the prosecution witnesses including two police officers. The judge eventually summoned up enough courage to have the courtroom cleared. Which gave me the chance I'd been waiting for."

He smiles at the memory.

"What did you do?" I ask.

"I fixed it so that someone jostled me. I floored two of the mob and handcuffed another two. This stiffened the backs of my younger colleagues who waded in and broke a few heads. The rest of the skins fled. Back in court, judge and prosecution took heart and handed down three year jail terms. Unfortunately Szarka's mob have appealed and are still out and about doing mischief."

"I'd like to have seen that," I say.

"It's not the right way to solve the problem, Charlie. Even I accept that. But it'll have to do for now."

Ubul peers over my shoulder. "Well, well. Look who we have here."

Two young men hover a few feet away. They're dark and handsome. One wears the sort of trendy clothes that only those with money and taste can afford.

The other is a police officer in uniform.

"You don't recognize me, Mr Barrow?"

I do a double-take.

"Coro. By all that's wonderful."

I rise. We shake hands. Ubul is rearranging the chairs.

"Can I introduce Joska Makule?"

More hand-shakes.

"Joska is Roma, Charlie."

"Works with me," says Ubul.

"How did all this happen?" I ask eagerly.

"I got myself an education," says Coro.

"He's an advocate," Ubul explains. "The best."

"One of the few Roma lawyers in the country," Coro adds with a sly smile.

"And Joska," says Ubul, "is one of the few Roma who've decided a cop's life isn't so bad after all." Ubul loves this. He knows I remember his old prejudices. He winks.

"Coro has just won a famous victory," he says.

"We got the Supreme Court to force a gang who'd attacked a Roma family to pay compensation. One and a half million forints."

"Case goes back a long way," says Ubul. "The mob threw a petrol bomb through the window of a house in Szolnok. Most of them were put away on criminal charges."

"But this was a civil case," Coro explains. "The first where someone's had to cough up damages for racism."

Joska hasn't said a word. He's too shy. But he's big for a Roma.

"How's Kalman Olah?" I ask.

Coro's face clouds over. "He died last year. Heart attack. Probably all that tobacco. Jenoe's in charge now. They're still playing their music. I think they're in town this week but I don't know exactly where."

"And Judit?" I ask tentatively.

He laughs. "I'm getting used to living in a house with a wife and two children."

Coro says he and Joska must go but will catch up later. "Work, Mr Barrow."

"Don't overdo it," I call as they take their leave.

"Come on," says Ubul. "Let's stroll up Memory Lane. He pulls out some notes and sticks them under an empty glass. The bar in the Art Otel hums with chat and canned music. Through the plate glass window we watch Coro and Joska climb into a Volvo. I look hard at Ubul and catch a sharp return glance.

"And Kovacs?" I ask.

"I knew we wouldn't be able to avoid that one," says Ubul.

"So?"

"They found the parts from three bodies in the wreckage. Just about managed to identify Kozma, Bokor and Kovacs. But it took 'em weeks. And you'd left by the time we were able to assemble enough to give him a decent funeral."

"Where's he buried?"

"He isn't. He was cremated and I scattered his ashes from the Chain Bridge."

"Kozma and Bokor?"

"Kozma's remains were taken to his home village somewhere near Balatonfured. He had no family, Charlie. Not a single relative. Two ministry officials buried him."

"Bokor?"

"Oh, they didn't believe the evidence we gave against him. He got all the honours his university could afford to give him. Buried in Rakoskeresztur Cemetery no less – not far from Imre Nagy. What an irony. I can't fight things like that, Charlie."

"But you're doing OK?"

"So they tell me."

We take a cab back into Pest. I ask the driver to cross the Danube via the Chain Bridge. I take in a panorama that brings tears to my eyes, the broad, grey river, Parliament and Margit Island in the mists beyond. In Rakoczi, we get out and walk. I weigh up whether to invite Ubul and Rozsi to the Kispipa for dinner. Before I can make up my mind, Ubul says, "I've got something to show you."

I take in all the familiar landmarks, the Odry Theatre, the tiny church in front of Saint Rokus hospital, shops and cafes, smells and sounds, and people, the newly prosperous and the poor, an obvious pickpocket, a whore plying for early trade, the *tabak* selling papers, smokes and metro tickets.

"It's a great city, Ubul."

"Want to come back?"

"It can be arranged," I say lifting an eyebrow.

"Remember Mitzi's, Charlie?"

"That was your pub, Ubul, not mine."

"It isn't mine any more. Take a look."

There, on the opposite side of the road is an establishment announcing itself as The American Sports Bar.

"Videos of that funny game they call football," says Ubul. "And bloody awful beer."

He leads on.

"See that street sign?"

I register the word *Erzsebet* in place of *Lenin*. A boulevard renamed in line with the times.

"Out goes the icon of the Soviet state. In comes a Christian saint. What do you call her in English?"

"Elizabeth."

"Ah, the queen."

"Two queens. This one and one of her predecessors. No saint even if she did claim to be a virgin."

Ubul laughs and spreads his arms wide.

"And there, my friend, is what used to be the 'Troika', the source of all our troubles."

I gape.

"They do a good plate of ham and eggs and decent coffee. Come on."

We cross Rakoczi, dodging the traffic and elbowing our way through crowds swarming out of a supermarket.

"McDonalds, Charlie. The land of milk and honey. You can have both with waffles."

"Ubul, Do me a favour. Come and eat at the Kispipa tonight. It's still there, isn't it?"

"It's still there. But it's not the same. No jazz these days. They've got a Gypsy band. Three brothers and their sons. They play authentic stuff, I'm told. And not too loud."

"Ah, well," I sigh.

Ubul laughs again. "We'd be delighted Charlie."

He pulls up suddenly. Two boys have chosen an empty cab rank for a quick game of makeshift soccer. One swings his foot at the ball. It flies straight at Ubul who catches it and holds it fast. The other boy gawps, then frowns.

"So?" Ubul looks down, hanging on to the ball.

"You're police, aren't you?"

Ubul waits. Then poses his own question. "How do you know?"

"Just do."

The boy shrugs, his small, pasty face waiting for the ball. Ubul lobs it to me and I drop-kick it back to the boy.

"But it's all right," he pipes. "As long as we can go on playing here."

Ubul lets his face crease into a smile and moves on.

THE END

EPILOGUE 1

The Hungary of 1990 was a country way behind the times – politically, economically and technically. In those days, I hardly ever saw a mobile phone or a lap top, which was why I used a typewriter, albeit an electric job, to fashion my copy for Fred. Kovacs was the only official I ever saw wrestling with a computer terminal, although Kozma and his mates had acquired a few. There were some Mercs and Opels around but your average Budapest taxi was a Lada or a Skoda belching the stench we always associated with communist Europe.

Yet rapid change was just around the corner. The people braced themselves for something better. After all, what had 1956 been about? A fight for freedom cruelly crushed by Soviet tanks and undermined by the treachery of the country's politicians. It was time for Russian troops to go home and for Hungary to rejoin Europe.

And so, one year after the fall of the Berlin Wall, the death of Janos Kadar and the reburial of Imre Nagy, many Hungarians shrugged off their pessimism and looked hopefully to the future, some with innocence and naivity. Free speech, a free press, freedom to read, view and listen to what you liked, even freedom to travel if you could afford it. Others saw freedom differently – freedom to own property, freedom to farm, grow crops and vines, raise cattle and horseflesh, freedom to invest, buy up state assets and make a blindingly huge profit.

And yet others didn't want freedom at all. They didn't want communism. But they wanted authority – a return to the illusion of discipline and respect fostered by the Horthy regime in the 1930's, a regime where people knew their place, master and servant, landowner and peasant, employer and worker, priest and parishioner.

And they wanted a Hungary restored, the return of territories lost to Romania and Slovakia. They demanded abnegation of the Treaty of Trianon. And a racially pure Hungary – no Jews, and no Gypsies.

Stir that pot and you got chaos, endless swings from Left to Right and back again. Some had a great time – bought Audis and Golfs and Bosch refrigerators, built themselves nice villas in the countryside or moved into the smarter suburbs of Budapest. They ate well, went to concerts and the theatre. To hell with the politicians, they said. Life's too short. But others lost out – prices rose and wages fell. Out of the window went free health care and full employment even though in communist times many of the jobs hadn't been jobs at all. Three million Hungarians lapsed into abject poverty. And as Kovacs spelled it out to me, that was a recipe for seemingly unstoppable crime and corruption.

And now we have it from the horse's mouth.

In 2006, a Hungarian prime minister – Ferenc Gyurcsany, socialist and former leader of the communist youth movement – admitted they'd fucked up, lied day and night and done nothing significant in the four years they'd been in office. When this secretly recorded speech to party members was broadcast on Hungarian radio (and which enterprising right-wing journalist managed that little coup?), there were riots on the streets of Budapest. The police waded in and fired rubber bullets. There were injuries and claims that this was as bad as the brutality of '56.

Bullshit.

Many with a passion for violence were of the Right – the ultra Right, waving the Arpad flag, under which the Arrow Cross did the Germans' bidding in 1944.

They'd helped to transport thousands of Hungarian Jews to Nazi extermination camps. The respectable Right kept its distance but it didn't hold back from parading a list of fifty politicians branded as unpatriotic Jews. Old habits die hard. In any case, the respectable Right has performed in government little better than its opponents.

All Hungary's politicians have let the country down, leaving it with massive debts and social problems to which their only answer is, "tough shit – that's what capitalism's all about".

But Hungary swims with the pack. It's joined the European Union and NATO. And Hungarians continue to hope that this will solve their problems.

And despite all, I love the place. I love its people, their hospitality, their good humour, their food and their culture. Not many countries with populations as small as ten million have produced geniuses like Ference Puskas and Bela Bartok, and a hundred others. Look up the list for yourselves.

Which is why I went back.

EPILOGUE 2

Take the metro to Oktogon. Walk fifty metres away from the city centre. You're standing outside Andrassy ut 60, branded these days the House of Terror, a museum to what the guidebook calls "two shameful and tragic periods" in the history of Hungary in the 20th century. In 1944 it was the headquarters of the Arrow Cross, Hungary's Nazis whose reign of murder and torture, sanctioned by Hitler, was only brought to an end by the Red Army advancing westwards across eastern and central Europe.

When Hungary swapped Nazi terror for Stalinism, it was the communist secret police who took up residence in a building which began to bear a different name. The House of Fidelity – or Loyalty to the regime. The irony is in its 19th century stateliness and style, besmirched and defiled by the use to which it was put. It was a place where those who opposed or questioned their rulers were taken for interrogation and torture. Imre Nagy was only one of many who languished in dank basement cells until they were subjected to the farce of a trial and executed.

Today the schoolchildren of Budapest are taken on a tour of four floors, passing through rooms exhibiting Arrow Cross and Nazi uniforms, the office of the sadistic AVO boss Gabor Peter, until he himself was jailed in 1953 in an anti-Semitic purge, and a replica of a courtroom made more spinechilling by the repeated showing of a Kadar era film depicting the trial of Nagy and his supporters in 1958. But perhaps the most terrifying episode for visitors to the House of Terror is the descent from the first floor to the basement in a slow moving lift. As this drops to the torture cells, you are forced to watch another film, an interview with a hangman, the one who dispatched Nagy and others to their deaths.

Dispassionate, matter-of-fact, unconcerned by the job he was given to do, the man tells his story with a blandness and objectivity that freezes the soul. He neither gloats nor smiles. He could be your favourite uncle.

Even more chilling in a way, despite the exhibitors' best intentions, is the ground floor of the House of Terror with its lounge, cloakroom, toilets, café, smoking area, bookshop and gift counters. Normality, banality and indifference among a collection of horrors. I couldn't get out fast enough.

ENDS

About the Author

Jack Thompson was born a long time ago in the north of England. After spells as a teacher, bus conductor, industrial spy and pianist in working men's clubs, he joined the BBC where he eventually landed the job of foreign correspondent for the World Service. He reported from south-east Asia, the Middle East, eastern Europe and the former Soviet Union. He followed the Vietnamese army into Cambodia as it overthrew the Khmer Rouge and saw the grisly aftermath of Pol Pot's killing fields. He was nearly blown to bits by militiamen in Lebanon and verbally pilloried by Saddam Hussein's information ministry for a report on human rights abuses in Iraq. His bosses at the BBC described him as "curmudgeonly and subversive", a badge he wears with pride. He left the BBC in 1995 and became a newscaster with Deutsche Welle TV in Berlin. Since 2002, he's devoted himself to writing, playing the piano again and trying to help with the upbringing of his grandchildren. In March 2006 he won the Scottish Association of Writers Pitlochry Award for Crimewriting with his thriller A Wicked Device. He lives in London with his wife, Kathryn.

Printed in the United Kingdom
by Lightning Source UK Ltd.
135787UK00001B/4/P

9 781438 916156